THE VAMPIRE ALWAYS RISES

Katie MacAlister

When writing dedications, I always try to think of who had an impact on me while writing the particular book. During the time I was writing this book, and the twelve years before it, my beloved girl dog Kelsey was my constant furry white companion. In 2016 she lost her brave fight against cancer. I miss her every day.

PROLOGUE

"Well, if it isn't Merrick." Two men emerged from an alley, pausing outside a run-down building.

The second man turned to where the first had pointed. "What? Where? Why, so it is, so it is. And he doesn't look happy to see us."

"Not happy at all. Why isn't he happy? I wonder," the first man asked, and removed a toothpick from his mouth, grinning to expose teeth that were crooked and stained the color of mustard.

The second man grinned, as well. It was about as pleasant as when his compatriot did so. "Vampires have strange ways, Henri. They most definitely have strange ways. But we could ask him why he is so angry-looking. Would you like to do the honors, or should I?"

"I would, Jens, but if I recall correctly, the last time we had speaks with Merrick, he called us lowlifes." Henri, the man with the toothpick, affixed a hurt expression to his unlovely face.

"Lowlifes! Shocking," Jens said, shaking his head. "Shocking is what I say it is when an old friend like Merrick has that to say about us. It's as if he didn't know us at all, not at all."

Merrick Simon halted in front of a rooming house located in an unsavory part of Prague long enough to give both men a considering look. "What did you call me here for that couldn't be handled via text messages?"

"Now, don't be hasty, Merrick, old friend," Henri said smoothly, jabbing the less-than-pristine toothpick toward Merrick. "You're the one who told us that secrecy is of the utmost importance."

"That he did, that he certainly did," Jens said, nodding his head, moving to a spot behind, which Merrick assumed gave Jens a false impression of security. "We're just doing as you asked."

"Giving you information you said you wanted," Henri said quickly.

"And now you look angry at us for doing our jobs," Jens added, leaning nonchalantly against a railing behind Merrick. "It's sad, it is."

"Get on with it," Merrick said, fast losing his patience. "What is it you have to show me?"

"You said you wanted to know of any movements of that man. Rex, was it?" Henri asked.

"Victor," Merrick said, well aware of Jens standing behind him. He wasn't a fool—he trusted the men about as far as he could spit, but that didn't mean he wouldn't use them if they really had information.

"That's right, Victor." Henri opened his eyes very wide. "It seems his right-hand man traveled to Prague two days ago, and hasn't left."

"Right-hand man?" Merrick frowned. It was the first he'd heard of his nemesis having a partner. "Who is that?"

"Don't know his name," Henri said from behind him, absently picking his teeth with his toothpick.

"We heard through the grapevine that he was doing some work for Rex."

"Victor," Jens corrected.

Merrick glanced at the house, unsure of whether to believe the two men. "Who passed along this information to you?"

Obligingly, Henri held out his mobile phone. "You can read the text yourself."

Merrick read, his frown smoothing out when he saw the sender's name. "That's Nico's informant. The one he has watching the airports."

"And he told us, so we told you," Henri said smoothly. "We figured if a man who works for the Four Horsemen says something, it must be true."

"The right-hand man is inside," Jens added, pulling out a small pocketknife and paring his nails. "Top floor. First on the right. We thought that was worth coming out to see."

"It is indeed," Merrick said, giving them a curt nod. Something felt off about the whole thing, but there was no denying the text Henri had shown.

Henri jerked his head toward the blue door. "You going in?"

"Yes." Merrick shifted his weight so that he was better balanced, and gave Henri a look that appeared utterly unaware of anything around him.

"Alone?" Henri asked.

"Unless you wish to join me."

"Now then, you know we prefer to keep a low profile," Jens said, and snapped his switchblade closed.

"He should know that about us," Henri said conversationally, which was all the warning that Merrick needed. "He should know that we don't like to get involved in these little disputes."

Merrick felt the air behind him stir, heralding movement, and spun around, grabbing Jens from where he leaped forward, the now-opened knife poised to stab Merrick in the back. Merrick slammed Jens into the wall, spinning around to land a kick on Henri's chest, pain burning through his left arm when the gun Henri held spat twice.

Henri flew back several yards before colliding with a trash bin, the gun spinning away from his hand and skittering along the pavement until it came to rest against Merrick's shoe.

Merrick scowled at the blood leaking out of his arm, ignoring the pain to bend down and pick up the gun. "If you ever attack me again, it will be the last time we meet. And yes, that is a promise. I'll send the bill for the bullet hole repairs to you," he added to Henri, before removing the magazine from the gun and tossing it into the trash can.

Jens sprawled against the wall, a bloody streak indicating his path down to the ground. He moaned, and twitched slightly, reassuring Merrick that he wasn't dead. The last thing he wanted was another death on his conscience, albeit that of a man whose actions had guaranteed he wouldn't be missed. Merrick pushed those thoughts from his mind when he entered the rooming house.

The small, dimly lit entrance hall was rife with scents that seemed to be engaged in an all-out war on the senses—boiled cabbage mingled with urine, with a top note of rodent droppings, and what Merrick suspected was the scent of freshly butchered mammals.

He didn't stop to wonder at how the inhabitants of the rooming house lived in such squalor—he ran up the cluttered wooden staircase to the third floor, his senses heightened. He wouldn't put it past his two so-called informants to have set up a trap.

At the top of the house, he paused outside the first door on the right and listened at it, but there was no sound beyond that of a radio from somewhere on the second floor.

His nose wrinkled. The smelling of butchery was stronger here, giving him a spurt of adrenaline that manifested itself into action. Without knocking, he kicked open the door and rushed inside, dreading the sight that he suspected would meet his eyes.

He stopped in the middle of the room, relieved to find that no Dark Ones were being killed. In fact, the room itself appeared to be empty, and he frowned in confusion. He'd never heard of Victor having a second-in-command. Had he taken on help?

The hairs on the back of his head stirred, but this time, he wasn't fast enough. Two men emerged from the shadows and leaped on him, one of them slamming what felt like a cricket bat down upon his head.

Dimly, he heard one of the men say that it was a shame that they had to kill him. But even as the words processed in his brain, the abyss claimed him, pulling him into its depths with inky fingers.

After an indiscernible amount of time, the blackness seemed to part. Had it been hours? Days? Merrick had been sinking through subsequent layers of unawareness, his body languid and tired, and knew he was dying. The effort to fight for life was simply too much to make, and he allowed himself to sink deeper and deeper, even as he hoped the man who took his place in the Four Horsemen would have better luck.

That was when he realized that he would not drift to death alone. Someone else was there, someone who cast a golden red glow that started in the distance, and which grew stronger until it took the shape of a woman's form. The glow seemed to be more than just light, since it permeated his being when she glided over to him. Her face was that of a goddess, with wide-set gray eyes, a little snub nose, and a rounded chin that for some reason made him want to smile.

His body had other ideas, however, and when she leaned over where he was lying, he had the worst urge to pull her down onto him.

"Don't," she said, her voice a whisper that seemed to be more a thought than a sound. "Now is not your time."

He frowned a little, confused by her words. He expected better from goddesses. "What do you mean?"

Her hair, a curtain of wild red curls, fell alongside his face and filled his mind with the fragrance of wildflowers warmed by the afternoon sun. "Don't die."

Her lips touched his when she spoke, her breath soft and warm.

"I can't help it," he said by way of an apology, and put his arms around her, pulling her down onto his chest. She was soft in all the ways women should be soft, the mounds of her breasts pressed against his chest in a manner that, had he not been dying, would have made him as hard as granite.

His penis disregarded the likelihood of imminent death, and promptly became fully erect, demanding that he provide access to the lovely glowing goddess.

"It's not your time," she repeated, the weight of her on his body doing amazing things to him.

He angled her head, kissing her with a passion that was surprising, given that he had spent his entire life effectively stripping emotion from his being. Her mouth was as sweet as her breath, but hotter, oh, so much hotter, and with the touch of her tongue to his, the hunger that growled around inside him roared to life, demanding that he claim her, and take from her that which only she could give him.

"Go ahead," she said against his mouth, her hands tangled in his hair, her knee slipping between his in a way that put exquisite pressure against his interested penis. "Feed, Merrick."

He nuzzled her neck, breathing in long, gasping breaths that dragged her scent deep into his lungs, his fingers busy trying to extricate her from the satin nightdress she wore, wanting—no, needing—to feel her soft, warm flesh.

"Feed," she said again, filling his head with the word until it reverberated with every beat of his heart. The hunger swelled up and blotted out all other feelings. He kissed a spot on her neck, and opened his mouth to bite, ready to fill his body and mind and being, to join his body with hers in the most fundamental way a man could ... and then she was gone, melting away into nothing.

He clutched at the air desperately, his body singing a dirge of loss, but there was nothing left to hold, nothing but the endless darkness that seeped into his pores, extinguishing the light, and filling him instead with despair.

He would die alone, unloved, and unmourned. The golden

red goddess would never know just how much he would have given to be with her.

He released the last little shred of hope, and let himself sink down into oblivion.

CHAPTER ONE

"Underwear, check. Toothbrush, check. Brand-new cosmetics, check. Gin for Allie, check."

"Gin for Allie?" Ellis, a friend since we were both shy, geeky kids in grade school, wrinkled his nose in the manner that a former boyfriend had told him was utterly adorable, and gave the bottle I held a scornful look. "Why are you taking gin to the Czech Republic?"

"I'm taking this bottle of expensive and hard-to-find gin because my aunt Roxy's friend Allegra supposedly likes gin, and it's my way of thanking her for hooking me up with whatever vampires are in the area." I rolled a couple of pairs of yoga pants around the bottle, and wedged it in the bottom of the suitcase. "I figured it was the least I could do. OK, that's it for me. Are you set?"

"Darling, I don't leave for another week," Ellis said, giving an airy wave of his hand. He was currently lounging on my recliner, sipping the bottle of wine he'd brought to bid me *bon voyage*, and offering criticisms of my wardrobe, packing technique, and general outlook on life. "I'm not the sort of person who makes lists like you do. I toss a few well-chosen and exquisitely cut garments in a bag, and then I'm off to face adventure with a style and panache not seen since the days of William Powell and Errol Flynn."

"That 1930s movie class has really changed you," I said, chewing my lower lip for a second over the last couple of items laid out on the bed. "Hmm."

"What are you *hmm*ing about?"

"Swimsuit." I said the word with the distaste it deserved.

"What about it? You know, this rosé is really quite drinkable. I wasn't sure about it because rosés can be so temperamental, but this is tolerable."

"The 'hmm' was whether or not to pack it. The swimsuit, that is, not the wine you brought." I held up the swimsuit. "Do you think it's too ... revealing?"

"I couldn't possibly comment unless you were wearing it."

I stared in horror at him. "I'm not going to let you see me in a swimsuit."

"Why not?"

"Because!" I said, sputtering a little and turning bright pink at the very idea. "Because you're—"

"Gay?" he asked.

"No! I don't care about that. But you're ..."

"A man?"

"Well ... yes, I guess that's part of it." I flapped my hands around helplessly, trying to think of how to explain one of the many weird hang-ups I'd had to deal with. "But mostly it's because you're my friend. What you think matters, you see, and if you think I look pudgy in my swimsuit, then I'll be crushed."

"Pudgy?" He tipped his head and considered me. Instantly, I sucked in my gut. "I wouldn't say 'pudgy' is the word to describe you. 'Titian,' now, that's a good word. You've got the red hair and the lush curves to stand up to the most nubile of Titian's ladies."

"That's sweet of you," I said, relaxing a bit. "I just ... it feels weird to let a man see so much of my body."

He snorted into the wineglass. "If I managed to keep from succumbing to your many and various charms in the tenth grade when we sat behind the gym and necked, I think you're safe now."

"That's because you don't like women in a sexual way," I pointed out, and wadded up the swimsuit and stuffed it into a corner in the case. It was followed almost immediately by the oversized man's shirt I used as a cover-up. "The necking was just you trying to figure out who you were. Rats."

"Where?"

I sighed and dug out of my nightstand drawer a battered and somewhat dusty box. "If I'm going to wear the swimsuit, I'm going to have to ... er ... deforest."

"Deforest?" Ellis did the nose-wrinkling thing again. "DeForest Kelley, from *Star Trek*?"

"No, deforest, as in prune the lady garden."

He stared at me, the glass of wine held motionless at his mouth.

I sighed even louder, and waved the box toward my crotch. "Wax my pubes, you boob."

Enlightenment dawned at last. "You mean you're not already spruced up down there?"

"No, of course not." I held a protective hand over my pubic mound, and consulted the box of wax strips. "That sort of thing is for special occasions, isn't it?"

He shuddered delicately, and took a long pull on the glass of wine. "Darling, I couldn't in a hundred years imagine being with someone without first removing everything unsightly."

"Uh-huh," I said, reading the instructions.

"There is no sensation quite as delightful as that of a shorn scrotum. You're not listening to me, are you? Tempest. Tempest!"

"Hmm? What does this mean? 'Once the strip has been applied, pull it off quickly in the direction opposite of the hair growth.' Pull off quickly like pulling a bandage?"

He gawked at me. "You can't possibly mean ... when you said special occasion, you didn't by any chance mean that you've never waxed?"

"No, but—"

"Not once?" Horror was rife in his voice, a fact that irritated me. It wasn't as if my pubes had anything to do with him.

"No. You know what my life was like. Can you imagine what my father would have said if he found out I was waxing my pubic hair?" I shuddered at the rage I knew such a thing would generate in my late parent. "He locked me in my bedroom for three days just for shaving my armpits. Waxing pubes would have given him a coronary."

"How you lived with that tyrant for all those years ..." Ellis shook his head. "Why don't you go to a salon like everyone else and have it done?"

"Ugh. And let some stranger touch me? No thanks. I bought this box of hoohaw wax strips when I turned eighteen, and I fully intend to use them. *Finally.*"

He made a face. "Are they even still good?"

"It's just sticky wax. That can't go bad, can it?"

"No clue, I'm afraid. Why didn't you use it when you bought it?"

"I never found the perfect opportunity, and then I hid it away under a floorboard so no one would find it."

He made a sympathetic moue. "I suppose I can see the wisdom in you hiding it. I can't imagine that the cult would like you waxing things."

"There wasn't very much they *did* like. But that's in the past. Let's focus on the here and now."

"Your bucket list?"

"My bucket list," I said, nodding, and returned to silently mouthing the wax-strips instructions to myself.

"You're the only woman I know who has tearing out her pubic hair by the roots on her bucket list, but then"—he rose and poured himself another glass of wine—"you're also the only woman I know who is taking a sizable amount of her inheritance and using it to find vampires."

I grinned at him over the top of the wax box. "Papa is probably rolling over in his grave at this very moment knowing that I'm using his precious money to enjoy myself."

"No doubt, given how little enjoyment you've been allowed. I have to admit that I've always thought it was a miracle you didn't turn out like the other women in your sect."

"Browbeaten and mindless?" I shrugged one shoulder. "I probably would have been if it hadn't have been for Mom. Her tying the custody terms so that I had to attend public school was the best thing she did. Well, that and pay to have her letters smuggled in to me. I probably would have believed everything that Papa and the Elders told me if it wasn't for those two things."

"I don't know why you've never been angry for her not taking you when she left the cult," Ellis said.

"Oh, I was for years. And then one day Papa told me that when she was getting ready to leave, the cult Eelders threatened to hunt down her family and harm everyone if she took me, so he begged her to leave me with him."

"Yes, but it's a cult!" Ellis protested. "How could she do that?"

"There was one thing Papa never bad-mouthed, and that was Mom," I answered, getting a bit nostalgic. "I think that's why he never fought her slapping so many requirements on the custody ruling—it was his way of reassuring her that he would take care of me."

"Different strokes," Ellis said, shaking his head.

"Definitely. OK, I'm going to go do this before I lose my nerve. Have the wine ready for me. I have a feeling I'm going to need it!"

Ellis lifted his glass to me, and pulled over the spiral-bound notebook that served as my journal. I disappeared into the bathroom, leaving the door open a bit so I could talk to him.

"Just how many items is your bucket list up to now?" he asked.

"Over a hundred, but most of those have to do with the trip to Europe."

"*Number twenty-eight: fly on an airplane. Twenty-nine: sing to myself in public. Thirty-two: drink several airline bottles of booze. Thirty-three: mile-high club.* Darling, I hate to tell you, but that last one isn't going to be easy to do when you're flying by yourself to the Czech Republic."

"I know. I don't have to do all the bucket list things right away. Besides, I've crossed off a bunch already. Grape juice!"

"What? Where?"

"No, no, not literal grape juice. Just ... *grape juice!*"

"You know, now that your father is gone and you're no longer a member of that weird-ass religious group, you can say actual swear words instead of substituting generic phrases."

"Swearing like a sailor is number seventy-eight on my list, actually. Boy, this is awkward. How are you supposed to put these little strips on?" I twisted around on the toilet, where I was attempting to position the super-sticky wax strips in the manner illustrated on the instructions, but the strips kept adhering to the edge of the toilet seat.

"I sit on the floor to do it. It lets you get full access to the zone, if you know what I mean," he said. "Where are your crossed-off—oh, here they are. *Sell Papa's house, and don't give one red cent to the church. Get cute apartment. Spend vast quantities of money buying clothes instead of making shapeless dresses. Read books Aunt Roxy sent.* Those were the vampire books, I take it?"

"Yup. The Dark Ones series by C. J. Dante, who is a close, personal friend of Aunt Roxy's. She promised me she'd introduce us." I got comfortable on the plush blue bath mat, and with a hand mirror propped up against a knee, applied the sticky strips to one side of my groin. I had images in my head of what I wanted, a nice tidy pubic area without any of the wild, deranged red curls that matched the ones on my head.

"I'm surprised your father let you read those books."

"Oh, he didn't. He made the school district show him every book I checked out, so that he could have approval of my reading matter. The vampire books I read after he died."

"Didn't your mother smuggle some decent literature in to you?"

"A couple, but one of the Elders found them and made me burn them in a ceremony of shaming in front of the entire church." I wondered if a razor wouldn't be better, but figured I'd made it this far—I'd just soldier on.

"That must have been hair-raising, to say the least."

"It was awful, but it wasn't like I was a stranger to being punished in front of everyone. It seems like at some time or other I broke every one of the basic tenets of the True Believer Church of the Apostles of the Armageddon. I danced in my bedroom, and dancing was a sin. I wanted to join choir at school, but of course, singing was a sin. I tried to swim in the lake behind the compound, but all hades broke out at that, because swimming is super sinful. And I can't count the number of times I was sent to sit in the corner with the punishment hood over my head while everyone ate dinner because I talked back to a male. Grape juice, this stuff is really sticky."

"It's a wonder you don't need deprogramming, darling," Ellis called.

"That's what I have you for. I'm so glad I found you on the line after Papa died."

"Online, dear heart, not *on the line*. And I'm glad, as well. It's been a delightful three months getting reacquainted. How's it going in there?"

"All right, I guess. I'm supposed to rub the strips in, then rip them off. Seems kind of ... sinful. Wait, is that the church talking?"

"Absolutely. There is nothing sexual about ripping out your pubic hair. Hurry up and deforest, or else I'll end up drinking the rest of this bottle."

"OK." I took a deep breath, grabbed one end of a strip, and, bracing myself mentally and physically, jerked the strip off my private parts.

The resulting scream that echoed around the bathroom almost deafened me. Ellis came running into the room, skidding to a stop at the door, one hand over his mouth as he stared at my crotch. "Dear god, what did you do to your coochie? Why is it bright blue?"

"Ack!" I screamed again, flopping over onto my front, my legs together tight. "What are you doing in here? You can't see my naked parts!"

"Darling, I'm staring at your bare ass, and let me tell you, it's nothing I haven't seen before."

"Eek! Stop looking at it! At me!"

"I can hardly help it, sweet thing. It's a full moon rising from where I'm standing. Why did you scream?"

"Because it hurt like hades!" I said, gritting my teeth. I pulled a large bath sheet off the towel rack, and swathed my lower parts with it before rolling over, tenting the towel to peer in and see how bad the situation was.

"Well, of course it hurt. You're pulling your short and curlies out. Do you want some medication?" He moved over to the mirror and flipped it open to look at the shelves inside. "Something soothing, I'd say, something aloe vera–ish. What do you have in here? Hmm. I don't think menthol rub and a yeast infection cream will give you the relief you want."

"I'll ... be ... fine ... ," I said, grunting a little as I wrestled with the towel, trying to get to the affected area so I could assess the damage. Unfortunately, my thighs appeared to be glued together, and what was worse, the bath mat seemed to have adhered itself to my legs. "Oh, this is just what I need!"

"What is the problem—holy shit!" Ellis stopped speaking for a second and pointed a wavering finger at the floor next to me. "What the hell is that?"

I snatched up the furry red blob of tape that I'd successfully ripped off my nether regions, and instantly, my hair snaked out and got stuck on an exposed bit of waxy glue. "Ignore that! Oh, darned socks! Now it has my hair."

Ellis doubled over, and for one horrible moment, I thought he was going to vomit on me. I tried to scoot backward across the bathroom floor, but stopped when the noise emerging from him was gales of laughter.

"It's not funny!" I said, glaring at him as I tried to get a hand in between my thighs to pry them apart while still maintaining the decorum of the towel covering me. "My legs are glued together!"

"They're what?"

"Stuck together!"

"I thought you pulled the strip off?"

"I did, but that was just one side," I said, scowling fiercely at the tears of hilarity streaming down his face. "Really, Ellis! A little empathy wouldn't be out of place here!"

"My dear, I'm as empathetic as I can be, but if you could just see you ..." He burst into another round of laughter, collapsing onto the toilet, pulling toilet paper to mop at his face. "Sitting there like a burrito with enough red fur to cover a large mouse hanging from your hair ... oh, where's my phone? I must get a picture of this."

"You do, and you'll never walk straight again," I threatened, looking as mean as I knew how.

It just made Ellis laugh harder than ever, and it took a full five minutes before he managed to regain his self-control.

"All right, darling, let's see just how bad it is," he said, kneeling next to me and reaching for the towel.

"It's Papa! I just know it is!," I moaned. "This is his curse. He always said he wished he had a way to keep me pure, and I just know he's done this from beyond the grave!"

"Deep breath, girlfriend, deep breath. I doubt that even your father has found a way to blight your coochie from the misty veil."

"You don't know how deranged he was," I said, pulling toilet paper from the roll to mop up my face and nose. "I wouldn't put it past him."

"Going in," Ellis warned, digging his fingers between my glued thighs. He didn't get any farther than I did.

"What are we going to do?" I said, my words definitely a bit wobbly.

He got nose to pubic mound and examined the situation

for a few seconds before getting to his feet. "Sit tight. I'll be right back."

"Where are you going?" I asked, panicking when he padded out of the bathroom. "You're leaving me?"

"Just to get some ice and the phone. Calm down, darling. I won't leave you in this destined-to-be-a-virgin-for-the-rest-of-your-life state. Hello? Are you the Girl from Ipanema Waxing Kit technical help people? I'm glad you're still in business. What do you have for someone who was raised in a cult, and doesn't know that you shouldn't glom fifteen-year-old wax strips onto your choochita?"

A half hour later, Ellis returned from a visit to a nearby pharmacy to pick up bottles of baby oil and mineral oil, both of which we drenched over my parts and thighs, which luckily allowed me to get my legs separated. There were still bits of blue bath mat fuzz decorating my private parts, which were enlivened by red, angry welts from the glue strips, but at least I had the blasted thing off.

"I feel ridiculous," I said a short time later, an ice pack pressed against the tender parts.

"Mmm. Well, if you ask me, it's not so much ridiculous as gullible," Ellis said.

"Huh?"

"The vampires, darling. You don't know any better because of your upbringing. Where the rest of us were growing up to *Star Wars* and Steven Spielberg movies and *Buffy the Vampire Slayer*, you were stuck reading some misanthropic version of the Bible."

"You don't believe vampires are real, do you?" I asked, giving him a sidelong look.

He shrugged. "Does it matter if I do or don't?"

"Not really." I was silent for a moment, then added, "I can't help shaking the dream I had last night. It had a vampire in it, and he needed me. I mean, seriously needed me. Life-and-death sort of needed me, and then he started kissing me, and after that ..."

Ellis sat up. "And after that what? Don't stop now, darling. I love a good erotic dream."

I waved away the comment. "And then nothing. Just when I thought it was going to be good, poof, it was over."

"That's all vampires are, my precious. Just dreams."

I shook my head, more to clear it of the remembered dream than to negate Ellis's comment. "My aunt Roxy swears they're real. She said there's a whole group of them that no one knows about. Only a few people know who they really are, and she happens to know the head honcho of the vampire organization."

"I'm sure you'll have a very nice time in the Czech Republic, and will be relaxed and ready to enjoy yourself in Italy with me." He smiled and, with a sigh at the clock, got gracefully to his feet. "I'd better get home or I'll be just dead tomorrow. Smooches, darling, and I hope Miss Thang down there feels better tomorrow. E-mail me when you get settled with your aunt's friend."

"Thanks, Ellis, I will," I called as he swayed toward the door, grateful that I'd picked an apartment on the same block as him. "Don't get run over by one of those strange metal horseless carriages that you heathen folk use."

He stopped at the door to give me a look. I giggled in response.

"I'd say you're going to hell for that blasphemy, but I suspect it's a little too close to what used to be home. Kiss kiss, darling. Happy flight tomorrow."

I curled up on the couch after he left, an ice pack strategically positioned, and one of C. J. Dante's deliciously wicked Dark Ones books at hand. I dipped into the book at random, and thrilled at the tall, dark, and decidedly sexy description of the hero.

"This is going to be the best vacation ever," I sighed to myself, and gave myself up to the joy of sinfully desirable vampires.

I just hoped they'd be as good as the one in my dream.

CHAPTER TWO

"I'm here!" I announced to my aunt Roxy almost twenty-six hours later. "Jet-lagged and hungry, and confused by the language, but I'm here in the Czech Republic, and I'm waiting on the train to take me out to Blanskso. How is Australia?"

"Gorgeous. Both the scenery and the men, but that's a tale for another time. Did Allie text you? I gave her your number and she said she'd try to get in contact before you arrived."

"Not that I saw. Thank you again for asking her to take me in."

"Pfft," Roxy said. "What are old friends for if not inflicting nieces upon, even if they are nieces you've only talked and written to, and not met in person because your sister's husband was a nutjob? Oh, sorry, Tempest."

"No apology is needed, and I'm looking forward to seeing you in person just as soon as we're both back home. Love to Uncle Richard."

"And to you. Just be sure to give Allie and Christian a kiss from me, only don't go wild on Christian, because Allie will take you down. Laters, kiddo!"

"A real vampire," I sighed to myself a few hours after that, peering out of the windows of a taxi on my way to Drahanská Castle. "I hope this vampire has some single friends. Just one would do. That's all I ask for, just one needy vampire."

"You want something?" the woman driving the cab asked, glancing at me in the rearview mirror. "You want stop?"

"No, no, keep going. I was just talking to myself."

"Hokay," she said, and turned up the volume of the radio, which was pumping bright, tinny music into the car.

Fifteen minutes later, we drove past a gatehouse, and started up a winding gravel road. Lining the road were torches, actual burning torches, not the electric kind.

"This is just awesome," I said, peering around first one way, then another at the torches. The trees blocked my view of the castle itself, but the flames dancing in the breeze set an eerie, anticipatory mood that I reveled in.

We rounded a curve, and my breath caught in my throat. Ahead of us was the castle, its bulky shape inky black against the night sky. Several small buildings were adjacent to the road, including one giant vault of stone that was topped by two massive eagles, their wings outstretched, and their heads thrown back in what looked to me like a victory howl. "Assuming eagles howl, that is," I murmured to myself, just about twisting myself in half as I peered back at the beautiful, but frightening, building.

I knew from my guidebook that along the front side of the castle were immaculately groomed lawns and a formal flower garden where the GothFaire would hold their All Hallows' Eve festival. As the gravel drive curved around toward the back of the castle, we passed all sorts of black, menacing shapes that indicated outbuildings.

"Here is castle," the driver said, pointing at the large building in front of us.

"So I gathered." I leaned forward and rolled down a window, so I could stick my head out to better see the approaching behemoth. Spires jabbed upward into the indigo sky, offsetting gabled towers that sat on either end of the building. The blank back of the castle—we were approaching from the service side, the front evidently being taken up by an elaborate garden—bore numerous tall, narrow windows framed in a softly glowing white stone. Or so it seemed to me, with the light of the moon falling on that side.

The taxi stopped at two large wooden doors recessed into the wall, flanked with torches. I got out, my mouth open, and my eyes bugging with amazement as I tipped my head back to try to take in all five floors of the building. "That is truly amazing. OK, I want my vampire to have a castle. I could so live in that."

"Here is castle," the driver said again, a bit more forcefully, and added, "Twenty-five euro."

"Oh, sorry. Sure. Here, I think I have ... yeah. Here you go." I doled out the appropriate money, gave her a sizable tip, and, with my suitcase in hand, approached the doors.

Each door bore a huge wrought iron knocker in the shape of a heart pierced with an arrow, but a discreet little button set beneath a metal speaker caught my eye just as I was about to pound on the door. I pressed the button, almost dancing with excitement. I was going to meet Aunt Roxy's vampire! I had so many questions for him, so many things I desperately wanted to know after reading his steamy books. And now I was about to meet—

A voice spoke in Czech from the metal grille above the doorbell. I was momentarily disappointed by the fact that it was a woman's voice, but pulled my wits together enough to answer what I assumed was a query as to who I was, and what I wanted.

"Hello. My name is Tempest Keye, and my aunt is a friend of Mr. Dante's. She was supposed to let him know I was arriving."

"Tempest?" the woman asked, the voice tinny and distorted. "Your name is Tempest? That is storm, yes?"

"Yes to both. Is this Allie? Roxy said she talked to you about me visiting."

"Am Tilda. Am housekeeper. You wait."

I waited, disappointment dampening my joy. "Stop being a baby," I told myself. "Patience, virtue, and all that. Oh, hi."

The door opened to reveal a small, dark woman with salt-and-pepper hair. "Come," she said, taking my suitcase. "You have yellow room. Dante and Allie not here. Will come later. You go with me."

I followed her up a staircase and across a dark-paneled hall complete with medieval weapons on the wall, banners hanging from the ceiling, and several toys of the Big Wheel variety. There was also a bike, a small doll's house, and an elaborate Star Wars Lego setup. We climbed another flight of stairs, then went down a dizzying number of hallways until Tilda stopped at a door, and opened it to reveal a room done in various shades of yellow and red, with gorgeous Japanese paintings on the silk hangings.

"You wash, or go to library now?"

"A library in the castle?" I asked hesitantly, wanting to make sure she wasn't shunting me out to the town's local library.

"Yes, yes, Dante's library. You come."

I left my suitcase and hurried after her, afraid that if I lost sight of her, I'd be forever wandering the halls. We went down a flight and, after a couple of twists and turns, emerged into a large room lit by soft golden light that seemed to gild the spines of books contained in the massive mahogany glass-fronted bookcases. There were several low display cases along one wall, as well, but it was the sheer number of books that had me gasping in pleasure.

"You stay here. I bring tea, then I leave. Allie and Dante home soon," Tilda announced.

"Oh. You don't live here?"

"No." She was gone before I could say anything more. I wondered if I was going to be nervous at being alone in a big old medieval castle, but then it occurred to me that I might not be alone after all. A place this size had to have a full-time staff.

When Tilda brought me in a tray containing a pot of tea, some cookies, and a couple of crustless sandwiches, I realized just how hungry I was. "Thank you for this. It looks wonderful. Oh, can you tell me who else is in the castle?"

She paused at the door and glanced back at me. "Who else?"

"Yes, whatever other ... uh ..." I didn't want to say the word "servant," since it sounded far too snobbish. "Whatever other staff is here?"

"Is me. I leave now. Dante home soon."

The door closed on the last of her words, leaving me feeling, for a moment at least, remarkably alone.

"Don't be stupid," I chided myself aloud as I sat down at the table at which Tilda had set the food. "How many people get to eat a vampire's sandwiches in his very own library? Not very many, that's who."

That little pep talk kept me going a couple of hours while I perused C. J. Dante's books. I was super excited to find he had a collection of not only his own vampire books but a large number by other authors, and happily dipped into several books that were new to me. By the time the little clock on a massive desk that took up one corner of the room chimed eleven, however, I was exhausted, no doubt due to residual jet lag.

I wandered out to the main hall with its toys, and wondered where my hosts were. "And should I stay up to be here when they finally roll in, or should I give in and go to my room to sleep, so they don't find me slouched in a chair sound asleep and drooling on myself?"

The mental image of that was enough to drive me up the stairs, but not before I left a note on one of the tables in the hall saying that I'd arrived, but gone to bed.

"I hope nothing's happened to them," I murmured, climbing into the bed. I could imagine any number of horrible accidents that would keep someone from arriving home safely, but was comforted by the fact that vampires (and their mates) were very hard to kill, and even if they were in a car accident, they were probably fine.

The dream started with a bird flying around at night, zipping in and out of a forest of tall fir trees, his shadow flickering on ground lit by a huge silver moon. Just as I was enjoying the bird's graceful moves, it swooped down toward a snake ... only it wasn't a snake—it was a winding dirt road, and along it one man dragged another by his heels.

The two men stopped before a set of beautiful dark doors with hearts carved crudely into the wood. They were the doors to the castle, I knew, but oddly, the rest of the castle seemed to be missing. The mobile man dropped the other one in a heap at the door, and reached up to pound on the door.

I wanted to point out to him that there was no building to go with the doors, and all the man had to do was to walk around the doors to get behind them, but my attention was focused on the man lying brokenly across the stone steps leading to the door. I bent over him, distressed for some reason, knowing somehow that the man was about to give up his hold on life.

"Don't," I whispered, my nose almost touching his.

"What do you mean?" he asked, his voice deep and yet so soft I wasn't sure I didn't imagine it.

"Don't die."

The pounding continued behind me, irritating me.

"It's not your time," I said, irrationally determined to keep the man's attention.

"I can't help it." He sighed then, a wordless expression of so much despair, it made me want to weep, but at the same time, I wanted to yell at the man behind me who was still beating on the doors. I looked up to tell him that he was wasting his time, but at that moment, the prone man grabbed my wrist.

"Don't open the door," he said, his eyes a beautiful indigo with little black streaks coming from the pupils, his gaze seeming to sear right through me to my soul.

"Why?" I asked in a whisper, leaning down over him so that my hair hid us from the man at the door.

"I am death," the pretty-eyed man said, his body going limp, and his eyes closing. I knew he was on the verge of dying if I didn't do something, and leaned down until my lips teased his.

"I'll save you," I promised, not in the least bit concerned with how I was going to do that.

His arms came around me, pulling me onto his chest at the same moment his mouth claimed mine—and it was a claiming, an act of dominance despite the fact that he was very nearly dead. His lips were hot and sweet and spicy all at the same time, and when his tongue ran along my lips in a silent plea, all my dark, secret parts seemed to come alive.

I gave in to needs that swamped my mind, kissing him back with everything I had, my hands tangled in his hair, my breasts sensitized and heavy as I squirmed against him. His hands swept up my back, causing me to move restlessly against him. I wanted more of him, more than just his mouth and hands, and pulled back to tell him so, completely oblivious to our surroundings.

I kissed the man's jaw, his cheeks, even his closed eyes, wanting to bury my face in his hair, all at the same time he kissed a line down my throat to my shoulder. I shifted, trying to figure out what it was I needed to do to save the man, but a stab of pain interrupted my thoughts, pain in my shoulder that quickly faded away into the most erotic sensation I'd ever had. I was on the verge of an orgasm, spiraling up to it, desperate to meet it and yet not wanting the feeling to end. And just as I was about to burst into the light, into the glorious burning blaze of rapture, I woke up.

The pounding noise was real. I thought at first it was my heart thumping in my ears as I tried to come down off the single most erotic dream of my life, but then I realized the dull noise had its source outside of my body.

"Christian Dante and his wife!" I said to myself, snatching up the sheer chiffon robe that matched my satin negligee. "Bet they locked themselves out."

I ran for the stairs, mindless of my bare feet on cold wood and marble, racing down the hallways and stairs until I reached the double doors, one of which I flung open with an anticipatory smile on my face.

The man who turned to face me was a disappointment, not at all what I had expected C. J. Dante—and a vampire—to look like.

He was dark, wiry, with spiky hair dyed pink, several facial piercings, and a rainbow flag tattooed on his neck. He said something in what I thought was French.

"I'm sorry, I don't speak French."

"You American?" He sounded oddly nervous. "This is for your master. He is not quite dead, although he should be since his blood was drained, but I didn't think it was right to kill him just because he was a vampire, you know? So instead I brought him here to your master."

"My what?"

The man turned around and hauled something up the couple of stairs to the door, laying it at my feet. "Do not tell anyone that I brought him here, or my master will have my head." He glanced around fearfully. "You did not see me. You don't know who I am. I was never here. You understand?"

I stared in horror at the object at my feet, dimly aware of the man at the door vanishing into the night.

"What ... who ... glorious grape juice! Vampire? Dead? Did you say ..." I looked up, but the man was gone. "Hey! Mister? Hey!" I stepped over the body and ran down the front stairs, but a white panel truck was barely visible zooming off down the drive. I ran after it a few yards, but it was too far off to see the license number.

With a shiver at the cool night air, I clutched my robe and dashed back into the house, hesitating over the body of the man. He was lying facedown, his black clothing matching his jaw-length hair.

"Now what am I going to do?" I asked, kneeling down and trying to rationalize what had happened while the wispy remnants of my dream still clung to me. "How do you bring around an almost dead vampire?"

Gently, I rolled the man over, stumbling back when I got a good look at his face.

It was the man in my dreams, the one who had told me he was death.

And now it seemed he was speaking the truth.

CHAPTER THREE

"I don't know ... oof ... how many people ... grape juice! ... have had to drag a full-grown bull vampire ... ow! ... any distance, but you, sir, are not the easiest weight to shift." I straightened up from dragging the vampire, and rubbed my back. The man didn't look like he was made up of anvils, but he sure felt like it.

"Well, I could leave you here, but ..." I glanced around the hall. It seemed so uncaring to just abandon him in a cold hall surrounded by a Lego Millennium Falcon. Even if he was dead, which Spiky Pink Hair said he wasn't. Although he sure seemed like he was dead. I'd felt for a pulse and found none, nor was his skin warm to the touch. I frowned down at him. "At least your head is still on, so no one had pulled a Highlander on you, and there is no sign of blood anywhere. That's two in the non-dead column, but if you're still alive, why don't you feel alive? Oh well. Dead or alive, I can't leave you here like a bag of dog food that someone dumped on the doorstep. But how I'm going to move you is beyond me ... hmm."

A glance around the hall didn't show me any handy vampire-moving tools lying around, but I'm pleased to say that it didn't take me long to realize an important fact: an antique Persian throw rug on a beautiful marble floor is the perfect vehicle for transporting almost-dead vampires across vast spaces.

"At least until the marble runs out," I grunted, hauling the vampire-bearing rug down what seemed to be endless miles of hallway until I reached the library, a room that I knew had a gas fireplace. It was also fully carpeted, but after a quick examination of the handsome almost-dead vampire to make sure I wasn't hurting him, I more or less rolled him across the short stretch of floor until he came to rest before the fireplace. "And now we'll get you warmed up, since you feel like an icicle, and I'm freezing in this skimpy nightie."

I turned on the gas fireplace, made sure the man wasn't too close to the flames, and, clutching my gauzy robe, dashed back to the entrance, hoping that a car would be pulling up with the castle's owner inside. He'd surely know what to do with a possibly dead vampire. Unfortunately, there was no one outside, not even a hunchback servant named Igor. All there was outside was a whole lot of inky darkness lightened only by a faint glow of the moon, and the still-flickering torches.

"Rat pickles," I swore softly to myself, closing the door carefully before I made my way back to the library to check on the probably-wasn't-really-dead vampire. "Where's Igor when I need him? Someone has to be out there keeping those torches lit. Right. I'd better see what I can do with Mr. Handsome."

I didn't even bother asking myself if it was wise to take it upon myself to rescue the vampire lying on the library floor—ever since I'd read Dante's books, it had been my greatest wish to meet a vampire, but hidden behind that was a secret desire, one so wicked that I hadn't been able to face it fully. I did so now.

"I want to feed him," I whispered to myself when I entered the library. The man lay exactly where I'd left him. "I want to feel all those things that Dante says women feel when they offer themselves up to their sexy vamps. I want to feel what it's like to be joined with a man on a level that transcends primal. I want to do something that no one else can. Hey, mister." I gave the vampire's shoulder a little shake. "Do you want me to save you?"

There was no answer, of course, and as I sat on my heels next to him, I considered how best to go about saving him. I laid my hand on his neck. The flesh was cool, but not cold or clammy, and still without a pulse. I thought about that for a minute. Did Dark Ones have pulses? I wasn't absolutely sure about that—Dante never mentioned it. I shook the man again. "Hello? Are you in there? Oh, grape juice, Tempest, that's a stupid question. Of course he's in there. OK. I need to get a grip. He needs blood. You want to give him blood. Therefore, you should just do it."

I leaned down over the vampire's face, pulling my curls back to expose my throat. *"Bon appétit,"* I said, pressing my neck against his lips, and bracing myself for the bite.

There was none.

"Hmm." I sat up again, frowning. "Maybe I need to get the process going. Let's see. I'll start by opening your mouth."

My tongue snuck out to the corner of my mouth while I carefully wiped my fingers on my negligee, then gently pried open the man's lips. There were no fangs visible, which I felt was a bad sign. Everyone knew a vamp had to have his fangs out in order to feed. Feeling more than a little bit awkward (and not a little like I was baiting a lion), I carefully eased his mouth open an inch. With a quick prayer that I wouldn't get my fingertip snapped off, I slid my index finger into his mouth to feel around for his tongue. I knew from a school first aid course that tongues had to be moved out of the way whenever oral aid was rendered, and was trying to remember what steps I should take next when I encountered a warm, moist blob.

"Warm," I said to myself as I pressed the blob down. "Your tongue is warm, which is a good sign. It means you aren't dead. OK, mouth open, tongue down. Now let's get a little blood into you. Er ..." I put my wrist over his opened mouth. "I don't suppose you'd like to take over from here?"

He didn't care to. I sighed, and got to my feet to investigate C. J. Dante's desk, returning with a wickedly sharp-looking letter opener. I held it over a finger, telling myself that a quick stab was all that was needed, but I've always had an aversion to blood, and I just couldn't bring myself to draw my own.

"OK, you're going to have to help me," I said, wedging the handle of the letter opener into his armpit, so that the sharp end pointed up at me. I raised my hand over it, turned my head, and, bracing myself mightily, brought my hand down.

I completely missed the letter opener, of course. I tried again ... and again ... but some sense of self-preservation kept me from so much as glancing the tip of the opener off my hand.

"Oh, for mercy's sake!" I said in exasperation, snatching up the opener, and of course, grabbing at a sharp, pointy object in a haphazard manner had exactly the result you'd expect. "Ouch! Rat pickles! Oh! Wait ... this is good." I squeezed the tip of my finger to encourage the few drops of blood to grow, feeling vaguely sick at the sight of the welling mound of crimson.

"Ugh. I sure hope this works." Without looking at my thumb, I maneuvered it between the man's lips, and waggled it around on his tongue, pushing away thoughts of germs and infection, and focusing on the anticipation of the joy that was sure to be mine any second now.

Any second.

Any ... "Well, pooh." I withdrew my thumb and leaned over the man, my nose touching his as I watched closely for signs of life. "Maybe it wasn't enough?"

A faint exhalation seemed to emerge from his still open mouth, brushing over my face. "Mister? Do you need more? If so, you're going to have to do the honors yourself, because it makes me queasy to do it mys—"

The words were stripped right out of my mouth when two arms suddenly wrapped around my back at the same instant I was pulled down onto his body, my mouth colliding with his in a way that I knew immediately wasn't an accident. His tongue had come to life, sweeping into my mouth like it owned the place, his spicy taste somehow both foreign and strangely familiar.

Without being aware of any movement on his part, I found myself on my back, the warmth of the carpet and the heat of the fire dancing along my nearly naked flesh, the man pressing down on me a solid but not uncomfortable weight, his hands not moving, but holding firmly to my hips.

Only his tongue moved, twining around mine as it tasted me, teased me, its movements seeming to stir fires deep inside me that echoed with the memory of my erotic dream. "Oh, Glorioski," I moaned when I managed to pull my mouth from his. I felt light-headed, like there was no oxygen in the room, but it was a feeling I wanted to go on and on.

The man's mouth moved along my jaw, pressing hot kisses to my flesh, his touch making me shiver with both anticipation and sexual excitement. I couldn't believe I was reacting this way to a man I didn't know, let alone who wasn't, strictly speaking, conscious, but I knew vampires had the ability to make women swoon just with their touch. "Man, C. J. Dante didn't get this wrong at all," I said, my breath catching in my throat when the mysterious vampire's mouth moved down to my neck. My heart beat madly, while intimate parts of me woke up and began to express interest in the proceedings. I clutched his shoulders, waiting, hoping for the bite, sure it was to come, and equally sure that when it did, it would be the last thing I'd ever feel.

The pain was over almost before my brain could process it, the sting sharp and swift, but easing almost immediately to an erotic sensation so strong that I writhed beneath his body in my attempt to get out of my underwear, every inch of me a sensitized erogenous zone. I was simultaneously hot and cold, the hunger within me blotting out everything but the need I had, a need that had to be fulfilled or else I'd simply fade away to nothing. My fingers weren't in the least bit gentle when I pulled at his clothing, the sound of cloth ripping as I exposed his chest, then struggling with the leather belt buckle, all the while my legs moving restlessly against his. I could do nothing but make incoherent moaning noises while I tugged at his clothing, releasing the hot brand of him into my waiting hands.

His mouth moved on my neck, and I caught a flash of beautiful blue eyes when he shifted, his body urgent as he bit me again, this time on my shoulder just as he'd done in my dream, the sensation of my blood flowing into him almost pushing me over the edge.

"Please," I whimpered, wrapping one of my legs around his. "I'm going to break into a billion pieces if you don't."

My hands were desperately pulling at him, under his shirt stroking the still cool flesh of his back, my hips doing a sinuous dance of enticement, my whole being focused on this desperate need that I felt to take life from him. And when he gave in to my urging and moved into me, it was as if my own personal heaven had opened and choirs sang down on us. I moved in ways I'd never moved before, matching his thrusts into my depths, reveling in both the stretching feeling and the sensation of my tightness upon him.

So ... hot.

"Oh, yes, so very hot." I arched back when his mouth moved again, and he kissed a burning path over to a spot just below my ear. "No wonder women do this. It's ... it's ..."

Exquisite.

So exquisite. I feel like I'm going to jump into something.

Jump, goddess, jump.

The sting on my neck did the job. My body tightened and seemed to explode into minute little pieces of sunlight as I gave way to the orgasm that had been hovering ever since he'd bitten me.

His breath was hot on my throat as he groaned and gave way to his own climax, the sense of it rocking me. And as I lay beneath him, panting, my mind reeling with the experience I'd just had, I realized something important.

I'd just had sex with a stranger.

OK, mind-blowingly fabulous sex, but still, sex with a man whose name I didn't even know.

Oddly enough, I wasn't bothered by the fact that he drank my blood—that seemed to be of lesser importance than the fact that I had given myself—really, demanded that he take me—to a man I'd known a total of fifteen minutes, and none of those minutes had he been conscious.

"Um," I said, turning my face into the ebony strands of hair that caressed my cheek. He had collapsed on me, his breath hot on my shoulder, his breathing just as wild as mine. "Excuse me, but this might be a good opportunity for us to introduce ourselves. I'm Tempest. Did you call me a goddess?"

I hadn't meant to ask that last question, but it had been trembling on the tip of my tongue ever since I'd recovered my wits. "I've been called Red before—just about everyone seems to think they have to point out that I have red hair, like that escaped my notice—but never goddess. So, what's your name?" There was no answer, just the rapid, hot breath on my shoulder. I gave his shoulders a shove. "Hello?"

My word seemed to echo, and came from a distance. I froze, listening intently, holding my breath as if that would help me hear better.

"Hello? Tempest? She must be in bed. Jakob, you do not need to check on Mr. Pibbles. He'll be asleep in his warm, comfy stall, and if you open the barn door, it'll let the cold air in."

"Someone is here," a baritone Spanish voice declared in a dramatic manner. The voices were distant, but perfectly audible, probably something to do with the way the hall was shaped.

"Roxy's niece is here, Antonio. I told you that. Christian, would you let Esme loose?"

Eeek! It was C. J. Dante and his wife! I struggled to get out from under the deadweight of my nameless lover, and managed to roll him over onto his back.

"No, no, it is a man. A foul one, like the one 'oo possesses you. I shall find ' im and smite ' im."

"There is a Dark One here?" That was another man's voice, but this man had a deep voice with a faintly Germanic accent, and a note of authority that fit perfectly with my idea of the owner of a castle. I pulled my nightie down, snatching up the tiny panties that came with it, and hurriedly pulled them on.

"Yes. I will find. You go to bed, old one."

The voices sounded louder, filling me with a sense of panic. I glanced over to the vampire and was horrified to see that not only was his shirt open and pulled out of his pants in a way that laid bare an extremely attractive chest, but his naughty bits were lolling right there for everyone to see, and the wetness glistening thereupon made it pretty clear what we'd just been doing. I stuffed his penis back into his pants, and yanked up the zip.

"Goodness, thank you, dear Christian. Mr. Woogums and I were most tossed around in your pocket. It's so nice to be back in my regular spirit form. Allegra, where is Antonio going? Mr. Woogums, no! You are not to follow him. You know he gets into all sorts of trouble."

I ignored this new voice, which was that of an Englishwoman, instead working frantically to get the vampire's belt buckled, and his shirt tucked back into his pants. He didn't so much as twitch as I worked over him.

"Antonio says there's a vampire here. Girls, go up to your room. Jakob, did you hear me when I said you were not to go out to the stable?"

That was the woman who had to be Allie speaking again. A door slammed in response to her demand. I turned my attention to buttoning up all the buttons on the shirt worn by the man next to me. There were three buttons missing, but I was hoping if I got the others together, it wouldn't be so noticeable.

I'd just finished, and pulled the unoccupied bit of rug over the man, when I felt a sudden swirl of wind. A man in Elizabethan garb rushed into the room, a rapier in his hand.

"Stand! I 'ave you now, you ... oooh." He looked taken aback for a second; then his expression changed from fierce to a leer. He swaggered forward, his eyebrows bobbling like mad, a smile on very red lips. "'Ello, my fiery one. You have very much beautiful breasts."

I looked down, found my scant robe had come undone during my struggle to dress the prone vampire, and had just pulled it closed when several people entered the room, including two girls of about four—obviously twins—and a tall, gangly boy of about seven or eight. He had a shock of black hair and silver eyes that were almost identical to those of the man who seemed to dominate the room the second he entered it.

My skin prickled with more than cold, causing me to wrap my arms around myself, very aware that I was in the presence of a man who wasn't going to stand any shenanigans. He stopped in front of me, his frowning eyes going from me to the man next to me.

"Hello. You must be Tempest. I'm Allie." The woman who was on Christian Dante's heels limped forward, greeting me with a warm smile. She had oddly mismatched eyes, but that just made me like her more. "I'm sorry we're so late. There was an accident on the train line, and they didn't get it cleared for hours. I hope Tilda has made you comfortable. Is this a friend of yours?"

She nodded toward the vamp next to me, who was still unconscious.

"No," Christian said, giving me a suspicious look before striding forward to peer down at the man. A surprised look flashed in his eyes before a shutter seemed to come down, blocking out all visible emotions.

"I didn't do this," I said, getting to my feet, holding my robe tight across my front.

"Esme, dear," Allie said, her voice light and apparently unconcerned. "Why don't you take the girls upstairs to their room, and help them into their jammies."

"What an excellent idea," the woman named Esme answered, nodding so fast her fat gray sausage curls positively bounced. "Come along, Julia. Iris, dear, leave the dead man alone. You don't know where he's been."

She left, accompanied by the two little girls, both of whom started chattering about what they were going to do when Mr. Woogums had kittens.

"My darlings, I'll leave that talk to your parents," was all that Esme said as their voices drifted away.

"The woman killed the evil one?" the Elizabethan man asked, eyeing me with a combination of speculation and lust. "I shall punish 'er for you. Slowly. With my hands. And possibly my mouth."

"And that's it for you tonight, Antonio," Allie said, glaring at the man. "Go away and let us deal with this."

"But I am your protector!" he protested.

"Go," she said, but there was a note of steel in her voice.

"You cannot just disperse me like I am nothing but the poof of steam," he said, sniffing.

"Look, we took you and Esme with us tonight because you guys said you wanted a night out in Prague, but that doesn't mean we need you underfoot now. Go watch a movie, or visit with your friends out in the mausoleum, or do something, so long as it's not here."

He looked like he was going to protest, but before he could, Christian Dante strode over, and waved his hand in the air. To my surprise, the Elizabethan faded away into nothing.

"Thank you," Allie said, giving her husband a smile.

"You could have done that yourself," he pointed out.

"I know, but it always feels so rude. Now, about this man ... who is he?"

They both turned back to the man before the fire.

"I don't know. I found him like that," I answered, assuming she was talking to me.

"I'll tell you later," Christian said in a low voice, turning to face me. "What exactly happened here?"

"Nothing!" I spread my hands and tried to look like I hadn't just enjoyed the single most erotic experience of my life with the unconscious man on the floor behind me.

"What do you mean, nothing?" Christian frowned and suddenly realized his son was still in the room. "Jakob, it is past your bedtime."

"I'm hungry," the boy said, his eyes grave as they considered me.

"Then you may go out to the stable and drink from one of the cows, but do not play with your pony."

"Awww," the boy said, and did a good approximation of a dirt kick.

"And put on your coat," Allie said absently, her eyes on the man before us. She knelt and touched his wrist. "It's chilly outside, and I don't need you getting a cold."

"I've told you ever since he was born that he can't get sick with mortal illnesses," Christian said, addressing his wife. "Why do you persist on ignoring that fact?"

"Because I'm a mother, and as such, I'm legally obligated to say things like that. Tempest, when you said that nothing happened here—"

"I meant that. Nothing happened. Nothing at all. He was just ... uh ... there. And I was here. We weren't together. Not even remotely. And ... that's all." I coughed and wondered if it was possible to die of shame. Perhaps my father and his cult had been right all along. Perhaps I really would go to hell for having sex.

With a vampire.

One I hadn't even met.

I sighed, and felt my shoulders slump.

"You just came out of bed," Christian asked in an extremely stern tone, his eyes flickering over my negligee, "and discovered this man?"

"Yes. Well, not really. I mean, I did find him, but not here." I decided it was safe enough to tell them the truth about that part of the evening. "I was dreaming about ... well, that's really not important. I mean, it could be, but probably isn't. So, I heard pounding and woke up, and someone was at your front door banging on it, and when I went down to answer it—I figured you guys must have gotten locked out somehow—a man was there with this guy. Oh. I just realized what that man meant."

"I'm confused," Allie said, moving over to pull the rug from where it was draped over the prone vampire. "Is there one Dark One, or two?"

"Two. Wait—I don't know if the pounding man was a vampire or not. Do you think he was?" I asked Christian, since he seemed like the best source of information concerning potential vampires.

He looked momentarily startled. "I have no idea. So there *were* two men?"

"Yes, poundy Pink Spiky Hair man, and the dead vampire."

"Dead?" Allie make a little sound of horror.

"Oh, he's not dead," I reassured her. "I gave him some blood. He hasn't woken up, but he's most definitely not dead."

"You fed him," Christian said, making it a statement, moving over to gaze down at the man before the fire.

"Yes. It seemed like the thing to do. I read in one of your books that vampires can't be killed unless you cut off their head, or they suffer some horrible injury, and since he didn't seem to be hurt in any way, I figured he was just nearly dead. So I nicked my finger and got a little blood on his tongue and that seemed to do the job, because the next thing I knew, he was at my throat and ... well ..." I coughed again, and tried hard to look like the modest, pure woman that my father's cult wanted me to be.

"I see." There was a strangled note to Christian's voice that smoothed itself out with his next words. "Then we have much to thank you for, Miss Keye. Who is this other man you mentioned? The one who was at my door?"

"I don't know—he never told me his name, but he did say ..." I paused, closing my eyes to remember his words. "He told me not to tell his master that he had not killed this man, or the master would cut off his head. Spiky Pink's head, that is. He had spiky pink hair, in case you are confused."

"I know I am," Allie said softly, her eyes on her vampire. "What do you think it means, Christian?"

He didn't answer her. Instead, he turned to me, giving me a little bow. "You are no doubt cold and tired and wish to return to bed. I'll have Allegra send up some cocoa to help compensate for your ... donation."

"Oh, that's OK, I feel fine," I said, waving a hand around with airy indifference to the loss of blood. "I take it that the message meant something to you? Do you ... er ... know who this man is? Not that it matters to me, but you know, it's always kind of nice to know the name of the man you just ... uh ..."

"Fed?" Allie asked.

"Yeah." I smiled a brilliant smile, all the while calling myself names for almost telling them just exactly what had gone down here less than a half hour before. *Just play it cool,* I told myself. *They'll never know how shameless you are.*

There's nothing to be ashamed of, wafted gently through my mind, making me shake my head.

"Is there something wrong?" Allie asked, watching me closely.

"No. Not really. It's just ..." I made a face. "Sometimes it's hard to shed the dictates that have been pounded into you for years, even though you know they're wrong. And that you're an adult, and if you chose to do things adults do, that's your right, and it doesn't automatically mean that it's sinful and you're going to suffer a thousand torments for it."

She opened her mouth, closed it, then opened it again with a little half shake of her head. "I'm not quite sure what you're talking about, but I'm going to guess it has something to do with the cult that Roxy said you were a part of."

"Against my will," I said quickly. "It wasn't like I believed in the stuff they did. And then I had to stay because my dad was sick, and I didn't want to leave him to Elder Wilhelm's idea of homeopathic care. I got Papa to see proper doctors, even if he complained the whole time about seeing non-church people, and—"

"Regardless of your sacrifices, I'm sure you'll feel better once you have had some rest," Christian said, and without realizing it, I found myself marching up the stairs, heading for my bedroom.

But not before I heard Allie say, "This isn't one of your Four Horsemen, is it?"

I listened intently even as my feet carried me upward.

"He was. The question is, will he survive whatever Victor's Revelation has done to him?"

CHAPTER FOUR

"Merrick."

He frowned. He didn't wish to come out of the floating black sea of unawareness that had held him in its tight embrace for what seemed like an eternity. It was rather pleasant there. He didn't have to worry about anything.

"Merrick, you've had enough blood for two Dark Ones. You must wake up now."

He was given blood? That must be why he was feeling relatively well.

"Merrick, by the saints, if you don't wake up now, Allegra will be back, and she will insist on bathing you, and that will just end in another argument where I have to forbid her from handling your naked self, and she will accuse me of being jealous. Wake the hell up so I don't have to be jealous."

Merrick cracked an eye open. "It's not my problem if your woman prefers my manly form over yours."

The man sitting on the bed next to him glared at him, but at the same time, his mouth twitched. Christian Dante, Merrick knew, had a stern appearance that he used to hide his sharply honed sense of humor. The fact that they both knew Christian's wife, Allie, would never so much as look at another Dark One had nothing to do with the ease with which Christian spoke, and Merrick answered.

"How long have we known each other?" Merrick asked, his mental and verbal filters slightly awry from the time spent floating in the soft blackness.

Christian frowned. "Is that a pertinent question to ask after you've nearly died on my library floor?"

"I wouldn't have asked it if it wasn't."

Christian looked thoughtful. "It must have been in the fourteenth century. You were in Constantinople, and I was passing through on my way to the Far East."

"Ah, yes, that's it. I make that 1314 or thereabouts. So a little over seven hundred years." Merrick thought about that. "Time passes quickly, does it not?"

"It does when you are lying insensible, drained of blood," Christian answered in what Merrick thought of as his patented dry tone of voice. "What happened? Who did this to you? I assume it was the Revelation?"

"Yes." Merrick felt the back of his head, but the lump that he assumed must have risen when he'd been struck was no longer there. "I went to Prague after an informant told me one of Victor's procurers was there. I didn't think I would have trouble taking him, but there was more than one, and they got the jump on me. I'm surprised they didn't kill me outright."

"I gather they were supposed to, but one of them had a change of heart and brought you here, instead."

Merrick grunted an acknowledgment of that. "How much blood did I lose?"

"All of it, from what I can tell. You were nearly gone when Allegra and I returned home. Luckily, there was someone here to keep you from fading away."

"Ah." Merrick nodded, the faint memory of flowers flitting through his mind. Clearly, the goddess must be one of Christian's staff, and she had found him and given him enough blood to keep him alive. "And how long has it been?"

"Three days."

"Three *days*?" Merrick sat upright. "Since the Revelation took me, or since you found me?"

"Since you were deposited at my door." The amusement that had been in Christian's eyes faded as he spoke. "You were more dead than alive, and I feared for the worst until we fed you sufficient blood that you once again had a heartbeat."

A small cold ball of anger grew in Merrick's gut. "I'll get Victor if it's the last thing I do. And the two informants who set me up."

"We're making progress," Christian said, rising from the bed and strolling to the window. "You and the others have brought seven procurers to justice. You have saved countless mortals from being turned."

"It's not enough," Merrick said, the small ball in his stomach turning into a burning sphere. "For every mortal we save, there are a handful the Revelation reaches. I must contact the other Horsemen. We have to do something beyond simply capturing random members of the Revelation. We need to strike at the head."

Christian turned back as Merrick rose and somewhat clumsily pulled on his clothing. "Have you had any word of who that might be?"

"No." Merrick's legs felt a bit rubbery, but he ignored the sensation. There was so much to do, so many people who were counting on him to save them from eternal enslavement. "Not yet. But we will."

Christian's silver-eyed gaze watched him closely for a few seconds. "Do you still believe that Renata's death lies at their door?"

"Yes." Merrick donned his shoes and a long black duster, placing a black felt fedora on his head in a way that would shade his face from any errant sunlight that might try to catch him as he ran for whatever car Christian would allow him to borrow. He pushed down the pain that automatically rose at the mention of Renata, not needing the memory to fuel his fury.

Not now. Not when there were Revelation members to capture, and a leader to punish.

"You look ... grim."

"I *am* grim." Merrick slid Christian a look from the sides of his eyes. "You know as well as I do what is at stake."

The two men walked in silence for a few minutes. "Allegra said you need a ..." Christian stopped, cleared his throat, and started again. "Allegra has pointed out that perhaps you could use a break from hunting the Revelation members."

"Your Beloved has no input on my life," Merrick said flatly.

"She means well. She worries that you have isolated yourself from contact with others to the point where your focus is too narrow, too uncompromising."

"You expect me to compromise with murderers and abusers?" Merrick asked, outraged.

"Of course not. But I agree that a more well-rounded life might allow you to serve with a bit more mental ... balance."

Merrick stopped abruptly and faced his old friend. "Now you call me insane?"

"Not that." Christian's expression showed both concern and frustration. "But when is the last time you took a step back to examine your life?"

Merrick snorted disgustedly, and would have continued onward toward the garage had not Christian stopped him by holding his arm.

"We have only your interests at heart, my friend. Since Renata died, you have been a man driven to the point of exhaustion. You cut everyone out of your life, left your friends both old and new. You live in isolation, keep yourself in solitary purgatory, and have no interaction with anyone not connected to the pursuit of the Horsemen. When is the last time you laughed? Took pleasure in a lover's touch? Found joy in the simple embrace of another human being?"

Merrick waited impatiently for Christian to finish. "None of those things are important. Finding Renata's killer *is*. Bringing down the Revelation *is*. Those are the only two focuses in my life now, and they will continue to be so until I find the answers I seek."

"I fear for you," Christian said, shaking his head as they started forward again. "Down that path lies nothing but sorrow."

"I live with sorrow every day of my life," Merrick said abruptly. "I do not fear it."

"What can I do to help you?" Christian asked after a few more moments of silence.

"Nothing other than giving me the use of a car. I have no idea where mine is, and until I can find it, I will need transportation."

"Of course," Christian said, leading Merrick from the room. "You will take your pick of the cars. All of them have tinted windows, although I would ask that you not take the Tesla. It is Allegra's favorite. But what are your plans now?"

"First, I must contact the others."

"Ciaran left a message for you," Christian said as they descended, pulling out a small piece of notepaper. "Evidently, he is leaving San Francisco tomorrow for somewhere in Quebec."

"Yes, he's following a trail that he said should lead to the main organization that fuels the Revelation. Han is also in the States, in Chicago."

"And Nico?" Christian asked. The two men exited the castle through a side door, running the few yards to a nearby stone building that served as a garage.

"He was in Singapore, although I believe he said something about going to Russia." Merrick shook his head. "Nico is never overly willing to share his plans."

"You are the Four Horsemen," Christian said, a warning note barely evident in his voice. "You protect Dark Ones and mortals alike. You are a unique force that *must* communicate with each other; else you cannot work together as one unit—"

"We do and we are," Merrick interrupted. He considered the row of six cars, and picked the most innocuous one, a black BMW. He liked to lie low, to be hidden from sight, and the car suited his needs. "It's just that sometimes the trails we follow don't give us time to check in with the other three. But you have no need to worry, Christian. Three of us have been doing this job for ten years now. We have each other's backs."

"That had better be true; else you might end up on my doorstep beyond our help."

Merrick smiled a small, grim smile as he took the keys Christian offered, and entered the car. "Don't worry, I won't be so careless again. Please offer my thanks to your staff member, and offer her any reparation if it is desired."

"My staff member?" Christian looked puzzled.

"The one who gave me enough blood to keep me alive until you could attend to me." Merrick gunned the engine, waving when Christian stepped back. "The redheaded one with the big eyes. For some reason, I thought she was a goddess, but now I realize I was near death and delusional."

"I'm not sure who—"

"The woman who fed me. And ... well, you know what happens when we feed. I would have you give her my gratitude."

Christian's eyebrows rose. "Ah. Yes. Just so. I don't believe the lady had any complaints about your ... reaction."

"Good. Let me know if she requires anything. I am in her debt."

"I will, but she wasn't a staff—" Christian said, but the rest of the words were lost in the sound of the tires hitting the gravel drive.

Merrick's attention was already focused on the job at hand. First, he needed to return to Prague to try to locate his car, and to pick up his possessions from where he'd left them at a hotel. And after that ... his eyes narrowed as he reviewed his plan to locate the people who ran the nefarious organization responsible for creating new Dark Ones from innocent mortals, and using them for profit.

Uppermost on his mind was locating Jens and Henri to find out who had paid them to trap him, and after that, he'd go to Genoa. With luck, he'd find the house where Victor was supposed to spend some time. And then, he'd be one step closer to bringing down the biggest threat to mortals and Dark Ones alike.

It was just too bad he was in such a dangerous line of work. He wouldn't mind thanking the redhead himself for saving him.

He pushed away thoughts of her, her elusive flowery scent, the feel of her skin against him, her heat surrounding him, and most of all her sweet mouth. Such things had no place in his life. Not while Renata's murderer still walked free.

Not while he was a marked man.

CHAPTER FIVE

"Hello again, Aunt Roxy." I was delighted to see her name pop up on my cell phone's display. "Are you still enjoying Australian men?"

"I was, but then Richard got called back to work three days early, so now we're home. What did you mean by your text?"

"Which one?" I asked, setting down a pamphlet advertising a boat tour around the La Spezia harbor.

"The one where you said that Allie kicked you out of the Czech Republic. What on earth did you do? You didn't try to ... oh lord ... tell me you didn't fling yourself on Christian, did you? I know he's adorable and has a voice that sounds like velvet, but trust me when I say that he's not for you. I told you about Beloveds, didn't I?"

"Yes, but—"

"I told you how for every unredeemed Dark One there's just one single woman out there—or two, if you're Christian and one of those women is Joy, but we'll ignore that because really Joy was crazy picking Bob over Christian."

"Joy?" I asked, not recognizing the name.

"Another friend; you don't know her. And I don't want you thinking that I don't love Allie, because I do, and I think she's just perfect for Christian—where was I?"

"You were telling me the rules about Beloveds. Not that I need you to, because I've read the books, and I know about the steps—"

"The steps! That's what I was going to tell you. Each vampire goes through these seven steps that tell him the woman in question is his Beloved."

"I know about the steps—"

"The first one is marking, and then there's protection from afar, followed by a spit swap—actually, it's any bodily fluid, but Allie says that most vamps do that by kissing—and then a few more steps. Somewhere in there is the woman saving the vampire from his darker self, which I think is just the most romantic thing ever. I mean, who wouldn't want a sexy vamp after you saved him from his bad self?"

"Aunt Roxy—"

"I'm just explaining why Allie got upset when you made a move on Christian, that's all. Don't take it personally."

"I didn't try to do anything to Christian!" I almost yelled into the phone, immediately dropping my voice when I realized the French doors to the balcony were open. "I barely said hello to the man before he was bustling me out of the castle and insisting I go off to the Italian Riviera, where I'm supposed to meet my friend Ellis in a week."

"Oh." Roxy was silent for a few seconds. "Then what did you do to piss off Allie?"

"I don't know!"

I spent the next fifteen minutes giving her an account of my movements in the Czech Republic, excluding the sexual hijinks that the nearly dead vampire and I got up to.

"Well. You have had a time. Hmm." Roxy mulled over my story. "You know what I think it is? I think it's you being at the wrong place at the wrong time. Christian is the head honcho of all the vampires, and I bet you got caught in something that was going on, and they got you out of there for your own good."

"Yes, but now I'm ahead of schedule. I'm here in Italy seven days ahead of my friend Ellis, although I suppose I can move up the meeting with Cousin Carlo."

"Cousin Carlo? I don't recall having a cousin with that name."

"He's one of Papa's cousins. Mom suggested that since I was now free of the cult and could see anyone I wanted, that I reconnect with family members. That's why Ellis and I are in this part of Italy—so I can meet Carlo."

"Ah, that makes sense. And good for you for stretching your familial wings that way."

I sighed. "The problem is that this was supposed to be my vampire time, not Cousin Carlo time. I don't suppose you know of any Italian vampires? I'd be willing to travel to see one, although I realize that sounds kind of desperate. Oh, just ignore me. I'm acting like a baby because part of my plans fell through."

"You're not acting like a baby at all. I'd be disappointed if I went to Europe to see Dark Ones and didn't get to do more than be hustled out of Christian's castle ... although, to be fair, he did that once to Joy and me ... but I'm afraid I don't know of anyone you could ask for help other than Allie."

My heart sank. I flopped down in one of the plastic white chairs on the balcony, enjoying the warmth of the sun even as my spirits took a nosedive. "I guess I could call her. Even if I was in the way while I was there—and honestly, I can't see how that is possible since I was only there for one night—she wouldn't hang up on me, would she?"

"No, of course not. Call her. Worst-case scenario: you be a tourist until your friend gets there."

We chatted for a little while longer, but Roxy was anxious to get unpacked, and I wanted to talk to Allie.

"I'm sorry you feel like we didn't want you," the latter said a half hour later, when I managed to get her on the phone. "I assure you it had nothing to do with you, and everything to do with Christian being overly cautious."

"You said that yesterday when you bundled me on the train, but I still don't understand why he would think I was some danger to the vampire who was left there."

"It's not that at all. He was thinking of your welfare, since the pink-haired man saw you."

I grimaced at nothing. "If Spiky Pink Hair would hunt me down because I knew he saved a vampire's life—and I can't imagine he'd do that, since he seemed more concerned about himself—I am certainly no threat to him. Even if I wanted to tattle on him, I don't know his name or who his boss is."

"No, but ... it's complicated ..." Allie hesitated, then said softly, "Oh, to hell with it. I'm going to trust you with the truth. After all, you're Roxy's niece, and when she asked if you could visit, she swore up and down that you were as trustworthy as she is."

"I am, I really am," I said, both flattered that my aunt would think so much of me, and intrigued by Allie's statement.

"Hang on a minute."

There was a rustling noise and a brief muted conversation, immediately followed by the sound of footsteps lightly running down what I imagined was one of the castle's stone hallways.

"OK," Allie's voice came hushed and somewhat breathless. "I'm away from the kids. I'm going to tell you what happened, but you have to promise not to talk about it to anyone else, because it involves the safety of four men. Four Dark Ones."

"I promise I won't breathe a word," I exclaimed, glancing around my little balcony to make sure no one could overhear me. Since I was the only person crazy enough to sit out in the midday sun, I was safe enough from eavesdroppers. "And thank you for trusting me. I won't let you down."

"There is this group of people called the Revelation."

"Revelation like ... in the Bible?" I asked, confused.

"No, evidently it's the name of some corporation. An *evil* corporation. Anyway, a few years ago we started hearing about this group called the Revelation. They were advertising at folk festivals and similar events about vampires who would come to your party and entertain."

"Like clowns?"

"No, do vampire things for the entertainment of those present."

"Um ... do you guys do that?"

"No! Not real Dark Ones, anyway, but you know how it is—there's a huge vampire fandom out there, and lots of people like to live the lifestyle and believe they are vamps when they really aren't. Anyway, we just assumed it was that, but then one day Merrick's sister went to one of the parties, and wasn't seen again."

"Who's Merrick?" I asked, having lost track of the players.

"The vampire you found on our doorstep. His sister Renata was seeing a man who we only know as Edward, who evidently was one of the high mucky-mucks in the Revelation. He invited her to attend one of their parties."

"What happened to her?" My gut tightened. I had a bad feeling I wasn't going to like the answer.

Allie was silent for the count of fifteen. "Her body was found two months later. She'd been raped and ... brutalized."

"Oh my goodness," I said, sick at the thought, of both the poor woman having gone through such a horror and her family dealing with the tragedy. "That's just appalling."

"Renata is a Moravian—a female Dark One. Do you know about them?"

I thought hard. "They don't have to drink blood like the males, but can if they want, right?"

"Yes. Merrick found Edward, and ... well, you can imagine what he did."

"Glorioski. He didn't kill him, did he?" Had I bonked a murderer? No wonder my father wanted to keep me away from men—clearly I lacked any sort of ability to discern evil from good.

"No, although I gather it was a near thing. Merrick brought Edward before the Moravian Council, the group that polices Dark Ones. He was tried and convicted, and is currently imprisoned in Merrick's villa."

"What a relief," I said without thinking, slumping back into my chair.

"I beg your pardon?" Allie sounded mildly outraged.

"Oh, I just ... I meant because I ... we ... uh ..." I gave a little cough and stopped.

"You didn't by any chance engage in some carnal activities when you fed Merrick?" Allie asked, the outrage changing to amusement. "Don't be embarrassed if you did—it's a very common effect, given the nature of the feeding. I mean, what could be more intimate? Although generally it's limited to Beloveds, it can happen when the respective parties are not engaged otherwise."

"Oh, good," I said, slumping even more. "I was worried I'd have to have my lady garden exorcised or something. Although if Merrick didn't kill anyone, then the point is moot. I don't blame him for hunting down his sister's killer."

"No more do I. Regardless of our feelings, the Revelation is now threatening Dark Ones, and the Four Horsemen specifically."

"The Four Horsemen of the Apocalypse?" I asked, startled.

She laughed. "No, although I take it that was the source of their name. The Four Horsemen is the name that Merrick and three other Dark Ones have given themselves. They are more or less an elite police force that tackles any threats that affect vampires and mortals alike. Right now they're focused on the Revelation."

"Gotcha. How ... er ... how is Merrick?"

"He was fine when I last saw him. He's gone now."

For some reason that I couldn't pinpoint—and admittedly didn't particularly want to analyze—my spirits dropped even lower at that news. I had a sudden yearning to see Merrick again, to look in those lovely eyes, and to feel the cool silk of his hair on my cheek ... not to mention other parts of him visiting parts of me.

I shifted in the chair, and tried to think of something intelligent to say, but Allie covered the phone and murmured something I couldn't hear, then came back and said with false brightness, "I'm so glad you're settled. It was a pleasure seeing you. Do come back and visit us another time. I must be off. Christian wants to take the children out, and it means loads and loads of sunscreen for him. Good-bye!"

She hung up before I could thank her for her thoughtfulness, leaving me with much to think over.

And think I did. For a day I kicked around the hotel and town, doing tourist things, but not really present—my mind seemed to be caught up with the idea of seeing Merrick again, and ... and ... "And what?" I asked myself the following night, staring at my reflection in the bathroom mirror. "And holding him? Offering him comfort for the pain of losing his sister in such a horrible manner? Having incredibly awesome sex again?"

Inner Tempest liked that idea a whole lot. I told her she was a shameless hussy, and pretended I didn't wholeheartedly agree with her. "What you need," I told my reflection, "is something to distract your hoohaw from the idea of Merrick and his hoohaw. Hmm. Do men have hoohaws? Maybe they have a manhaw?" I sighed, and padded out of the bathroom, and onto the bed, punching the pillow a few times to make it comfortable.

"Let's see. You have six days before Ellis arrives to distract you from your complete lack of vampire in your life. One of those days was going to be for Cousin Carlo, but I guess I can see if he wants me early."

One pleasant if slightly awkward phone conversation later, I was packing for departure to Carlo's house in Genoa the following morning. Once there, I had to admit I was impressed how my father's Italian side of the family was doing. The house had a huge fence around the perimeter of what looked like a large estate sitting high on a hill, with a view of the glittering sea beyond, white ships dotting the deep cerulean of the water.

I showed my passport to the security camera at the gate, and after a few minutes, my taxi was allowed to enter the grounds, and deposited me at a solid white stone villa, all colonnades and large windows.

Beyond the house, hills rose, dotted with olive and orange trees, brilliant red and yellow flowers, and the odd occasional palm tree swaying with stately grace in the breeze that lifted off the harbor.

"Hi, I'm Tempest," I said to the man who opened the door. "Are you Carlo?"

"No," the man said. He was a little taller than me, but built like a wrestler, with no neck, thick shoulders, and a barrel chest. He also had a nose that had clearly been broken more than once. But it was his eyes that sent little shivers of worry down my arms. They were a dull hazel color and completely devoid of any humanity. It was like looking at a photograph of eyes.

This must be what a sociopath looks like, Inner Tempest commented. I had to agree, but, despite that, forced a smile to my lips and entered the cool darkness of the house, stumbling blindly for a few seconds until my eyes adjusted from the dazzling sunshine to the dark interior.

I was taken to a room that was lined with floor-to-ceiling windows, the white drapes fluttering in the breeze, a full view of the sea beyond. Sitting behind a desk that was cluttered with two laptops, several stacks of spreadsheet printouts, and a variety of what looked like medieval torture instruments was a man who bore absolutely no resemblance to my father.

"Hello. You must be Cousin Carlo. I'm Tempest."

Carlo was probably twenty years older than me, balding with a rusty brown fringe of hair, and a thick Mario Bros. mustache. "Ah? Oh, Tempest." He stood up and came around the desk to shake my hand. "You are welcome, very welcome. I'm pleased to see Raymond's daughter at last. You had a good trip out? Yes? Good. You admire the view? Yes? Good. Giovanni! My cousin's daughter will have a room that will give her a view of the sea. You will like to swim every day? Yes? It shall be as you desire. Giovanni will ensure a car is at your disposal."

The man with the flat eyes took my luggage and, with a murmur in Italian, left the room.

Carlo embraced me, kissing both cheeks. "It is very good to have you here. You like Italy, yes? There is a pool you may also swim in. You swim? Yes? Good. You will wish to see your room." With an arm around me, he spun me around and marched me out of the room, and into the main hall, where a wrought iron and marble staircase curved upward in a graceful arc. "There is much to see in Genoa. You will wish to see it all, yes? Giovanni will see to anything you need. Dinner is at eight. You need not dress for it—we are very informal here. Ah, there is Giovanni now. He will see to it that you lack for nothing."

Before I could do more than say hello and offer up a few stunted syllables as replies, which were summarily ignored, I was hustled up the stairs and deposited in an airy room with French doors that opened onto a lovely balcony.

My brief experience with Cousin Carlo pretty much set the standard for the rest of the day. Whenever I tried to have a conversation with him, intent on getting to know him, he seemed affable enough, but almost immediately fobbed me off onto Giovanni with an offer to go sightseeing, or shopping, or sailing, or any of the myriad other options available to tourists.

Needless to say, I dreaded time with Giovanni and his dead eyes. By the following morning, I had learned to stop trying to converse with Carlo, and kept to myself.

By that evening, I wandered through the grove of olive trees, wondering if it was something about me personally that Carlo objected to, or if he had a dislike of women in general. There were no other females in the house; I'd seen only two other people, both men, one of whom was the cook, and the other some sort of handyman-gardener.

"It's got to be me," I said morosely. "Or it's Papa. Maybe Carlo found out about the cult, and figures I'm as crazy as Papa. In which case, what am I going to do?"

"Suffer," a man's voice said from behind me. I spun around, but a black bag was pulled down over my head and upper body. Before I could scream, the breath was knocked out of my lungs when the man picked me up and flung me onto his shoulder. "Suffer like you've never suffered before. And after that, you will tell me where I can find Victor. If you refuse, you'll die."

Anger washed over me, a foreign sort of anger, one fueled by a great sadness tinged with a sense of loneliness so profound, it left me speechless with despair.

CHAPTER SIX

"Who are you?" I managed to ask after I caught my breath, which wasn't easy, given that my abductor was apparently jumping over a bunch of ruts. Or at least, that's what it felt like from where I was slung over his shoulder. "Why are you doing this? And who's Victor?"

"Do not play games with me. It will get you nowhere." The man's voice was deep, with an Irish twang that sent little ripples of pleasure down my spine despite the fact that he'd just kidnapped me. I tried a kick of my legs, since my arms were plastered to my sides inside the bag, but he slapped my behind. "None of that."

"Hey!" I yelled through the bag, spitting out a bit of material that was in my way when I inhaled. "Stop touching my behind! I will not be mauled by anyone, least of all a brutish kidnapper."

"I am not brutish," the man said, bending down in a way that almost had me falling off him. Luckily, his arm tightened around my legs. "I did not savage you as you deserve. In fact, I have treated you quite well."

"I do not deserve to be savaged! I'm a nice person! And if you call jamming a bag over my head and picking me up like I'm a bag of bark treating me well, then I'd hate to see what you think ... hey! What the bejeepums are you doing? Let go of me!"

My voice rose in outrage when he bent again, this time letting me slide off his body, but not before his hand cupped my derriere again. I gasped when he whipped off the bag, and found myself staring up into familiar indigo eyes.

Behind me was a black car, but it was the man in front of me who held my attention. He stared right back at me, his eyes narrowing as I gaped at him, my Inner Tempest cheering and urging me to grab the man by his head and kiss the dickens out of him.

"It's you," I said stupidly, then realized the inanity of my comment. "Merrick, isn't it?"

His eyes narrowed further until the blue glinted ominously. "How do you know me? Was it Victor? Did he tell you about me? Where is he now?"

With each sentence, he moved forward, forcing me to back up until I bumped into the car.

"Whoa, now," I said, holding up a hand and pushing on his chest. He didn't budge, just stood there, toe-to-toe with me, his nostrils flared slightly as if he was trying to catch a scent. Holy moly, was he impressive when he was standing upright. "Less of that bossy tone, if you don't mind. I don't know anyone named Victor, not that I'm sure I'd tell you if I did, what with you abducting me without so much as a *Hi, hello, how are you, mind if I pick you up and fondle your derriere?*"

An exasperated look flashed across his face, and he actually backed up a step, letting my hand drop from his chest. "It wouldn't be much of an abduction if I chatted you up first."

"Just because you're a brute doesn't mean you can't be polite," I said with a serenity I was far from feeling. My insides were all fluttery from seeing him again and feeling the warmth of that hard chest beneath my hand. I wanted nothing more than to slide my hands beneath his shirt so I could stroke the muscles. With a start, I realized he was speaking and I hadn't heard a word. "Er ... sorry, what was that?"

He looked outraged. "Asking me to repeat myself needlessly is not going to make things any easier for you."

"It's not needlessly. I was ... er ... woolgathering."

He looked even more outraged, if that was possible. Then an oddly martyred look filled his gorgeous eyes. "Are you trying to goad me into killing you? Is that it? You think that you can escape me through death? It won't work. I refuse to kill you."

"Good," I said, and actually smiled at him. It struck me that I wasn't frightened of him, not really scared, not like I would be if someone else had shoved a bag over my head and carried me off somewhere. This wasn't anyone else, though. This was a vampire, one whose life I flattered myself to think I'd saved. And even if I hadn't exactly saved him, at least we'd had the single most erotic experience of my life.

I was musing over the oddness of my reaction—lots of women had erotic interludes with men who turned out to be abusive or evil—when I realized that he'd been speaking, and once again I'd missed what he had said.

"Sorry, what was that? I was ... er ... thinking of something."

"You're doing this on purpose," he growled—actually growled the words at me. "Well, it won't work. I refuse to allow you to anger me."

"Awesome!" I said brightly. "Anger is so overrated, don't you think? I mean, if anyone has a right to be angry about all the crap—pardon my French—that's gone down over the years, it's me, and I learned long ago that it doesn't do any good. So I'm glad you're not mad and don't want to kill me, because I don't particularly feel like courting death today. Maybe another time, but not now that I've seen you."

"You will explain how you know me," he started to say, but a shout from behind him, from the region of Carlo's house, had him casting a glance over his shoulder. We stood outside the gate, which was closed (and had me momentarily wondering how he'd gotten us through it), but before I could ask, he opened the car door, and more or less shoved me inside.

"What the—" My protests were cut off by the slamming door.

He started around to the front of the car. I opened the door and jumped out, racing to the gate. Inner Tempest asked me what the dickens I thought I was doing, but I told her to mind her own business, and also, that I wasn't going to take being kidnapped without protest, not even when the abductor was the handsome-eyed vampire who'd given me so much pleasure.

He was on me before I even reached the gate.

"No," was all he said, swinging me up and marching back to the car. This time, he tossed me into the backseat before taking his place behind the wheel.

"Gah! Stupid kid locks," I snarled, trying to open the back door.

"Who were you trying to warn?" he asked, putting the car into gear and zooming off into the night with such speed that I was thrown back against the seat.

"No one. I've always felt that if I was ever abducted, it would be mandatory to try to escape. Why are you kidnapping me?"

"I saw you in Victor's garden. Clearly you are his woman. Thus, I took you so that you can give me information on him."

"I don't understand who this Victor person is, but even if I did, why didn't you just say, 'Hey, I want to talk to you—can we have a little chat over here?' rather than stuffing a bag over my head? You're lucky I don't have an elaborate hairstyle." I ran a hand through my tangle of hair.

His eyes met mine in the rearview mirror. An odd expression of speculation took hold of his face, almost as if he was trying to figure something out. *Who are you?*

"Do you often kidnap people you don't know?" I shook my head. "You're never going to get ahead that way."

"What are you talking about?" He made a noise of annoyance, and pulled the car to a stop at an overlook. There wasn't much of a moon, but what there was glinted on the now black sea. "I *know* who you are. You are Victor's woman."

"I don't know anyone named Victor," I repeated, hitting the back of the seat in frustration. "My name, in case you are wondering, and you should be if you aren't, since it's only polite to know the name of your abductee, is Tempest Keye."

"That name means nothing to me," he said slowly.

"Thanks for that," I said, then, with an irritated click of my tongue, started climbing over the seat.

"What are you doing?" he asked, reeling back.

"Climbing up front so I can talk to you rather than the back of your fat head."

"My head is not fat!"

"I meant that figuratively rather than literally. Ow. Would you move your arm—ow! Stop trying to help!" I managed to get over the seat into the front without flashing too much leg. "If I'd known I was going to be doing this, I'd have worn pants rather than a sundress. Whew. OK. Now we can talk."

The look he gave me was one of mingled puzzlement and exasperation. "You are not at all what I expected."

"Since you evidently have me mistaken for someone else, I'm not surprised." I stuck out my hand. "Let's do this properly, shall we? Hi. I'm Tempest, and I don't know anyone named Victor."

He looked at my hand for a moment, then reluctantly shook it. "I am Merrick Simon."

"I know." I smiled at him, getting a good look at his face when he switched on the interior lights. He had a slightly Slavic look about him despite his Celtic accent, with high cheekbones, a sharp jawline, and a narrowly squared chin. I had the worst urge to reach out a hand and draw a line along that jaw, wondering if the hint of stubble felt as nice as it looked. Inner Tempest urged me to do just that, but I told her to turn off her motor, and stick to what was important—like why the vampire whom I'd fed was now kidnapping me.

"*How* do you know?"

It was on the tip of my tongue to tell him that Allie had told me all about him and his three Horsemen buddies, but remembered in time that she'd asked me not to mention it to anyone. I didn't want to get her into trouble after she'd been so honest with me. "Um. That's ... I can't tell you."

He squinted at me. "Why not?"

"Because I promised someone I wouldn't. But you can take it from me that it was someone nice. That is, someone who isn't a bad guy. Why did you kidnap me? Why didn't you just talk to me? I mean, after what we've been through, you can't think I'd yell or scream at seeing you."

"What we've been through?" He looked downright confused now, and it struck me with a blow that was almost physical that he truly had no idea who I was. He didn't remember me! We'd shared the most profoundly important physical relationship I'd ever had, and he didn't remember it.

My brain whirled around trying to process this fact, and it wasn't until he placed a finger under my chin and gently pushed upward that I realized my jaw had dropped at the realization. I blinked at him a couple of times, unsure of what to say that didn't sound either bitchy or extremely needy.

"I ... I ... " I stammered, and came to a halt. "We ... uh ... we've met," I finished lamely.

"When?" He gave me a visual once-over. "I don't remember meeting you."

"We have, regardless."

His gaze settled on my hair, an odd expression on his face. "Your hair ..."

I touched a curl. "It's red."

"Yes. There's something ..." He closed his eyes for a few seconds, clearly trying to remember. I held my breath, waiting for him to tell me that he recognized the face of his savior, but all he did was shake his head, opening his eyes to reveal nothing but vague suspicion. "It's not important."

Oh, he did not just say that, Inner Tempest gasped in horror. I fought back the desire to tell Merrick just how we'd met, but my pride had me keeping silent. It was bad enough that I wasn't memorable enough to remember having sex with me, but I'd be horn-chicken-swoggled before I went for the pity points and told him I'd saved his life. *No,* I told Inner Tempest, *we've been hurt before, and we managed to get through it. This rejection is no different than any other. We will maintain our diginity.*

Dignity can be overrated, came the thought wafting into my brain as if on the breeze.

"What?" I asked.

"*What* what?" He frowned at me.

"Did you say something?"

"Not right before you spoke, no." Merrick started the car again, and swung out onto the road without another word.

"Where are we going?" I asked, wondering if I should be worried, and then being concerned because I wasn't the least bit disconcerted by the fact that he was taking me away from Cousin Carlo's villa.

Shouldn't I be bothered? I was hurt because he didn't remember me, but shouldn't I be worried that he was a deranged ax-murdering rapist vampire with a fetish for Americans, even if C. J. Dante knew him?

Surely wisdom decreed I should not be feeling calm and collected in this situation.

Why not? came the question on that same sort of odd wafting breeze of thought.

"OK, now you did talk," I said, snapping the seat belt into place before poking him on the arm.

"I did not."

"Don't try to make me think I'm the odd one in this car, because you're winning not only the tiara but the cape and bouquet when it comes to that."

He sighed a martyred sigh and muttered something under his breath in a language I didn't know.

"And now you're saying things about me in a language I don't speak, which is all shades of rude." I crossed my arms and looked out of the window at the passing night. "I would never speak behind the back of someone I kidnapped."

"I apologize. Next time, I will abuse you to your face."

"Thank you," I said, giving him a smile that I didn't wholly feel he deserved, but it's always better to give people the benefit of the doubt.

He cast me a quick startled glance before focusing on the road. "You're serious, aren't you?"

"Yes. Wouldn't you rather know what's being said about you than having people hide it?"

Sometimes, it's best not to know.

"Oh, I don't buy that at all," I told him, watching with interest as we joined a highway that led south and east.

"You don't buy what?"

"That it's best not to know."

He slammed on the brakes, causing the car to fishtail wildly for a couple of seconds. At the same time, he rammed his arm across my torso, keeping me from snapping myself painfully against the seat belt.

"What on earth?" I gasped, the air having been knocked out of my lungs with the movement.

He pulled off the road, and turned to look at me, flipping on the interior light again. "What did you say?"

"I said 'what on earth,' as in what on earth do you think you're doing?" I touched my neck where the seat belt had rubbed. "Man alive, Merrick! Could you warn me when you're going to do that again?"

I will, if you promise to answer a question.

"What question?"

He was silent, watching me with an intensity that I found equal parts exciting and worrisome.

You ought to be worried.

"I don't see why ... hey. Your lips didn't move when you said that. Are you a ventriloquist?"

"No."

"How did you do that, then?"

You can hear me.

"Of course I can."

No one can hear me. Not like this. His eyes narrowed. *Who are you?*

"I told you. I'm Tempest Keye."

Why can you hear my thoughts?

I gasped and stared openmouthed at him for the second time in a few minutes. "Holy shish kebab! Is that what I'm doing?"

How are you doing it?

I don't know.

You must. There has to be a reason for you to be able to do this.

I gasped again. "You heard me, too? Jeezumcrow! We can mind-read each other! I read about that in C. J. Dante's books, but I thought it was a bit of literary license on his part. Cheese and crackers! We can mind-talk!"

He froze solid, just like he was a block of extremely sexy vampire.

His nostrils flared slightly. "You find me sexually attractive?"

"Gloriana, you heard that?" I slapped a hand over first my mouth, then, when I realized that didn't make any sense, my ears, just as if that would hold in my wicked thoughts about his naked self. "Ack! Pretend I didn't have a smutty thought about you, OK?"

Another one of those indescribable expressions passed over his face. "I cannot help it when you project into my mind. If you don't want me hearing them, then do not be so brazen with your thoughts."

I dropped my hands. "Oh, I am so not projecting! I wouldn't know how to if I wanted to. You're eavesdropping, that's what it is. And eavesdroppers never prosper, so you can put that in your pipe and smoke it."

Now he just looked confused. "What pipe?"

"There's not … it's a saying … oh, never mind." I thinned

my lips at him. "The point is that people who deliberately listen to other people's thoughts about how sexy they are deserve what they get. Wait ... that came out wrong."

He made an exasperated noise and glanced over his shoulder, then pulled back onto the highway.

I felt oddly deflated for a few minutes before realizing that he hadn't responded to my comment.

I smacked him lightly on the arm. "Don't you know what this means?"

"Yes. I will have to practice my mental barriers more."

"No, I mean what the implication of it is. Don't you read C. J. Dante's books? Boy, and you're a vampire. You'd think you'd know this stuff."

He slammed on the brakes again, pulling over, much to the annoyance of the car directly behind us. The face he turned to me was filled with suspicion. "Who. Are. You?"

"We've been over this like a dozen times," I said, somewhat exasperated. "OK, three times, but still. I'm Tempest Keye."

"How do you know I'm a Dark One if you are not Victor's woman?"

"I can't say. Wait, actually, I can't discuss *all* of it, but I can tell you that I was at C. J. Dante's castle and saw you there."

"You know Christian?"

"Yes. Kind of. Mostly he asked me to leave, but I did see you there. For a little bit."

"What else did you see?" His voice was gritty, and I could tell he was trying to intimidate me.

"Nothing. There was a conversation about you, but as I said, I can't talk about it because I promised I wouldn't."

He leaned forward, menace rolling off him. "And if I told you that I would make you sorry if you did not tell me?"

"I'd tell you the same thing," I said, swallowing back a little spurt of fear. Maybe I wasn't so comfortable with him as I first thought. After all, what did I know about him other than he was a hell of a lover, and evidently on a crusade to rid the world of some bad people? "A promise is a promise."

He sat back after giving me a long look, and pulled back onto the road. "It is a rare woman who holds true to her word."

"I can only hope that's not a slur against women, because I don't tolerate that crap."

I assure you, the same applies to men.

"Good. To answer your question—to the extent that I can—I know you're a vampire because I had a dream about you."

"Dark One."

"Sorry?"

"We prefer the term Dark One."

"Yeah, but that sounds so ..." I waved a hand around in a vague gesture. "Hollywood. 'Vampire' is sexy and dark and brooding and big box office, whereas 'Dark One' sounds kind of demonic, you know what I mean? I meant to ask C. J. Dante about it, but I didn't get the chance. Where are we going? I don't mind taking a little trip, but I don't want my cousin Carlo to worry, and all my stuff is back at his house."

Merrick said nothing, just drove on with a grimness that was worrying.

"So, this mind-talking thing. You are aware of how that works, right? It's one of the steps."

His jaw tightened.

"There's seven steps that you vamps have to go through before ... glorious grapefruit! Do you know what this means?" I punched him on the arm. "It means I'm your Beloved!"

The protest I was waiting for didn't come, which more than a little surprised me ... and, to be honest, somewhat disappointed me. In every Dark Ones book I'd read, the vampire always protested at first that the heroine wasn't his Beloved, before finally coming to his senses. And yet, here was a real live vampire, and he didn't bat an eyelash at finding out that I was the woman who was put on this earth to save him.

Me! I was a savior! My mind boggled at the serendipity of it all.

"I don't need saving," he said, his attention focused on driving. "And if I did, you would not be my Beloved. As you pointed out, there are steps that must be taken."

"Yes, well." I gave a little cough and ignored my warm cheeks. "As it happens, when I saw you at Dante's castle, I might have ... there was some ... uh ... medical aid given. And we might have exchanged some body fluid."

"You kissed me while I was unconscious?" he asked, disbelief dripping off every word.

"You kissed back," I pointed out.

He said nothing, but his jaw worked a couple of times.

"Anyway, it all boils down to the fact that I'm your Beloved because you're unredeemed, right? According to Dante's books, that means you don't have a soul, and only your Beloved can get it back for you. So that makes me your soul-finder. It's like this was meant to be all along! Why else would my aunt give me Dante's books if I wasn't supposed to be here at this exact moment, poised to save your eternal self? Hoo! Sometimes life really takes your breath away, doesn't it?"

I sat back, my pleasure at how life had worked out fading when he didn't say (or think at me) anything more.

"Well?" I asked him when the silence became too much for me.

"What do you want me to say?" he asked irritably, flashing me an annoyed glance.

"A little excitement wouldn't be out of order," I said, perilously close to snapping at him. What was wrong with him that he wasn't happy at finding me? "Out of all of the millions of people in the world, over all the years you've lived—wait, how old are you?"

"Seven hundred and eighty-two."

I gawked at him, just let my jaw drop and gawked. "You're not!"

"I just said I was." He flashed me another irritated look. "Why do you contradict me? It is annoying, and I don't like it."

"You don't look a day over seven hundred," I told him, ignoring his bossiness. I've found that is the best way to deal with people who try to dominate you. "Where was I? Oh, yes, if you think about all the people in the world who've lived over the last seven hundred and eighty-six years—"

"Seven hundred and *eighty-two*."

"—then it has to boggle your brain that we've managed to come together. According to C. J. Dante's books, not many of you guys find your Beloveds."

"Not every Dark One needs a Beloved. They are a weakness, and some of us must remain strong." He looked nobly martyred, something I wanted to point out, but decided he'd take the wrong way.

"That's one way of thinking about it. Here's another: There's strength in numbers. Two have to be stronger than one. Oh my goodness, I cannot wait to tell Ellis about you! He didn't think vampires existed, not really. He's going to go gaga when he finds out I have a Dark One of my own."

"I am *not* yours. I do not belong to anyone. I am utterly and wholly alone, and I wish to remain that way," he growled.

"Sure you are," I said, going over just what I'd tell Ellis. "This is going to be so awesome, although I have to say, I wasn't planning on coming to Europe to get married."

The look he shot me was filled with disbelief. "Did I, at some point that I'm unaware of, slip into a mental fugue or catatonic state, during which time I asked you to marry me?"

"No, but—"

"Then I believe I have the right to say, without you feeling spurned, that I have no intention on marrying anyone, but most of all you."

"Well!" I said, miffed. "Why me most of all? I'm your Beloved."

"You are *not* my Beloved. What you are is an extremely opinionated woman who doesn't seem to understand the world you've stepped into. That's assuming you're as innocent as you claim to be."

I let the miffed feeling go, having learned long ago not to hold on to negative emotions. I'd seen too much how that affected people, and had made it my personal motto to not give in to negativity. "I don't recall telling you I was innocent."

He sighed heavily. "You said you are not Victor's woman despite being in the location that I found you."

"That was my cousin Carlo's house. There's no one there by the name of Victor."

He gripped the steering wheel tightly, and muttered under his breath.

"You're doing it again," I said conversationally. "You said you'd abuse me to my face next time, and you haven't."

It took a moment for him to speak, because the muscles in his jaw kept flexing, but at last he got them unclenched. "I said that conversation with you was like talking in circles. I never know what you're going to say next."

"Yes, but that's a good thing," I pointed out, and sat back in my seat. "It'll keep us from getting bored over the centuries. Oh! I get to be immortal, too! Hoobah! That's going to be a kick in the pants! Except, of course, for outliving all your friends, but we'll have each other, and that's what is important."

Silence filled the car, a pregnant sort of silence. It lasted for the count of twenty. ""Now that I'm a Beloved—"

"You are not."

"—I'll have to tell Ellis." I sighed happily. "Ellis—he's my friend; you'll like him—doesn't get into the whole vampire thing, although he loved that movie with the sparkly vampires. He said they didn't have their shirts off enough, though."

Merrick grimaced. "I have never understood the mortal fascination with Dark Ones. Vampire lore has permeated modern society at all levels, from gangs of women roaming the streets on the hunt for us, to movies and books and even video games extolling our virtues. Perhaps you can tell me what the attraction is, because it has escaped me."

"Well ..." I bit my lip and considered the matter, sensing that he was speaking the truth. He honestly was puzzled by the fact that women the world over were ready to fling their clothing off and wrestle men like him to the ground. "You guys are all dark and dangerous and sexy."

"Other men are dangerous and sexy," he answered, and I caught an unreadable look slid my way. "Terrorists. Madmen. Homicidal ax-murdering rapists."

"Yes, but they're bad. You vampires are dangerous, but in a thrilling way. Dark Ones don't hurt women."

"I wish that were true, but unfortunately, there are bad Dark Ones just as there are bad mortals."

"Most of you don't hurt others," I amended, and he conceded that point. "And you are loyal, and protective, and have an edge to you that leaves a woman thrilled without being worried she's going to be hacked to pieces and left by the side of the road—stop!"

I shrieked the last word, causing him to once again slam on the car's brakes. Luckily, there weren't many other cars on the road, and he managed to pull over onto the shoulder without endangering us or anyone else.

"What is it now?" he asked, his voice dripping with annoyance.

I had the car door open and was out of it before he finished his sentence, calling over my shoulder as I ran down the side of the road, "There's a dog back there."

"So?" He was out of the car now, too, standing beside it and looking very annoyed.

"This is a fast road, so I can't leave a dog here to be hit. Here, doggy. Come here. Oh, there you are. Hi. You look scared."

The dog, some sort of a white shepherd, shied away and ran past me. I held my breath, wanting to yell lest it run right into the traffic, but luckily, the dog had enough sense to lope along the shoulder, straight toward Merrick.

"Catch it!" I yelled, hurrying after the poor creature.

He didn't need to. The dog ran straight up to him and tried to climb him in its terror. Merrick, with a look that would have made me laugh in a less dire situation, picked up the dog and stood waiting for me.

"Oh, good, he's OK. I thought he was going to run right into the traffic. Let's get him into the car." I opened the back door, gesturing toward the interior.

"You do not honestly expect me to place this stray into one of Christian's expensive cars," he said, his brows together.

"Of course I do. It's our duty to rescue those who need our help," I said self-righteously, and gestured again to the interior.

"Since when?"

"Since you developed a moral compass. Put the dog in, Merrick."

He considered me for a minute. *And if I don't?*

I'll never speak to you again.

That is supposed to be a threat?

"Of course it's a threat, you great big boob!"

He pulled himself up, his shoulders squaring even though he was holding a large white dog to his chest. "I am a Dark One. I walk the night, and am feared by mortal and immortal beings alike. I am *not* a boob."

"You are if you think that losing your Beloved isn't going to make your life a living hades," I pointed out, and tried to pull the dog from his arms.

"I've survived this long without you," he said dismissively. "I don't see any reason I can't go another eight hundred years."

"I am going to ignore how wrong you are, and instead, I will point out that you have to do what your Beloved says."

He gave a short bark of laughter. "In what world is that a rule?"

"In C. J. Dante's books!"

"Perhaps for a Joined pair, but we are not Joined," he said, but to my relief put the dog on the backseat of the car. "Despite your ability to access my thoughts, that does not mean you hold any sway over me. We will get along together better if you remember that."

He moved around to the driver's side while I tried to think of a good comeback for that statement, but my Inner Tempest failed me. She was too busy swooning over just how tight his shirt had been across his muscles while he was holding a dog who must have weighed at least eighty pounds.

I got into the car, and didn't say anything when he drove off, but I thought a lot of things.

Not *all* of them had to do with wanting to get him naked.

CHAPTER SEVEN

"I think the dog is going to be OK. He's curled up asleep back there. When we get to the next town, we can find a twenty-four-hour vet hospital, and have them scan him for a microchip. Maybe he's just lost, and his owners are frantic trying to find him."

The woman, Tempest, spoke just as if she was not in a dangerous situation, with a dangerous man, in a dangerous location. And yet, there she was, prattling on to Merrick about being his Beloved (he gave a mental snort at that idea), the stray she'd forced him to take, and every other subject that flitted through her mind.

"I love dogs."

Of course she did. He had no doubt she also liked butterflies, kittens, and rainbows. He felt quite certain that if he ever saw a rainbow, he'd dislike it intensely.

"My papa would never let me have one, because he said the dogs and cats have no souls, and thus aren't worthy of our love. I call bullcookies on that one. My friend Ellis has a cat, named Jose, who is the most soulful cat you'd ever meet."

She just had no clue about him. How could she sit there, periodically leaning over the back of the seat to check on the mongrel, and chat at him just as if they were going for a nice drive? Did she not realize she had been abducted by a man whom most beings feared?

"I hope we're going toward Tuscany, because I'm going to be meeting my friend Ellis in Genoa in four days."

Did she not grasp the basic concept of danger? Perhaps her mind didn't work that way. Perhaps she was too busy jumping from topic to topic to understand just who he was, and how grave was her situation.

"This is my first time in Europe. It's amazing how much it looks like northern California."

He did not like women who had such trivial thought processes. Even if he was willing to admit she was his Beloved—and he most definitely was not—he wouldn't claim her. She was all glowing brightness, the coppery redness of her hair casting an aura of light and goodness around her that simply would not work in his life. He was dark and shadows, the inky abyss of torment, and she was sunshine and happiness and a free-spiritedness that had no place in his life.

What a shame that was.

He squelched the thought before she could pick it up.

Pick up what? she asked.

He didn't answer her, more than a little discomfited by the ease with which she managed to find her way into his mind. No, he had to let go of such trivial thoughts, and focus on what was important.

He had to find the link to Victor. He knew it was out there, and if Tempest—what a fitting name that was for her; it was as if she were a storm that had come into his life, turning everything he knew upside down—if Tempest wasn't that link, then he needed to find who was.

"What were you doing at Villa Carlo?" he asked her.

"—was a friend from high school, but we lost touch for several years while I took care of my father, and we only just reconnected ... what?"

He repeated his question.

"Oh. I told you, didn't I? Carlo is my papa's cousin, and since I got to Italy early—I'm meeting Ellis here in a couple of days—I figured I'd spend the time until then with Cousin

Carlo. He's not really ..." She frowned while she thought out what she wanted to say.

Merrick didn't like it when she frowned. He much preferred her smile. That seemed to light up all the dark corners of his soul.

He squelched *that* thought, too. He didn't need to be dwelling on the woman's personality, or her wild curls that glowed like gilded copper, or the brightness of her gray eyes. He absolutely would not think about the way her legs had felt when he hefted her over his shoulder, or how enticing her ass was the two times he happened to brush his hand against it. Most of all, he would not remember the scent of her, sun-warmed and vaguely floral, a scent that seemed to sink into his skin and heat his blood.

"He's not really overly friendly. Not that he's not-friendly, if you know what I mean."

Merrick hadn't a clue, but since he enjoyed hearing her talk, he said nothing.

Dammit. Now he was dwelling on the sound of her voice. It was just a voice. She was just a woman. She was nothing to him other than a means to an end.

"He was always foisting me off on his buddy, and let me tell you, that I did not enjoy." She gave a little shiver. "Giovanni has to be a serial killer. Or at least a sociopath. Have you ever met a sociopath?"

"I *am* a sociopath," he said, giving her a look that would have scared the life from a normal mortal.

She smiled at him. She actually smiled, and it bathed him in a warmth that he found both satisfying and annoying.

He didn't want to be warm. He was a Horseman, one of the most feared beings in the Otherworld. He hunted, he captured, and if he had to, he killed. He was not a man to be warmed by a redheaded goddess's smile.

A goddess ... a vague memory wafted through his mind. There was something that had happened at Christian's house, something that just slipped past the grip of memory. He'd been a little foggy in the brain the day that Christian had awoken him, and didn't quite remember what had happened beyond the fact that the Revelation had caught him and almost destroyed him.

Christian had saved him, though. No, not Christian, one of his servants.

Her red hair making a flaming halo around her head as she bent down over him ...

He slammed on the brakes for the fourth time.

"Do you not know how to stop a car properly?" she had the gall to ask him, giving him a glare just as if he was a normal person. "I don't have a driver's license, but even I know you aren't supposed to come to a screeching halt every couple of minutes. For one thing, it has to be hard on the tires."

"The goddess. You are the goddess, the woman who fed me."

Her face lit up with joy. "You do remember! Oh, I'm so relieved! You have no idea how embarrassing it was for me to want to tell you, but it would seem like I was bragging, and then there was the whole thing where we had wild bunny lovin' all over the rug in front of the fireplace, and oh man, there was no way I was going to tell ... you ... about ..." Her voice trailed off as her eyes widened in horror. "You ... you *do* remember that part, right?"

Merrick allowed no expression to escape his iron control, but his mind was frantically digging around its memories. Unfortunately, with the exception of the memory of the woman's hair, and the sensation of life returning to him, there was nothing else.

And what a profound shame that was.

She gasped and covered her cheeks with both hands. "Glorious grape juice, you don't! That's it—I'm going to die of shame right here and now. You have your way, Papa! I had sexual congress with a man without being married, and now I'm doomed!"

Merrick only just managed to keep from rolling his eyes.

He did, however, not only pull back into traffic; he pulled an extremely illegal U-turn and started speeding back the way he'd come.

"What are you doing?" she asked, looking over her shoulder at the direction they had been headed. "Is it because we ... you know ... were intimate? Are you disgusted by me? If you are, then you can just bite my shiny pink behind, because I do not hold with double standards, and if you're disgusted by the fact that I'd engage in carnal relations with a man I just met, then you should be disgusted by yourself, too. In fact—"

"I'm not disgusted by you," he interrupted, annoyed that she'd think that of him. "On the contrary, I'm profoundly grateful that you fed me when you did. I will admit that I am unable to call to mind the exact proceedings that happened after the feeding, but such things are not unknown, and so long as you did not suffer by it, then I'm willing to forget it."

"Forget it!" She smacked him on the arm, clearly outraged.

He would *never* understand women.

"Well, of course you're never going to understand us if that's the sort of attitude you have."

Why are you so angry with me?

Because you want to forget the fact that we had sex.

I said I was willing to forget it because you were just stating that you were going to die of shame. You were distressed, and I simply wished to ease that state.

Oh. He could feel her thinking. "Oh. That's actually quite nice of you. Thank you. Why are we going this way? I thought you were taking me somewhere."

"I was, but that has changed."

She shot him a pointed look. "Because we had nooky time?"

"Because you saved my life. I cannot use someone who saved me."

"Use how?"

He sighed, and thought lovingly of just pulling over and forcing her and the mongrel out of the car, but knew that was not an option. "Because I owe you a debt. I will find another way to reach Victor."

"OK, let's go back over that, because I don't quite understand. Who is Victor?"

"A man who has killed many Dark Ones, and harmed even more mortals."

"Bad guy, then. And why did you think I have something to do with him?"

"You were in his car."

"I was? When?"

"Yesterday. I arrived to find a report from an informant that a man and woman were seen outside of Genoa traveling in his car. Photos were provided. You were in the photo. My informant traced you to the villa where I found you. Thus, you have a connection to Victor."

"But the house and car belong to my father's cousin Carlo, not Victor."

"Then Victor has some connection to him."

She was silent for a few minutes, and Merrick actually found himself missing her effervescent conversation. "I don't know what that could be, but admittedly, I've only been here for a day, and I don't know Carlo at all."

"Are there others in the house?"

"Just the sociopath Giovanni. Oooh! Maybe he's your bad guy? I can totally see him torturing and killing, and kicking puppies."

"Describe him."

She did so.

"He sounds like the man in the photos. I will show them to you, but I suspect your sociopath is not the man I want. There are no pictures of Victor, unfortunately."

"Pooh. So, what do you want me to do?"

He glanced over at her, surprised by her question. "What do you mean?"

She gestured at nothing in particular. "What do you want me to do to help you find Victor?"

"This is not your problem. I told you—I cannot use someone who has saved my life. I will return you to Genoa, where you will take a room at a hotel. Then I will fetch your things from your cousin's house, and you can continue with your vacation."

"I doubt if my cousin would be happy to have you show up to grab my stuff. If you drive me back there, that'll be fine."

"I won't leave you there. It's possible your cousin is Victor."

"It's also possible he's not."

"It's not safe there," he insisted, wondering why she didn't understand this important point.

"Fine," she said, heaving a dramatic sigh. "I won't stay there, but only because Cousin Carlo and I weren't really connecting like I'd hoped we would. I'll get my things and you can take me to a hotel, OK?"

He said nothing, but thought a great many things about her not doing as he instructed.

"You know," she said in a conversational tone that he just knew was going to pave the way to the most outrageous statement. "You're not actually the king of the world. You may think you are, and I bet people treat you like you are because you're big and bad and scary and have pointy teeth—wait, you do have fangs, don't you?—but the truth is that I've spent my life fighting authority, and I have the scars to prove it. So I don't buy this bullcookies about you telling me what I can and can't do any more than I accept being kidnapped."

"You *were* kidnapped."

The look she gave him was filled with pity. "Do you really think I would be here now if I didn't want to? The first thing on my bucket list was to take a self-defense class."

He was silent for a bit. He'd never met a woman like her, and didn't like the unbalanced feeling that she generated in him. On the other hand, he bet he'd never be bored with her, as he was with so many other people.

That's the nicest thing anyone has ever said about me.

Now you are eavesdropping. Stop it. I dislike it.

I don't know, it's kind of fun. Just think about it—when you're off at the grocery store picking up a few things for dinner, I can tell you about something I left off the grocery list.

You are not my Beloved. There will be no grocery list!

Fine.

He waited for the count of eight, knowing there was more to come.

We'll do a grocery delivery service.

"What scars?"

"Huh?"

"What scars do you have? You said you have scars to prove your point. Mental scars, emotional scars, or physical ones?" He pulled off the highway and into the suburb of Genoa where he'd tracked down Victor's villa.

"All of the above." She twisted around in the seat so that her back was to him, reaching behind her as best she could with the seat belt limiting her movements, and pulled down an edge of the back of her dress. "Elder Davenport, who ruled the sect, used to deal out the public punishments. Boys got whipped on their bare behinds, while girls were whipped on the upper back and shoulders. Papa used to protect me from most of the punishments, but there were a couple of times when he was called out to do work with a sister sect, and Elder Davenport made sure I got what he thought I deserved. Most of the whippings didn't leave permanent scars, but one time mine got infected, and left scars. You can still see a couple of stripes on my shoulders."

Rage filled him, red and thick and unbearable. "Where were your parents? Why did they allow you to be tortured so?"

"I told you that Papa was away—the Elders would never touch me when he was around—and my mother thought she was leaving me well protected by my father. Which was the case most of the time. Why are you so angry-sounding about this? It was my punishment, and if I've chosen to forgive the Elders for their stupidity and cruelty, then I don't know why you should sound like you are gargling with lava."

"I am angry because you mention this heinous act just as if it was nothing." He fought to control the rage, afraid of frightening her with the intensity of it.

She placed her hand on his knee. "That's really sweet of you to be so mad on my account, but, Merrick, there's no need. I've fought my whole life against the people of my father's cult, and I've finally made my peace with that past. What happened, happened. I refuse to live my life surrounded by anger and negative emotions when there is so much joy to be had in the world."

He glanced at her, unsure of how to process the emotions she was pouring into him. She truly was at peace with a past filled with abuse and what was little more than neglect, and didn't understand why he was so angry. The rage he still felt fueled a need within him, one that was heightened by her physical contact.

And suddenly, he couldn't cope with it any longer. He pulled the car under the gnarled branches of an old olive tree that hung over the road, and tore the seat belt from his body.

"What—," Tempest said, her eyes huge as he lunged for her, managing to get her out of her seat belt without hurting her or damaging the car. His mouth was on hers before he could think of what he was doing, the emotions inside him threatening to spill out. Her lips parted, allowing him entrance, the taste of her sending his mind reeling.

Yes. This was the taste of the goddess, the one who had danced through his dreams.

Grape juice, you are so hot! So … oooh, you can do that with your tongue? It's so sinful! I love it! Do it again.

He twined his tongue around hers again, the hunger inside growing until it pushed aside the rage. *I do not want to take from you if you are not willing.*

Glorioski, Merrick! She squirmed in his hold, sliding one leg around him and trying to pull him closer. *If you don't bite me right now, I'm going to bite you!*

That is interesting, and I will address that at some future

date, but right now—are you sure? You know what might follow.
Here? In the car? Where anyone can see us?
The tree hides us, the windows are tinted, and it's dark outside.
Hot potato! Bite me!
Only if you are sure—
BITE ME, VAMPIRE!

He managed to pull his mouth from hers, his brain swamped with all sorts of erotic images, things he wanted to do to her, wanted her to do to him, and possibly even some they'd do at the same time to each other, but uppermost in his mind was the hunger, the need to take what she so clearly was offering. He kissed a path along her jaw, down her neck, the red need blinding him to everything but the woman held so awkwardly in his arms. Just as he was about to bite, his lips touched a thickening of skin at the point where her neck met her shoulders, obviously one of her scars. He switched directions, and bit into her upper arm, the taste of her flowing into his mouth satisfying on a level he'd never experienced.

"Oh my good garden gnome, that's ... it stings for about a second, but then it's just ... hooo ... it kind of winds me up, you know. I mean, my breasts feel really sensitive, and my lady garden is just buzzing like crazy. No wonder this ends in sexy times. Although I just don't see how this is going to happen here in the car."

He pulled his mouth from her arm, swirling his tongue over the mark to help it heal, then, without speaking, lifted her up and slid underneath her, reaching down alongside the seat to pull a lever.

"The seat goes back? Whatever will they think of next! Oh, hi, doggy." She giggled at the dog, who obligingly scooted over to the other side of the backseat, allowing Merrick to fully recline.

"Last chance," he told Tempest, his hands sliding up her bare legs, adjusting them so she straddled him.

"To say no? Are you insane? You're a vampire! This is like the ultimate fantasy for tens of thousands of women the world over. Hundreds of thousands!" She rose up and, with fingers that he wanted to praise to the sky, got his belt unhooked and his fly lowered. "Golly. You're a bit bigger than you were before."

"I doubt that." He pulled her down toward him, the hunger not yet sated.

"It must be because you were deflated."

He paused in the act of nuzzling across the exposed upper slopes of her breasts. "I assure you that I'm anything but deflated."

"You were then. It's because you had no blood in you. You know, kind of like a deflated balloon. Am I supposed to do fellatio here? Because if I am, you're going to have to give me some help. I've never done it, and don't exactly know what to do. I mean, it's not the sort of thing I can ask Ellis, is it?"

Another time I would very much like to introduce you to the joys of oral sex, but I am close to the edge now. Kiss me.

Oooh, so demanding. She leaned forward, her lips teasing his in a way that just made him harder, if that was possible. Her mouth was sweet, though, almost as if she'd been eating honey, and wholly intoxicating. He groaned into her mouth when she shifted and positioned him properly, the heat from her body tempting him inside.

Thousands of little muscles seemed to grip him as he entered her, the feeling almost too much to bear. It fired the hunger again. He licked a path to a spot above her right breast, the drawing in his loins causing him to bite the tender flesh, her gasp of pain turning immediately into a moan of ecstasy. *This is ... are you sure we can do it like this? You're so right in there, and merciful heavens, you* are *bigger!*

If I am, it's because you are so hot.

Make me burn, Merrick.

He thrust upward as he drank from her, his body desperate to finish. He had to think of her, though. Evidently she was a neophyte at lovemaking, and he wanted to make it good for her. He reined in his emotions, holding them with an iron grip while he attempted to bring her pleasure. Just when he had himself in check, her sensations flooded his mind in a way that caused his control to go flying.

She arched back when he shouted a wordless cry of exultation, the thousand muscles rippling around him in a manner guaranteed to drive him to the brink of sanity.

"That was ... doggy, no, my face doesn't need washing. That was amazing." Tempest pushed herself up from where she'd collapsed on him, blowing back a few curls that had sprung free from her hair band. "I had no idea it was like that in a car. Is it better in a bed?"

Merrick lifted a wan hand, and wondered if it was out of line to suggest that they take a little nap right there. He'd never felt so drained—or satisfied—in his lengthy life, but he decided it was due to both his recent near-death experience and the unusual situation.

He opened his eyes to find the dog's face mere inches from his. While he glared at it, it licked his nose.

Tempest giggled. "You must be a good person. Even our furry friend there likes you."

"Then he is a poor judge of people. I am not a good person. I am death personified." He leveled his gaze on Tempest. "I am bound to my job, and have no room for anything else in my life. So despite what you think, we have no future together."

The light of humor faded in her eyes, and with it, he felt some corresponding bit of hope inside of him die.

CHAPTER EIGHT

"You can come inside and meet Cousin Carlo, if you like. It's only, what, eleven? I think he's a night owl, because he didn't get up this morning until noonish." I waited until Merrick pulled into the drive for Carlo's house before making that suggestion.

To be honest, I was a bit discombobulated about our recent carnal activities.

Why? You enjoyed yourself.

Stop eavesdropping.

But more than that, I was feeling somewhat deflated. Not by the experience itself—

Good. I made sure you enjoyed yourself.

Stop it!

But because of what he'd said afterward. That he could share something so wonderful, so ... primal ... and then tell me that we had no future together when clearly we did, well, that said a lot about the sort of man he was.

I've been telling you that all along. I'm sorry that you are disappointed, but I believe in honesty wherever possible.

"There's honesty, and then there's brutal frankness when there should, according to movies, be pillow talk." I pointed at the gate. "You don't have to buzz. It's open."

"There were no pillows involved, so I don't see the lack of pillow talk as worth commenting on."

"That's not what I meant, and I know you know that, because I can feel you thinking at me. No, don't bother objecting," I said, holding up my hand to stop his protest as he pulled up at the front of the house. "It's clear you don't want anything from me but blood and nooky, so we won't discuss it further. C'mon, doggy."

"One moment." He put a hand on me to stop me from leaving the car. "It's not safe for you to go in. Not until I've ascertained the true identity of your cousin."

"If he wanted to hurt me, he could have done so well before this," I pointed out. "And don't think I don't know that you're making this statement to distract me from the fact that you treated me pretty rotten after our car interlude, because I know you are. Doggy, heel!"

The dog obediently trotted after me when I stomped my way up the white stone steps to the front doors of the villa.

"I have no intention of distracting you from anything, although I will point out that I did ask you if you were sure you wished to continue before I fed and we had sex," Merrick said, following. "You agreed to my terms, if you recall."

"Here's the thing," I said, spinning around at the door to face him. Merciful marshmallows, he was gorgeous. The light from the sconces on either side of the double doors lit him with a warm amber glow, burnishing his dark hair, and emphasizing the line of his jaw.

I *loved* his jaw.

"I may not have had sexual relationships with an actual person before, but even I know that you don't set terms for what we have together. Whether you like it or not, we have a connection, and you grinding your teeth and insisting we don't isn't going to change that fact."

"Neither is embracing the impossible with open arms. Do not mistake me for one of the characters in Christian's books," he said, climbing the steps and standing so close to me, I could feel his breath on my lips. "I am not a romantic figure yearning for a woman to redeem my soul. What soul I might have had has been destroyed long ago because of the work I do. If I focus my attention on you instead of my job, people will die—mortals and immortals alike. Do you want to live with that?"

"No, but—"

"Then you will accept that we have no future together." He strode past me, and for a moment, I felt like slamming the doors and collapsing into a puddle of tears, but I haven't survived hell for most of my life just to give in when a pigheaded, annoying man doesn't know a good thing when it walks up and kisses the dickens out of him.

I object to pigheaded.

If the pig head fits, wear it, I said stormily, and pushed by him to enter the house and call out, "Cousin Carlo? I'm back. I went off with a friend for a little bit, but we're back now, and I want to introduce you."

Silence, thick and heavy, was the only answer.

"Cousin Carlo? Giovanni? Hello?"

"We will search," Merrick said, and went to the nearest door. We looked through every room on the ground floor, including the library where I'd first seen Carlo. The desk was still littered with papers, and both Merrick and I had a quick look at them. They appeared to be financial portfolio statements, as well as some prospectuses for a variety of investment opportunities.

"Bedrooms upstairs?" Merrick asked when we exhausted the possibilities downstairs. It certainly seemed like Carlo and Giovanni were gone, but the lights were all on, the front door was unlocked, and the gate had been left open.

"Yes. Mine is, at least," I said, leading him up the curving stairs. "What do you think has happened to them?"

"I don't know. If we find a laptop or a safe, perhaps we can determine what your cousin has been up to."

"You're assuming he's been up to anything suspicious," I pointed out. We started the search of the second floor, and after glancing into my room, Merrick opened the door to a small room at the back of the house. It was clearly a bedroom, but I didn't see anything exciting in it. "Probably Giovanni's room," I said, leaving the room after a quick glance around it. I opened another door, finding a desk in front of a wall with three large monitors.

When I turned around to tell Merrick about my find, I saw him hauling Giovanni's bed into the middle of the room.

"What on earth are you doing?" I asked, returning to the room.

"Finding this." Merrick pointed to the floor.

A black panel sat flush in the floor, the door of it open.

"Is that a safe? Wow. I didn't know people really had them put into floors. And Giovanni slept over it?"

"What better way to ensure it was guarded?" Merrick asked, kneeling and reaching down into the safe. "Looks like they took the contents. Which means your cousin isn't the innocent you believe."

I stared down at the empty black safe, and shifted my mental picture of Carlo. "I guess not. I found a sort of office, if you want to have a look there."

Merrick followed me to the small room and glanced around it. "Ah. I wondered where the security cameras fed to. This is clearly where your cousin monitored the property."

"Recognize someone?" I asked, pointing to the monitors.

He did a double take at one, then slid a look toward me. "You know what that means, I assume."

"The fact that a close-up of you standing with me next to your car is frozen on the screen? Yes, I assume that, coupled with my cousin's obvious hasty departure, is proof that he is the guy you're looking for." I sat down in a chair for a moment, trying to process the information that my cousin was clearly not what I thought he was.

"Or if not, he knows who Victor is," Merrick said grimly, and quickly searched the room.

"This just leaves me feeling ... I don't know. Disappointed. Kind of scared that I can be so misled. And really, really wondering if all of Papa's side of the family are off their rockers. Do you think this proves my cousin is Victor? Because I might just scream and burst into tears if it turns out I'm related to a world-class villain."

Merrick was silent for a few moments. "It's not definitive proof, no, but it's not an indicator of a selfless and altruistic nature." He stood next to me and looked down at where I sniffled back the start of a couple of tears. "You are hurt by this knowledge. I can feel the pain within you. I dislike you feeling this way. It will do no good, and will not help catch Victor. You will stop feeling bad now."

I hiccuped a little weak laugh. "I wish emotions were that easy to cope with. But I know what you mean, although you said it badly and super bossy. Crying isn't going to help, and neither is feeling betrayed. Cousin Carlo is what he is, just as Papa was what he was. I'm going to focus my emotions on helping you find Carlo so we can know for certain if he is guilty or not."

"I do not need your help finding him. It's not safe for you to do so," Merrick announced, and, without another word, left the room and headed downstairs.

"I'm seriously getting tired of you making obnoxious statements like that just like you're the king of the world. Hey, Merrick, wait up. What are you going to do now?" I asked, following him, the dog on my heels.

"Try to pick up his trail before it gets cold."

I grabbed his arm when he was obviously going to leave. "Hang on. Let me get my things. It won't take me but a minute, since I didn't really unpack."

He looked down at my hand on my arm, his eyes icy blue. "You aren't coming with me."

"Don't be silly. Of course I am."

He took a deep, outraged breath. "There are times when I wonder if I'm just talking to amuse myself. I've told you who I am and what I do. I've told you that mortals and immortals fear me, and that you are not my Beloved. Since your cousin is not here, I will arrange to have you picked up shortly and taken to a hotel where you will be safe."

"I know, I know, you're Mr. Denial," I said, waving a hand and turning around to dash back up the stairs. "But you're ignoring three important things."

I knew he wouldn't be able to resist that, and I was right. After a moment of inner struggle, he asked, "What three things?"

I paused at the top of the stairs long enough to throw him a smile and say, "One, you can't leave me here alone. Two, I *am* your Beloved whether or not you want to face that fact. And three ..."

"Yes?" he asked when I hesitated.

I shrugged. "I don't want to be left alone. I don't know anyone in this country, I don't speak the language, and I'm vulnerable. I need you."

His sigh was filled with antagonism, but I didn't let that worry me. I grabbed the few items of clothing that were laid on a chair, and stuffed them into my suitcase, saying, "If you have to go potty, doggy, do it now before we get in the car. I have a feeling Merrick isn't going to be happy with the idea of potty breaks."

The hall was empty when, five minutes later, the dog and I stumbled down the stairs, my two large suitcases bumping after me.

"Well, pumpkin rot!" I swore, going to the front door. Maybe Merrick was sitting in his car waiting impatiently for me.

The drive was just as empty as the hall. A little flutter of yellow caught my eye. A note was stuck onto one of the white stone columns. *It is not safe for you to be with me* was all it said. *A taxi will be here soon.*

Hurt pierced me, a hurt tinged with a deeper sense of betrayal than that caused by Cousin Carlo. I stood for a moment, the note in my hand, not believing that Merrick had really left. How could he just drive away from me? What about everything that Christian had written about in his books? None of those Dark Ones had been able to leave the one woman whom they loved above all else.

There is no love, Inner Tempest said sadly. *Lots of lust, sure, and some pretty impressive bow-chica-bow time, but no love.*

"Well, this is just the limit," I told the dog, slumping down on the steps, everything about me crestfallen, from my heart right down to my posture. "Cousin Carlo is most likely a bad guy and ran away from me. Merrick abandoned me. Criminy beans, how can he not realize that we're supposed to be together? Everything says we are. What an annoying vampire. Nowhere in C. J. Dante's books does he mention how downright annoying they are."

The dog licked my hand in obvious agreement.

"Now what are we supposed to do?"

A car pulled into the drive and came to a screeching stop in front of me before I could do more than wonder how much of a distance our mental link would work across.

"Get in," Merrick said, leaning over to open the passenger door.

I stared at him for a couple of seconds. "You're annoying. You are stubborn. You don't know a good thing when you see it. I'm not sure I want to go anywhere with you."

"And you're too cheerful, see the good in everything, and believe what you read in those damned books of Christian's. Get in."

I sniffed, thought about telling him to take a flying leap, but instead rose with infinite dignity, and let the dog into the backseat. "All right, but I want it understood that you hurt my feelings by leaving me more than my cousin did."

"I came back for you." He glanced at his watch. "I've only been gone four minutes."

"Doesn't matter. You left me, your almost-Beloved, behind. With a dog."

He looked like he very much wanted to roll his eyes, but instead got out and took my suitcases, tossing them into the trunk of the car. "I'm sure that thought will haunt me for years, but I will strive to overcome it and focus on the job of ridding the world of monsters like Victor."

"Hrmph," I said, and slid into the passenger seat.

Silence reigned for about ten minutes as we retraced the route that headed south.

You can't live without me.

He glanced my way. *I can do so quite easily, as a matter of fact.*

I read the books, Merrick. I know that once you find your Beloved, you can't distance yourself.

That's not true.

C. J. Dante says it is. Is that why you came back? Because you missed me? Or was it because you were hungry?

"Christian has a lot to answer for," he muttered under his breath, then said louder, "We aren't Joined, Tempest. Until then, I am not irrevocably bound to you."

"That's right, there are more steps. Let's see...we must be up to step four or so by now. More than halfway through them," I said with particular significance that he ignored.

"I doubt if we've done more than two steps," he said, his eyes moving between the rearview mirror and the road in front of us.

"There's the mind thing—that's marking, according to the books." I turned around as best I could with the seat belt on, and patted the dog, taking the opportunity to look out behind us. There were a few cars on the road at this hour, but not a whole lot of traffic. I wondered if Merrick saw something I didn't. "Then the kissing, which I have to say is pretty spectacular. How many lovers have you had?"

The look he sent my way was one of disbelief. "Why do you want to know?"

"Well, I was technically a virgin before we got together, although I ... you know ... have toys. I mean, I didn't have them before my father died, but once he was gone, I kind of ran amok in a sex toy shop. If you're ever in the market for a vibrator, I'm your girl."

"I will keep that in mind," he said without the slightest twitching of his lips, but I felt his amusement, and relaxed a little. I didn't want to spend the rest of my life with a man who didn't have a sense of humor.

"So it will be nice to know that one of us can bring lots of experience to the sexual table." I patted him on his thigh. "We can both contribute. I'll be the source of info as to which vibe carries the biggest bang for the buck, and you can demonstrate lots of positions and interesting sexual additions like blindfolds."

"Into bondage, are you?" Now he did look amused, although the expression faded almost immediately.

"No." I looked out of the window, noting absently the streetlights of cross streets blurring past us.

"You surprise me."

I said nothing, still watching the lights.

Have I said something to offend you?

Why would you think that?

Because I can feel your distress. Is it because I am not interested in your sexual toy reviews?

"Goodness, no. I'll give you those whether or not you want them, because I think you're closed to new experiences until you see how fabulous they are. You know, how you are with me."

"Then why are you upset?"

I picked through my words carefully. "One of the promises I made to myself when I was younger was that I wasn't going to be a victim. I wasn't going to dwell on what happened in the past. I was going to put it all behind me, and move forward."

"And that has something to do with sex?"

"No. It has something to do with being tied up as punishment." I kept my eyes on the lights, refusing to let the darkness that those memories brought with them fill me. I'd worked too hard to expunge the dark from my soul to let it back now. "Bondage isn't a fun thing for me. It's something to endure."

"I see." Anger burst through the car, a sort of red haze of anger that seeped into every pore. A spurt of adrenaline accompanied my brain's being filled with images of vengeance against nameless men.

Wait ... nameless men? Is this you getting so furious again? I told you when you got mad about the beatings that it was in the past. I've made my peace with it. I just don't happen to like being hit or tied up.

Merrick snarled into my head something quite rude.

Clearly, the situation needed to be lightened a bit. I did what I could to downplay the events of the past. "Buzzing bumblebees, Merrick! Why are you so angry because my father was part of a whackadoodle cult, and the Elders clearly had issues with women? It couldn't be in part because you know deep down I'm your Beloved, could it?"

"I dislike anyone being abused," he said self-righteously. "It's one of the things I have fought so long against, in case you missed that point of my repeated discussions of just what it is I do, and why I do not need or want a Beloved."

"Well, lucky you, you got one anyway," I said, and decided to put a little icing on the cake. I leaned over and gave him a loud kiss on the cheek.

The look of outrage he seared me with in response gave me immense satisfaction.

It wasn't long after that we found a twenty-four-hour vet hospital. The tech there kindly scanned the white dog's entire body for a microchip, but came up blank.

"The man says they can't take the dog unless you are abandoning him, and then there will be a charge," Merrick told me, translating for the tech. He reached for his wallet, and started pulling out cash.

"There's no need for that," I said loudly, glaring at him, and taking the thin emergency leash the vet hospital offered. "Kelso is coming with me."

"Kelso?"

"I just named him, now that I know he's not chipped.

Here, give him my number, and tell them to call me if the dog's owner comes looking for him." I walked out without another word to Merrick.

You can't keep a dog, he told me when I marched out to the car.

Why not?

Stranger in a strange place, remember?

Now I'm a stranger with a dog.

The next five hours aren't worth recording, since they mostly consisted of me sleeping, with one break while Merrick got gas in the car, and I took the dog for a potty break before taking my own.

"Where are we going?" I asked at that point, rubbing my face as I blinked at the bright neon lights of the gas station. Merrick shoved a bottle of water and a bag of chips at me before squatting down and pouring some water in a bowl for Kelso.

"To a small town you have most likely never heard of."

"Really? What's there?" Absently, I opened the chips and started munching on them, smiling to myself when Merrick offered Kelso a sandwich, which he happily wolfed down.

"My villa." Merrick returned to the car and waited for the dog and me to get settled before returning to the road.

"Why are we going to your house? And wait, aren't you Irish? Why do you live in Italy?"

He gave a mock sigh. *Do you always ask so many questions?*

Only when I want answers.

I was born in Ireland, but moved to Italy a few centuries ago.

Oh. Why?

Because I liked it!

Sheesh, I just asked. Silence filled the car for about five minutes. *Why are we going to your house?*

It's the only place where I can ensure your safety.

"My safety?" I shook my head, feeling like my brain wasn't functioning so well after the nap I'd just taken. "Why on earth do you keep imagining that Cousin Carlo wants to hurt me? He knew who I was before you kidnapped me."

"He didn't know your connection to me," he pointed out.

I rubbed my face again. I had a serious wrinkle from where my face had been pressed against the door. "That's right. He did have that picture of us together frozen on the monitor. I don't see that he'd want to hurt me, though. Not because I let myself be kidnapped."

"If he is Victor, then he would not hesitate to destroy you in order to get to me." There was something more to his sentence, but he must have been hiding his thoughts from me, because all I got was an echoing sensation in my head.

I went back to sleep not long after that conversation. By the time we reached Merrick's villa, the sun was coming up, my back was cramping from being in the car for six hours, and I had to pee again.

"What are we doing here?" I asked when Merrick woke me up. We were stopped in a small square parking area, lined on either side by gray stone walls. Ahead of us was a silver metal doorway apparently cut into a vertical rock face.

"This is my home." He got out of the car, and went to the trunk to get my luggage.

I got out slowly. "You live in a cave?"

"No, I live in a house eighty meters up. That's an elevator."

"Eighty meters ... that's like two hundred and fifty feet. Wow. I don't think I've ever met anyone who had an elevator set into a cliff just to get to their house. Come on, Kelso. I bet you're going to be happy to have a yard to run around in. Wait, you do have a yard? A fenced one?"

"There's no fence, but there is no way in or out of the gardens from the outside." Merrick cast a sour glance at the dog when we followed him into a small elevator. "Please confine him to the lowest garden. I don't need him soiling the other areas."

"Just how many gardens are there?" I asked, more impressed than I wanted to admit.

"Four. What is your birth date?"

"August eleventh. Why?"

He punched something into the panel on the elevator wall. "I've just set the code to zero eight one one. You will have to enter that to use the elevator."

"Nifty," I said.

The doors opened and I gasped at the sight that met my eyes. Floodlights shone up on the long front of a house painted the color of goldenrod, dotted with white shutters and French doors down the length, and bisected with a long narrow balcony that that was heavily covered in some sort of green vines. In front of the house, a lush green lawn spread out toward the sea, visible even though the sun was just starting to lighten the sky. "Criminy noodles! This is some sort of gorgeous. I bet the view is breathtaking in daylight."

"I wouldn't know," Merrick said drily, and unlocked a door. I released Kelso, who happily trotted off, his nose to the ground, the white plume of his tail waving gently in the darkness.

"Why not—oh! Vampire. Sunlight." I eyed him as we entered the villa. "So that's true? You burn up into little black blobs of nothing if you go out in the sun?"

"No, but it's not particularly enjoyable to be in sunlight."

"What happens to you?"

He set down my suitcases, and pulled out his phone. "We blister."

"Is that all?" I glanced around the room, pleasantly surprised. I don't know what I expected Merrick's home to look like—something out of a German expressionist's nightmare, all white and black and angles everywhere—but this room was Mediterranean cozy with pale acid-washed-jeans blue walls, darker blue sofa, love seat, and chairs, and, overhead, thick wooden beams that had been stained a honey oak color.

"It can be deadly if we are confined for a length of time in full sunlight, so, yes, that's all." He nodded toward a staircase. "You can use the room at the top of the stairs just on the left."

"This place is breathtaking," I said, noting a dining room beyond the living area. The house was clearly built to utilize the view, with lots of windows and French doors opening onto the lawn and the sight of the sea beyond. "How many rooms does it have?"

"Six." He finished with whatever text message he was sending, and took both cases upstairs. I followed after him, counting three bookcases in the living room alone. I couldn't wait to see what sort of reading taste he had. "There is a bathroom attached to your room."

I entered the room he indicated. A large bed sat against the wall, facing a bank of windows, which Merrick opened after setting down my suitcases. "Pretty room."

"I'm sure you are tired after being up all night." He nodded toward a bed swathed with mosquito netting. It looked like something out of *The Arabian Nights*.

"Not with all the sleeping I did in the car." I looked around. "This isn't your bedroom, is it?"

"No. Mine is down the hall on the right. I'll have some food brought in for you." He pulled out his phone again when it made a burbling sound. "And food for the dog. There's a key to the front door in the top left bureau drawer in the main room downstairs. If you like, I can have a rental car delivered for you to use."

"Thank you," I said, warmed by the thoughtfulness of his gestures. "That's very kind of you, especially considering you didn't want me to be around."

"Here is my mobile number." He pulled out a card and wrote a phone number on the back. "Although I would ask you not to call unless the situation is desperate."

"Desperate," I repeated, a suspicion slowly starting to dawn in my brain. "Situation?"

"If you hear from your cousin, tell me immediately." Merrick glanced around the room, then turned and left.

I stood staring for a few minutes, the suspicion growing until it propelled me out the door and down the stairs. I caught up to him at the elevator. "Wait a minute—you're leaving me here?"

"Yes." He stepped into the elevator and punched a button.

"You can't do that!" I objected.

"You need not fear for your safety. You will be safe here. You may have the run of the house and gardens. There's a pool on the side. The town is small, with few tourists, but you might find it interesting."

"You can't just dump Kelso and me like this!" I stuck my arm out to block the elevator doors.

He made an annoyed noise, and tried to move my hand. "I just told you that you will be safe here."

"Safety is not my issue with the situation. Where are you going?"

"I have a job to do." His gaze was level, but I could feel the anger within him. It burned white, different from the red hunger, but no less potent.

"And I want to help you with it! Don't give me that look— you're not thinking things through properly." I clutched the elevator doors tightly. "Who knows Carlo? I do. Who would recognize him if she saw him in a crowd? I would. Who can help you find him? That's right, me."

"How?" he asked, his expression wary.

I waved my hands around in an attempt to distract him from the fact that I really hadn't a clue what I was talking about. "He's ... he's family. That will help me find him."

Merrick gave a disbelieving snort and pried one of my hands from the door.

Desperately, I grabbed at the first thing I could think of. "What about eating? If you're going to be gone longer than a few hours, you're going to need to eat, aren't you? C. J. Dante says that now that we've hooked up, you can't feed elsewhere."

His eyes narrowed, and I could feel him thinking that through. I braced for him to deny again that we had a physical connection, but instead, he said, "There are other sources of food."

"Such as?" I asked, a spike of jealousy zinging through me.

"Animals. We can feed from them if we have to."

"Ew." I wrinkled my nose. "That sounds unpleasant, and can I point out how insulting it is that you'd rather eat from some cow or horse or whatever you find to guzzle in order to avoid me?"

"It's not ideal, but if it's what has to be done, then so be it." He pried my other hand off the door, but rather than pushing me out of the elevator, he wrapped both hands around me and pulled me up against his chest, his mouth on mine before I could even gasp in joy. Instantly, my body went into pure celebration mode, sending off little fireworks and starting up the brass band of welcome.

You sure do know how to kiss, I moaned into his mind at the same time I pulled his shirt out of his pants, running my hands all over the lovely planes of his back. *I'd like to thank each and every one of those women who you've had relationships with over all the centuries, because the work they did has paid off.*

Normally women are jealous of any past partners, he pointed out, a sense of amusement in the back of his head. *Trust you to turn that upside down and want to thank them.*

Why shouldn't I? It's not like you're cheating on me to go learn how to kiss. Also, could you please do that thing with your left hand again?

His hand, which had slipped down into the bodice of my dress, was currently engaged in tormenting my right breast, his thumb gently stroking my nipple while his fingertips grazed the underside of my breast.

"You must stay here," he said, his mouth hot on my jaw and neck. "I'll know you're safe if you're here."

"But I can help you. Oh, grape juice, not the spot behind my ear. That's ... it's like kryptonite. My knees go weak when you nibble there."

He nibbled, his arms strong around me when my legs gave way. He turned so that my back was up against the wall of the elevator, the cold of the metal on my back a stark contrast to the hot man pressing against me. *I won't be able to do my job if I'm worried about your safety,* he said.

I don't know why you're so convinced that someone is going to want to harm me, but I appreciate it. I also dispute it. Let me help you, Merrick. Let me help find my dad's cousin so he can be locked away where he can't hurt anyone. Let me do something good. Let me into your life.

You are in my life, he said with a growl, and instantly, I was filled with hunger, a need for him, for us to be joined together, for the life to flow between us.

You say that like it's a problem. Bite me!

His teeth pierced the flesh of my neck, that fraction of a second's pain fading instantly away to a heat that flowed down my neck and settled deep in my belly.

I squirmed against him, both hands now desperate to touch all of him. His hands left my breasts, and slid down my hips to my thighs, where they found their way under my dress.

"You don't—we're not—you can't—oh, merciful joy of all beings, yes! You won't hurt your back doing this?"

I writhed against him as his clever, clever fingers managed to divest me of my underwear. His mouth moved around to my shoulder, where he bit a second time, pushing me almost to an orgasm just by the pleasure that he was feeling from the act.

Luckily, he managed to get his fly undone, because I was a mindless ball of erogenous putty in his hands.

Wrap your legs around me, he instructed, lifting me up a few inches.

I've never done this standing up, I managed to babble into his mind, locking my feet together around his back. *This is so … so wicked! Can I bite you?*

His eyes flashed a pale icy blue at the moment he slid into my body. *Bite me where?*

I don't care. I want to do the blood exchange, Merrick. I want to be your Beloved properly. I want all the steps.

He kissed me, his hips working hard against me, the thrusts making the elevator shimmy a little. My tongue twined around his, one hunger diminished while the other raged unchecked. I dug my fingers into his shoulder muscles, my back arching when he increased his pace until I slipped over the edge. My legs tightened around him just as my intimate muscles did the same, which had him groaning with pure pleasure as he gave back the life he'd taken from me.

I held him tight as little aftershocks of pleasure swept over me, my brain having a hard time coming to grips with the sensations that he poured into it, acting like an echo of my own experience.

"That's amazing that you can do that standing up," I said in between gasps for air. I was pleased to note that he was breathing just as hard, feeling that if I was going to be totally wiped out by our lovemaking, it was only fair that he was, as well. "I'm not sure that I could hold up another person like that. I feel like my legs are made of gelatin as is."

He held on to my hips while I unlocked my legs and let them slide down until I was standing again. My inner thighs felt especially quivery.

"It's not my preferred venue for seduction, but it did the job," was all he said.

I stood with my hands still on his shoulders, looking deep into those eyes, now a dark sapphire blue. "Let me be your Beloved, Merrick. Let me redeem your soul from wherever it is—C. J. Dante was never very clear about that in his books—and make you whole again. You know as well as I do that what we have isn't something you can set aside. We were meant to be together. I feel that to the tips of my toes."

He said nothing, but an interesting array of emotions passed over his face, from male smugness to regret, longing, and finally anger.

"Merrick, don't do this," I warned, feeling his intentions if he said nothing. "Don't close me out. I can help."

"At the risk of your own life?" He shook his head, and put me out of the elevator. "I might be many things, Tempest, but I am not a man who willingly risks the life of innocents. And you, sweet goddess, are very innocent. The monster Victor would destroy you simply for the pleasure of corrupting your soul."

"If he wanted to do that, he could have done so earlier," I protested.

"He didn't know who you really were," he answered, and punched a button on the elevator.

"Who am I?" I asked him, confused about what he was saying. "His cousin, you mean? Or your Beloved?"

He didn't answer, the doors closing with a near-silent whoosh, but I felt the echo of thought in his head.

You are the hope that I cannot have.

CHAPTER NINE

The texts started almost immediately. I just knew Merrick wouldn't be amused by them.

To: Merrick
You may think you can run away after having extremely fabulous sex in an elevator—something I hadn't even thought of adding to my bucket list, but which I'm putting on now just so I can cross it off—but you can't deny the connection we have.

From: Merrick
Fifteen minutes. I'm surprised you lasted that long before using my phone number. What part of "don't contact me unless it's an emergency" was unclear?

To: Merrick
This *is* an emergency. I need to know where you are going.

From: Merrick
Why?

To: Merrick
Because I'm your freakin' Beloved, that's why. Well, almost. I would be if you had let me bite you.

From: Merrick
I'm going to Nice. That's all you need to know.

To: Merrick
Oooh. Nice is on the places-to-visit list that Ellis and I made up before I left. What are you doing there?

From: Merrick
Following leads and trying to find a thief taker.

To: Merrick
A what, now?

From: Merrick
It's the Otherworld equivalent to bounty hunter.

To: Merrick
Wow. You guys have that? Cool. Wait, are you driving while texting? You know that's super dangerous, right?

To: Merrick
Also, don't think I didn't notice you continue to refuse to address the connection issue. Re: us. Stuffing me in your fabulous villa on the gorgeous Italian Riviera isn't a solution.

To: Merrick
Your pool is seriously awesome, though. Kelso and I had a dip in it. Do you have the number of your pool cleaner handy? Kelso's shedding a bit.

The response to the last was something in Italian.

To: Merrick
I ran *che palle* through the translator, and I agree. *What balls* indeed. Hadn't figured you were the braggart type, though.

From: Merrick
Stop texting me, woman!

Fine. We can do it this way instead. Hey, what's the distance limit of mind-talking?
A sigh echoed in my head. *I have no idea.*
Merrick, we really do need to talk about this.
No, we don't.
I understand that you feel it necessary to protect me—
This conversation is over. If you think driving while texting is dangerous, try driving while grinding your teeth.
Hrmph.

The balance of the day consisted of me taking naps, receiving the grocery delivery that Merrick had obviously arranged for Kelso and me, floating in the pool while trying to mind-talk to Merrick (he didn't answer, so either he was ignoring me or he was out of range of my mental transmitter), and exploring the house.

"Let's go see Merrick's room," I told Kelso that evening, after we'd watched a gorgeous sunset over the water. We had explored the grounds, and now turned our attention to the house. The room Merrick had given to me was done in shades of delft blue and white, while the other guest room was papered in pretty pale olive wallpaper.

"I'm interested to see what his room says about him. I bet it's all monochrome modern furniture with straight lines and no curves, and possibly the heads of the bad guys he's captured mounted on the walls." I opened the door to the master suite, flipped on the light, and promptly sucked in almost all the air available.

The furniture was a dark wood, mahogany most likely, while the soft furnishings were done in a simple black-and-white stripe theme. Very minimal, very clean, and utterly emotionless, as I expected. Only the walls belied the true passionate nature that Merrick clearly hid from others: they were covered in trompe l'oeil paintings depicting the glorious view of the Riviera coast directly outside the windows.

"This is ... hoppin' hippos, this is just beautiful," I said aloud, slowly turning in a half circle to take in the artwork. "I wonder if it exactly matches the view."

I opened a pair of French doors and stepped out onto a small balcony, then leaned back inside to look at the walls. The landscape perfectly matched the paintings. They depicted a gorgeous sunny day, complete with the busy little port town down below, boats dotting the water, and seabirds wheeling overhead.

"What a clever idea for a man who can't go out into the sun. And it's just more proof that there's a whole lot more depth to Merrick than he likes people to know."

Kelso jumped on the bed, and curled up at the foot of it.

I pursed my lips at the sight of the bed, thought about my blue and white room, and two minutes later, having locked the doors and turned out the lights, snuggled down into Merrick's bed, the faint scent of him rising from the pillow.

Good night, wherever you are, I sent out into the Merrick-sphere.

There was no answer.

Three days later, I was zipping along in a red convertible, on a road leading from Genoa toward the French border, the wind whipping my hair around my face. "You're probably tired what with the jet lag and all, huh? We can find a hotel once we get to Nice."

"Nice?" Ellis looked around us as if he'd just noticed we'd left Genoa proper. "I thought we were going to stay in Genoa for a few days, then go to Florence?"

"Change of plans. We're going to Nice."

"Why?"

"I need to find someone who's supposed to be there. At least he was as of last night's text, when he admitted that he had trouble finding someone he was looking for, but that the person was supposed to roll into town today." I gave Ellis a sympathetic look. "You can take a nap while I'm trying to find my friend, if you like."

"Darling, I slept on the plane almost the whole way, thanks to my friend Brady's handy way with look-alike pharmaceuticals." Ellis stretched and leaned back against the car seat. "This sun is heavenly, though, just heavenly. It was raining when I left home. And isn't this road pretty! When did you learn to drive? I wouldn't imagine your overprotective papa would have allowed it."

"I had a lesson after Papa died," I told him, whipping around a corner, enjoying the speed and power of the car. Merrick certainly had excellent taste in vehicles, although I doubted if he got to use a convertible much.

"A lesson? Was that enough to get your driver's license?"

"Nope. I was supposed to do the whole course to get ready for the driver's test, but I got distracted by this trip."

The sound of the wind rushing past us was the only noise for the count of fifteen. "Pull over!"

"What?" I risked a glance at him. "Why?"

"Do as I say!"

Figuring he might suddenly be carsick, I pulled out onto one of the many overlooks that allowed people to take shots of the glittering blue water. "Are you feeling sick? I have some water in a cooler in the back with Kelso."

Ellis got out of the car and marched around to the driver's side, pointing at the seat he'd just vacated. "Move."

"Why?" I repeated, frowning.

"Because you don't have a license."

"So? I drove all the way to Genoa without a problem. I picked you up at the airport, and that traffic was brutal. I'm driving peachy keen, so I don't see why you're making such a big fuss."

"Move!" he said louder, his lips narrowed in obstinacy.

I sighed, and moved over to the other seat. "You're awfully bossy now that you're on the other side of the world."

"Self-preservation is not bossiness. Since I see you're puffing up to tell me that your driving wasn't going to kill us, I'll ask you instead how your visit went to your auntie's friends. Did you meet all the vampires in Europe?"

"Just two of them, actually," I said, looking over my shoulder to check on Kelso. I'd managed to find a pet store in Genoa that sold not only dog seat belts, but also canine goggles intended for rich people's dogs, all of which meant that my white furry friend was now strapped securely into the backseat, his blue goggles giving him a particularly dashing appearance as he happily snuffled the air while we zoomed along on the coast road.

"You're kidding!" Ellis turned a startled face to me, the sun glinting off his dark glasses. "Darling, this is me, your oldest friend. You don't have anything to prove to me. I've seen your coochie glued to a bath mat—there's nothing to be ashamed of just because you've found out that the books you love aren't based on reality."

"But they are! No, really, don't give me that pitying look—I met two vampires. Look, see where Merrick bit me last?" I lifted the hair from my neck, showing him that spot near my ear that made me weak in the knees when Merrick nuzzled it.

Ellis glanced quickly. "There's nothing there but neck, adorable one. Who's Merrick when he's at home?"

"He's one of the vampires. He's ... for lack of a better word, he's my boyfriend."

Ellis gawked at me, although he managed to keep his eyes on the road while he did so. I made a mental note to practice that, since my driving lesson hadn't covered the art of safety-conscious gawking. "You didn't!"

"I sure did," I said with no little amount of smugness.

"You hooked up already? Did you meet him on the plane or something?"

"Nope. Saw him for the first time ..." I counted back. "About a week ago. But he was unconscious that time. I saw him again soon after, and that's when I realized that he was a vampire, and I was his Beloved, and just as soon as he's willing to admit that, he'll fall in love with me, and we'll live happily ever after."

"There's nowhere for me to stop," he answered. "Do me a favor and feel your forehead. If you are feverish, you may want to lie down in the back with your furry friend. You didn't tell me how he came to join our party, but that can wait until we find out what recreational drugs you've imbibed."

"None, and I don't have a fever, nor am I insane, which I know will be the next thing you suggest. Merrick is a vampire, a bona fide vampire, and he's mine, although he doesn't quite want to admit that yet."

The look Ellis slid my way spoke volumes. "Sweetness, far be it from me to suggest that you're having some sort of PTSD thing going on after your time in the bizarro cult, but do you know if there is a mental health facility in Nice?"

I gave him a succinct version of the events of the last five days, leaving out the intimate details.

By the time we hit the French border, Ellis was fully briefed. "Lordisa, girl! Your life has suddenly gone all Hollywood. We should write this down and sell it to HBO. If only it was real! The cosplay alone for the vampire culture—but no, let's not think of that until we sell the rights to your life story."

"Well, I think it's been an interesting few days, but obviously, I'm biased. Oh, good, that sign says Nice isn't too far. We'll be there by lunchtime."

He cast a shrewd look my way. "Is your supposed fangy boy toy the one we're going to meet?"

"Not so much meet as find," I said, wrinkling my nose a little. "And there's nothing supposed about him, as you'll see.

But yes, that's the idea. I think you'll like him. He's a bit intense when you first meet him, but I think all the vamps are that way. C. J. Dante almost had me trembling—he was so... rawr!"

"Rawr?"

"Yeah. Scary as heckbeans. I could totally see him enslaving people just like it was nothing, except I think he's probably too nice for that. And Allie, his wife, wouldn't let him. She's very nice, although she has mismatched eyes. Merrick is scary, too, but in a different way. He's more like the feeling you get when you turn into a dark alley in the middle of the night, and it looks empty, but you just know something is lurking down at the end."

"Hoo. Sounds fascinating."

"Did I mention he's taken?" I asked. "As in, mine?"

"Subtle," he drawled, flashing a smile.

"Just reminding you."

"So what are you going to do about your father's bad cousin? And just what is this organization he runs?"

"I don't know, exactly. We're not even sure he is Victor." I worried my lower lip for a few minutes while I turned my mind to that subject. "I gather they are targeting the Dark Ones, and doing something horrible to them like killing them off. Kind of modern-day vampire hunters, only the vampires are the good guys, and this Revelation group is definitely the opposite. But why they're doing it other than they don't like vamps, I don't know. I also don't know how I'm going to help Merrick find Cousin Carlo. Merrick says he's going to find a supernatural bounty hunter to look for him, but I feel like I should be able to do more than a stranger can. I mean, he's Papa's cousin."

"You'd think, but we both know how family is, especially your daddy's side."

I grimaced. "They don't seem to be overly blessed with sanity traits."

"True that. Now, tell me about this so-called vampire you've fallen for."

"I haven't fallen for him," I was quick to point out. "It's all biological. C. J. Dante makes it quite clear that each Dark One's Beloved is uniquely perfect for him. It's something to do with genes, but I'm not sure what, because talk of genetics was tantamount to heresy at the compound."

"Darling, you forget that I know you. You have the softest heart of anyone I've ever met. You've fallen in love three times in the last month, alone."

"That was with actors," I said, waving away that idea. "And two of them were Hemsworths, which means I'm excused. Also, seeing movies is still new and exciting, so seeing half-naked men on giant screens is a bit overwhelming."

"They're filming a new James Bond," he said simply.

"And I'll be in the theater every day of the movie's run," I said, fanning myself a little. "So long as they have scenes where he takes off his shirt."

"You see? You're a hair-trigger romantic. You fall in love at the drop of a hat, and that's with fictional people. I can only imagine the state of your emotions now that you have your fingers on a real man."

I stopped imagining Merrick starring in a James Bond movie, and considered his point. "I like Merrick, of course. I like him a lot. But I'm not wildly, crazily, head-over-heels in love with him."

"You're not doing the fuck-buddy thing, are you?" he asked.

I glared at him. "No! Not that I'm sure what that is, other than extremely offensive terminology."

"Sorry. Let me rephrase: what do you get out of the relationship?"

I stared at him, confused. "I don't understand what you mean."

"Relationships are give-and-take, Tempest. If all you're doing is giving, then that's not a relationship—that's slavery. Emotional slavery."

"I'm not a slave," I protested. "Merrick gets me feeding him, and redeeming his soul, and I get ... I get ..."

He cocked an eyebrow. "Yes?"

"I get a super-hot man. One who's immortal, and who won't get old, and grow hair out of his ears, and develop a beer belly."

"And what happens when you get tired of this super-hot guy who just takes from you and doesn't give anything back?"

"Dark Ones usually fall in love with their Beloveds," I said slowly.

Ellis pounced on one word. "Usually? That means there are times when they don't fall for their salvation in lady form. What then? What if your Merrick never comes around?"

I stared sightlessly at the gorgeous scenery slipping past us as we headed for Nice, blind to the sparkling blue water, the scenic towns, the expensive villas and yachts and low-slung sports cars. What would I do if Merrick never realized just how perfect I was for him? I couldn't imagine a more hellish life than falling in love with a man, spending my life with him, being as intimate as two people could be, but never touching his heart.

Ellis patted my knee while I pondered this horrible future. "Don't worry sweet cheeks. Uncle Ellis is here to make everything right."

"I don't know that you can," I said gloomily, going back over everything Merrick had said to me. "What if he was using the protection thing as an excuse?"

"I don't follow."

I gestured vaguely. "He kept saying he wanted me safe, that I couldn't go with him because Cousin Carlo would hurt me, but what if that was just a nice way to tell me he didn't want me around?"

"Deep," Ellis said, nodding. "That's very deep. I can't tell anything until I meet this Merrick of yours, but never fear, I won't leave you to deal with the bastard alone. No one brutally and cruelly tramples your heart, gets into your pants, and then casts you aside without another thought while I'm around."

I slumped down in the seat, a pathetic ball of confusion, worry, and misery.

CHAPTER TEN

Merrick took one look at the thief taker, and knew he wouldn't like the man.

"Hi! I'm Savian Bartholomew. You the vamp who's looking for a mortal?"

For one thing, the man smiled too much. He was downright cheerful, his long face and English accent all but radiating genial good humor.

"Whew, it is hot here, isn't it? I don't know how you lot stand going around with those long leather coats and fedoras and sunglasses all the time. Well, the sunglasses I understand, but you must be sweltering under that duster."

Then there was his chatty nature. He stood right next to Merrick in the shade of the portal shop building, long tendrils of some blooming flowers drifting down from hanging baskets, effectively making a screen from the people shopping and meandering along the streets. Savian chatted away just as if Merrick was a normal person, and not one of the dreaded Four Horsemen. What the hell was wrong with this man that he greeted him like a long-lost friend instead of treating him like he was a pariah?

"My secretary—really my wife, Maura—she's a dragon, but she's a whiz at keeping records—told me that you're trying to track someone who was just down the coast near Genoa. Like to see a picture of Maura? Here we are at St. Moritz last winter. And here's the sprog. Attractive little beast, isn't he? Maura insisted he be named after me." Savian donned an expression that Merrick assumed was meant to imply modesty. "He's a clever little devil. Gets that from his mama, of course. Well, now! Here we are, and you need my services. Luckily, I just finished up a job in Vienna finding a troll who was wanted for some child support, and was able to take a portal out here. They really need to put in some portal shops in the north of Italy—it would have taken me forever to get here by train. But that's neither here nor there. Let's hear about what you'd like me to do."

It was Tempest, Merrick decided with an odd sort of martyred satisfaction. She was infecting everyone else until soon there would be no one left who feared and shunned the sight of him as was right and proper. "There is a man named Carlo who, until a few days ago, was located in the area near Genoa. We believe he is connected with the company known as the Revelation. You know of them?"

Savian gave a low whistle. "Yes, I've heard whispers about them. Not a lot of info is going around, but word on the street is that they're offering some pretty big sums of money for beings with special abilities to go to work for them."

"What sort of work?"

Savian shrugged. "No one seems to know. There's a story going that a mage tried to investigate them, and promptly disappeared. No idea if he's reappeared or not."

"Hmm." Merrick considered this new information. The Revelation that he knew wasn't trying to lure people in with offers of money—that appeared to be a new tactic. "If you hear of anything more, let me know. Information about the Revelation is worth money to us."

"Right you are. Now, who is it you want me to find?" Savian all but beamed at him.

Merrick found himself wanting to be back at his villa, where he could accuse Tempest of turning the world against him. Or rather, turning it *for* him, which was completely unacceptable. "The man is known to us only as Victor, although he might also be appearing as a mortal named Carlo Marcuzzi." Merrick gave the entirely too-happy thief taker the information he had gleaned from his sources, and the few items Tempest had mentioned.

Savian looked at his watch. "So it's been, what? Two days since you've lost track of Carlo?"

"That's about right."

"Hmm. I'll have my bloodhounds get to work on the trail, but that's a bit long, even for them." Savian grinned when Merrick frowned, and added, "Bloodhounds are what I call my team of sprites."

"You use sprites?" Merrick wondered if he'd made the right choice in calling in this particular thief taker. "The little balls of light?"

"That's only one of their forms. Most of them look perfectly human, since that's the preferred form. Attracts so much less attention than a sentient ball of light. I have four sprites around the world who I use to pick up markers on cold trails." Savian pulled out his mobile phone again and tapped out a text message. "The nearest one is in Paris, but she can be in Italy shortly via the portal."

"What do you do if the sprites are the ones finding the trail?" Merrick didn't like the idea of paying a vast sum of money to a man who simply used others to do his own work.

"They just find the signs that I can't see. Once they identify the marker the individual leaves, then I pick it up and follow the trail." Savian looked up from his phone. "You don't know what a marker is, do you?"

"Of course I do," Merrick said, bristling slightly. "It's my job to hunt people. Markers are a sign someone has passed by a location."

"Well ..." Savian rubbed his chin. "Yes and no. In your job, that's probably right. But for us, for thief takers, we use a different sort of trail. Every immortal has a certain marker unique to them. Dragons have dragon scales; you Dark Ones shed something we call sanguine, which is more or less an arcane-based blood residue. Trolls leave minute plant spores, and demons, of course, trail demon smoke everywhere."

Merrick couldn't help but glance down at himself. "I've never heard of sanguine, but I know that I do not leave any sort of a blood trail."

"Ah, that's where you're wrong, although I'm not surprised you haven't heard of sanguine. It's just the name we thief takers give it, and it's not something you can see unless you have a sprite pointing out just what to look for. Each Dark One's trail is unique, hence the need for the sprites."

"But Carlo might very well be human," Merrick pointed out.

"Well, if he is this Victor dude, then luck is on our side."

"How so?" Merrick asked, confused.

"If he's been around vampires, or any other immortal being, then he'll have traces of their markers on him. The fact that the marker is changed slightly by contact with him will clue Imelda the sprite into the fact that it's not the immortal itself who left the marker."

"So she finds the marker, identifies it to you, and then you follow the trail? Can you do that, considering that Victor left the house two days ago?"

"I'll give it a shot. If there hasn't been a lot of immortal traffic in the area, there should be some residue. Of course, the samples degrade over time, so the sooner we get to it, the better."

Merrick wholeheartedly agreed with that sentiment and, after a few more instructions, sent the thief taker on his way. He found a hotel room, and slept away the daylight hours.

He dreamed, though, dreams filled with images of Tempest that both aroused and enraged him. He woke at one point with an erection, and a determination to cut her out of his life at the first opportunity.

A gnawing feeling reminded him that it had been a while since he last fed, but an odd sort of reluctance gripped him.

"Eat," he told himself the following evening, scanning the crowd outside the hotel, looking for a likely subject. He prefered feeding from women, since men tended to be more aware of personal-space issues, but today, as he eyed the people outside an artisans' market, no one seemed appealing.

Except Tempest.

"I don't need her, no matter what she claims," he said aloud, garnering him some odd looks from passersby. Fine. If he didn't want a human, there were animals in the vicinity. He was sure to find some accommodating horse who wouldn't mind donating a little blood.

He grimaced even as the thought rolled through his head. He'd never before been overly picky about his food source, and now here he was making an issue out of nothing.

"This is just yet another reason why I can't have a Beloved," he informed his hotel room when he returned to it. "It provides yet another way someone could use her against me. Well, I'll have none of it. I simply won't eat until I get over this uncomfortable phase."

He wallowed in his righteous indignation for a bit, but distractions soon left him feeling hungry and grumpy.

"I can't believe you were so close to Victor and let him get away," Nico, one of his brother Horsemen, said some six hours later. It was almost midnight, and the four men had gathered together on a rare videoconference.

"Because I don't know for certain who he was," Merrick explained. Nico, the youngest of all the Dark Ones to belong to the Horsemen, had a notoriously short fuse, and always acted before thinking. "There is a chance that Carlo Marcuzzi is Victor, but it's far more likely that he's a front."

"I agree with Merrick," Ciaran said, rubbing his face. His blondish red hair stood on end as if he'd just gotten out of bed, which Merrick assumed he had, given the time difference between Nice and Quebec. "We've worked too hard to find Victor to rush forward when a little observation will tell us if this man is him."

"What do you suggest we do, Merrick?" Han asked. Behind him, Merrick could see the naked form of a woman lying in a bed, just barely covered with a sheet. Evidently Han had been dining when the call had come through. The faint sound of feminine snoring could be heard. "Do you want us to drop our lines of investigation and come to France?"

Merrick considered his options. It went against his nature to ask for help, even from his fellow Four Horsemen, but he had to put aside his pride in order to focus on their goal. "I have a thief taker working on Carlo's trail, but that aside, the informant who set me on to him insists that Victor is still in this region. It might be helpful to have more than one Horseman here. Nico, what trail are you following?"

"One that led to a Slavic genetics company, but it hasn't gone anywhere."

"A genetics company?" Ciaran smothered another yawn. "Why would Victor want to meet with them?"

"That's what my informant told me," Nico said defensively.

"And you see how well that turned out," Ciaran responded.

Nico's face darkened. "My informants are normally reliable, which is why we knew Victor was operating out of France and Italy to begin with. What have yours told us? Nothing, that's what. I don't even know why you're in Canada when Victor is in Europe."

"Calm down," Merrick interrupted before the two men got into an argument. "Ciaran is following the Revelation's movement of money in the States, and Han is tracking down the Dark One who supposedly got away from Victor."

"And I suppose you expect me to drop everything and rush to Italy now?" Nico asked, his tone still irate.

"I'm not telling you to leave Moscow," Merrick growled, close to snapping at the younger man. He knew Nico was dedicated to the cause, and had an uncanny knack of telling when someone was being deceptive, but his youth and inexperience rubbed Merrick the wrong way. "I'm simply telling you what I've found, and that an extra set of eyes might be beneficial. If you believe your contact will provide you a link to Victor, then pursue it. There's nothing to say we can't come at the man from different angles."

"I'll go to France," Han said, glancing back over his shoulder. "I'm done here, anyway. The man reported to us as having escaped appears to be a figment of someone's imagination. At any rate, I couldn't find proof he really existed."

"I can go to Europe, too," Ciaran said with a yawn. "It looks like the financial information isn't going to pan out as much as we hoped. I've found some references to money laundering through South America, but I suspect the federal officials are watching the accounts, since activity suddenly ceased last month." Ciaran spent the next five minutes detailing what he'd uncovered regarding transactions involving banks in Belize, the US, and Austria. Merrick disregarded most of the information about the transactions themselves, since it was the people behind them that interested him.

"If all of you are going to meet, then I might as well as join you," Nico said as soon as Han wrapped up the summation of his investigation. Nico's tone was tinged with petulance that Merrick thought was unworthy of a Horseman. "Although I don't see what good having all four of us together is going to do. If Victor isn't in the area, then all we've done is wasted time."

"If you have a better lead, then follow it," Merrick told him. "It would be foolish to ignore what could be viable information just to join the rest of us."

"I don't want it said that I didn't do my part," Nico said with a distinct edge to his voice, and disconnected from the video chat.

"Someone is going to have to talk to him," Merrick said. "And it can't be me, because he takes everything I say as a personal attack."

"He's young," Han said, running a hand through his hair. "I'm sure we were all just as fervent as he is when we were that age. Right, I'm off if there's nothing else to discuss."

Ciaran stretched, and rubbed the stubble on his jaw. "I have one or two things to tie up here, but nothing of importance. I believe Merrick is correct in saying the Revelation is focused on Europe, since all my leads here have dried up."

"It could well be that they put out some false tracks for us to follow away from the heart of the organization," Han added. "I'm inclined to agree that we should be focusing on Europe, Italy in particular. And Merrick knows that ground better than any of us."

"You wouldn't know it by my results," Merrick said, mentally damning himself for not having run Victor to earth by now. Invariably, his thoughts moved to Tempest, and the horror of what could happen should she fall into the Revelation's clutches.

"Don't be so hard on yourself. You've done more than all of the rest of us put together. You not only found two of their operatives. You were so much of a threat they almost killed you. You've done your part and more," Han said soothingly, and, with a stretch, signed off.

"You all right?" Ciaran asked Merrick, squinting at the computer screen. "You look tired. You're not still feeling the effects of your run-in with Victor's men?"

"No." He thought of simply ending the video call, but Ciaran was the Horseman with whom he was the closest, and some odd little urge prompted him to say, "I met the woman who saved me, the one who gave me blood after Victor's men dumped me at Christian's castle."

"And?" Ciaran asked.

"She thinks she's my Beloved. No, not just thinks—she demands that I make her my Beloved."

"One of those," Ciaran asked, with an exaggerated roll of his eyes. "Ever since Christian started writing those books, women have been crawling all over me to make them my 'dark consort,' whatever the hell that is."

"Exactly! She's a fan of Christian's books, too, and is constantly telling me what they say about us."

"Just like you needed to be told what these books say about Dark Ones. Not that we actually *read* them."

"No, of course not," Merrick agreed quickly, ignoring the spurt of guilt that came with the lie. He told himself it was only one or two of the books that he'd read, so that really barely counted at all.

"Women," Ciaran snorted. "They eat that drivel up because they don't know any better."

Merrick frowned. He didn't like the implication that Tempest consumed drivel any more than he appreciated the slur against Christian's books. They might not be great literature, but they weren't that bad, and certainly Tempest appeared to have enjoyed them.

"I like Christian as well as anyone, but I have never understood why he went out of his way to write those books."

"Well, we are interesting," Merrick said, feeling somewhat defensive. "Tempest—that's the woman who saved me—"

"Fed you," Ciaran interrupted. "In Christian's books, it would have been some woman who 'saved you from your dark self.' All this woman did was give you blood. We need to keep the line between fiction and reality clear."

Merrick's frown grew. "What Tempest did was more than just a feeding. She pulled me back from the brink of oblivion. I was ready to give up until she saved me."

Ciaran snorted again. "You really must have had some damage to that brain of yours if you think that. No, no, I can see by the way you're scowling that you're going to be all protective of this woman just because she fed you when you were desperate. We'll move past that, even if the woman can't. I just hope you haven't given her any encouragement."

Merrick cleared his throat and studied the wallpaper. "I had to ensure she was safe. I owed her that."

"Put her on a plane to somewhere remote, and forget about it."

"I'm not sure it's going to be that easy. She's ... she's fairly insistent that we've completed a few of the steps of Joining."

"Aren't they all convinced of that!" Ciaran said with a short bark of laughter. "If I've heard 'Oh, Ciaran, bite me and make me your eternal love' once, I've heard it a hundred times. I'd give anything to find just one woman who was intelligent enough to see through Christian's dreck."

"Tempest is a very smart woman," Merrick said firmly, a flash of fire giving his voice an edge that he struggled to smooth. "She is discerning, and there's nothing wrong with women reading books. Hell, a few centuries ago, women could have been burned at the stake for reading, and now you want to damn the lot of them for having the interest to learn more about us? You don't deserve a woman like Tempest."

"Good. I don't want her." Ciaran narrowed his eyes. "She sounds insipid and pushy."

"She is not anything of the sort," Merrick snarled. "She's a goddamned goddess, and I'm done with this conversation." He slammed the lid of his laptop shut, the sounds of Ciaran's laughter echoing in his ears.

How dare Ciaran judge Tempest's character? He had no idea what she was really like, none whatsoever. He didn't see the warm glow that she seemed to exude, or the way her eyes got misty with passion, and the teasing note in her voice when she was saying something outrageous just to get a rise from him.

He spent the rest of the night grappling with a desire to check on Tempest while he dealt with a report that a Dark One in the south of Italy had gone missing. By the time he'd taken a portal to Rome, driven to Pisa—where the Dark One was last seen—and returned to Rome, only to portal back to Nice, it was midday.

That's when the texts started.

From: Tempest
Hey, you awake? It's noon, so I don't know if you are sleeping or not.

To: Tempest
Yes, I am awake. Are you having an emergency?

From: Tempest
Not so much. Well, kind of. We're wondering what you're doing?

To: Tempest
Do I need to define the word "emergency" to you?

From: Tempest
Smart-ass. What are you doing? Are you in Nice?

To: Tempest
Yes.

From: Tempest
Good. Um. Any particular spot?

To: Tempest
Who is we?

From: Tempest
Huh?

To: Tempest
You said "we were wondering." Who are you with? Did you find Victor? You were supposed to tell me if you saw him! Has he harmed you? Is he forcing you to text to me? Why didn't we set up a duress word? Tell me where you are right now.

From: Tempest
Whoa now, that was like a wall of words. No, I haven't seen Carlo.

From: Tempest
We is Ellis and me.

From: Tempest
No one is forcing me to text you. Ellis wouldn't let me drive, so I have all the time to text without killing someone.

To: Tempest
Why are you threatening to kill someone? What the hell is going on?

From: Tempest
Henceforth, my duress word is: windowpane. I think I could work that into a conversation in which I was being forced to text you.

To: Tempest
ARE YOU WITH YOUR COUSIN?

From: Tempest
Such as, "here I am in a windowless van, one that doesn't even have a windowpane."

To: Tempest
Did you just use windowpane as an example, or did you use it because you are secretly under duress?

From: Tempest
I am not with my cousin. I told you that I was meeting my friend Ellis in Genoa today. You sound odd. Are you hungry? Are you missing me, but don't want to tell me that because you insist you don't need me, but in truth, you're hungry and crabby and don't get the humor in someone sending you a faux duress word text?

To: Tempest
Emergency (noun): a situation of dire peril, and not one in which you simply wish to text someone information about the picking up of friends from California.

To: Tempest
Although I will remember windowpane for future situations.

From: Tempest
What are you doing in Nice? Are you hiding from the sun somewhere like a hotel? If so, which hotel?

To: Tempest
I am ignoring all further texts from you unless they are emergency-based.

From: Tempest
OK, how about this, if you were going to recommend a hotel in Nice to someone, which would it be?

From: Tempest
Merrick? Hotel?

From: Tempest
You aren't really going to ignore me, are you? Because I'd never ignore you.

From: Tempest
Fine. Be that way. You only have yourself to blame for what happens.

To: Tempest
What the hell is that supposed to mean?

From: Tempest
Plbtbtbt.

Merrick sighed to himself. Tempest showed absolutely no respect for him, had no fear for her own situation, and was entirely too caring for his peace of mind. "She's coming to help me," he said aloud, and, with a few thoughts about how uncomplicated his life was before Victor's man dumped him on the steps of Christian's castle, went down to the front desk of the hotel.

CHAPTER ELEVEN

It took us an hour and a half of calling around hotels in Nice to find the one where Merrick was staying.

"Merci, merci beaucoup," I said into my phone, giving Ellis a thumbs-up. We were almost to Nice, and I made a note on a scrap of paper. "And you have a room I could book? Excellent. The name is Ellis Dawson. We'll be there in about half an hour. *Merci! Au revoir.*" I hung up and looked at Ellis. "You speak French. What does *devenir chèvre* mean?"

Ellis shot me a startled look. "Where did you hear that?"

"It's the name of the hotel." I glanced down at the note. "Hôtel Devenir Chèvre. That doesn't mean something rude, does it? Like Hotel Lady of the Evening? Hotel Scatological Content? Hotel Nose Pickings?"

"How your mind works!" Ellis said, laughing. "No, it literally means to become a goat, although colloquially it means to be driven mad by someone."

"The hotel mad goat?" I shook my head. "Whatever it is, it's not close to the water. It's on ... let's see ... forty-two rue Monteton."

Ellis choked. "You're shitting me!"

"I wouldn't poop on anyone, least of all you. Why would you even say that?"

"Monteton means 'my nipple' in French, my innocent one."

I was silent for a moment. "Trust Merrick to stay at the mad goat hotel on nipple street. They'd better have a place for dog walkies, since Kelso will have to go by the time we get there."

"You'd better hope your sexy vampire wasn't so suspicious by your texts that he left immediately."

I made a face. "He was still there as of a minute ago, so I think we're good."

"*You* might be, dear heart, but I am anything but good. Or at least, so I plan to be very naughty indeed on this exotic vacation. Tell me there's a pool at this goat hotel."

"I hope so. It is the French Riviera, after all." We chatted about what Ellis hoped to do during his vacation (mostly lounge on the beach and next to pools, and ogle the scantily clad males), and what things I wanted to do (ogle Merrick).

We rolled into town shortly after that, and went straight to the hotel, a gleaming white stone building that was almost blinding in the full sun. It was three stories tall, had a center courtyard that was partially covered by a second-story verandah, and which also sported lots of plants in pots, and black iron grilles on the windows.

"Hello," I said to the desk clerk when we arrived. Ellis was panting by the time he hauled his mammoth luggage in from the car. Kelso, having had a potty break on the green strip of lawn in front of the hotel, sat politely and gently wagged his tail. "I'm Tempest Keye, and this is Ellis Dawson. I reserved a room for him."

"Ah, *oui?*" The man sitting behind an old-fashioned reception desk looked up from a book. His gaze moved from me to Kelso to Ellis.

"Yes. *Oui.* I hope it has air-conditioning, because it's hot as blazes out there."

"Hotter," Ellis said, glancing around the small reception area. Off it, the cool darkness of a tiny dining room sat unoccupied. Next to us was an elevator and a flight of carpeted stairs. Ellis moved over to consider one of the portraits that hung on three of the four walls.

"Do you need a credit card?" I asked the desk clerk. "I'll pay, Ellis, since I brought you out here."

"Sweetness, you are spoiling me rotten, and I love every minute of it! I'd insist on paying my own way, but you know full well that IT pays nothing, and I just about bankrupted myself getting the plane tickets," Ellis said, stopping in front of one painting of a girl in a Georgian-era dress. "Is it just me, or does this chickie have three arms?"

The clerk graciously allowed me to pay, and asked for Ellis's passport.

"Passport?" I asked Ellis, going over to where he was leaning in squinting at a painting of what looked to be twin blond-haired boys. Absently, he pulled it out of his pocket and handed it to me before pointing to the painting and saying, "Can you see through those two boys? I swear they're transparent."

"Why would someone paint transparent twins?" I asked, and returned to the desk clerk, handing over the passport.

"The dog in this picture has a forked tongue," Ellis called over to me, pointing at a picture of a little girl and her panting dog. He looked again at the picture. "And so does the girl."

"What of Madame?" the clerk asked. "You are not staying with us?"

"I could swear this painting is of Barnabas Collins from that *Dark Shadows* soap opera that my mother loved so much." Ellis moved a plant in a pot in order to get a closer look at a painting of a man holding a cane.

The desk clerk raised an eyebrow at me, causing me to blush. "Oh. Um. About that." I tried very hard to not look like the sort of woman who shacked up with the first vampire she met. "I'll be staying with Merrick. Merrick Simon. I called about him, too."

"Monsieur Simon has not informed me about this," the clerk said, and sat down, picking up his book again.

"Well, he will just as soon as he knows I'm here. What room is he in? I'll go talk to him and he can tell you it's OK that I share his room."

"That I cannot tell Madame," the clerk said, not even looking up. "It is the policy of the Hôtel Devenir Chèvre to not release information. I am sure Madame understands this little problem."

"Madame doesn't," I said somewhat waspishly, and pulled out my wallet to extract a few euros. "Right, what'll it cost me to get Merrick's room number?"

"I'm going to look up *Dark Shadows* on YouTube," Ellis informed the room in general. "I know I'm right about this."

The man looked horrified at my attempted bribe. *"Pardon?"*

"You heard me just fine. How much for Merrick's room number?"

"Didn't Barnabas Collins have a cane? Someone on that show did—"

The clerk looked obstinate. "I cannot be bought, madame!"

"Fine." I picked up the handle of an old-fashioned phone that sat on the counter, clearly for guests' use. "I'll call him first, and then he can tell you to let me know. What room is he in?"

The look the clerk gave me was amusing, but not in the least bit helpful. "No, madame."

"Sheesh!" I shoved the phone at him. "You dial it, then."

"I cannot."

"Gah!" I switched tactics (I never was good at being bad cop). "Think of the good karma that will come your way for telling me. Merrick needs me, and by letting me know where he is, you'll make us both happy. Birds will sing, squirrels will dance with each other, and the galaxy will continue to spin on its way secure in the knowledge that you did the right thing."

The clerk looked unimpressed by the galaxy's good thoughts.

"You, sir, are most annoying," I told him, and turned my back.

Merrick, are you there?

Silence answered my question.

You're not ignoring me just because you're annoyed, are you? Because if you are, you need to stop. I really need to talk to you.

He didn't answer. I sighed, not sure if he was just being stubborn, or if, for some reason, we were no longer connecting mentally. Glumly, I went over to where Ellis was taking pictures of a portrait, while muttering to himself, "It *has* to be the same picture."

"It's a good thing there are two beds in your room, because I may be needing one of them," I told him.

"Hmm?" Ellis dragged his attention from the portrait. "Wait, what? You can't stay with me. What if I want to invite someone back to my room?"

"For what?" I asked before my brain, with a disgusted click of its tongue, reminded me that other people enjoyed sexy times as much as I did. "Oh, for that. Well ..."

"Why can't you stay with your fanged one?" Ellis asked.

"He won't tell me." I nodded to the clerk, who was pretending to be absorbed in his book.

Ellis sized him up, smiled, and said, "Leave this to me, darling."

I watched with amazement as Ellis sauntered over to the reception desk, and said in a drawl, *"Bonjour."*

The clerk looked up, and sat up straighter, his hands making little gestures that I interpreted as him being pleasantly flustered. *"Bonjour, monsieur."*

"I understand that you told my friend she can't see her boyfriend." Ellis leaned in and whispered something in the clerk's face. Instantly the man pursed his lips, and shook his head.

Ellis whispered again. This time, the clerk gave one of those Gallic shrugs I've seen in old black-and-white French movies, and wrote something on a piece of paper, which he gave to Ellis.

"You are the bestest friend ever," I told Ellis when he strolled over to me. "What room is Merrick in?"

"No clue." Ellis grabbed the handle of his behemoth suitcase. "Be a dear and grab my airport shop bags, would you?

Let's take the elevator. I don't think I'm up to hauling my suitcase up a flight of stairs."

"You didn't get the room number? Then what did the guy write down for you?"

Ellis grinned. "His number. I'm meeting him at nine."

I pulled out my cell phone. "I'm just going to have to text Merrick and ask him what room he's in, although he's bound to kick up a fuss."

To: Merrick
What is your room num—

A   movement at the hotel's glass door caught my eye before I could finish the text.

Standing just outside it with his hand on the door was Carlo. For the count of ten, we stared at each other.

"Ellis!" I shrieked, and pointed. "It's my dad's cousin Carlo!"

"What?" Ellis dropped the handle of his suitcase and hurried over to me.

Carlo spun on his heel, and was gone before I could blink. "Come on, we have to follow him." I clutched my phone, grabbed Kelso's leash, and bolted through the door, the heat of the day hitting me like a wall. The hotel itself didn't have a parking lot, but there was parking a half block away, and that's where I saw Carlo headed.

"Hurry!" I yelled, waving Ellis on. "You can run faster than me. Blast my vanity in getting heels. See where he's going!"

Ellis sprinted past me, leaving Kelso and me to run as fast as we could after him. I made a mental promise to myself never again to buy anything but flats. Kelso loped beside me, tongue lolling, evidently going with the flow of this new game we were playing.

"I should let you off your leash and send you to follow them, but I don't want you getting lost again," I told the dog in between pants. "You'll just have to ... whew, I need to take up jogging or something. You'll just have to put up with slow me."

Ellis disappeared around a large parked bus into the parking lot, and I set up a little chant of "don't get away, don't get away" before I dashed around the bus into the lot.

In front of me, a black car squealed to a halt. I didn't have to see who was behind the tinted windows before the door opened. I knew full well it was Carlo, and that he'd just set up the most obvious trap in the world—and I'd fallen for it. I turned quickly, whipping out my phone to call Merrick, but the text message screen was still open.

"Get the phone," a voice snarled from the car at the same time that Ellis warbled, "Run, Tempest, run!"

"Too late—ow! Stop pulling my hair. Hey, don't delete my text message! And don't you dare leave Kelso behind! He has abandonment issues!"

The man behind me—to my surprise, not Giovanni—was short and dark, but built like a bull. My struggles to get free meant nothing to him, not even when I tried some backward kicks to his shin. Kelso leaped around, barking wildly, evidently unsure of whether we were playing, but even that didn't bother the man. He just tightened his grip on my hair until tears stunned my eyes, and dragged me backward into the car, where he threw me onto the floor of the backseat.

"No!" I screamed, and pushed myself up off the floor, only to be slammed down again by a heavy weight. One that panted and licked my ear.

"Kelso, get off of me—hey!" I struggled to my knees, and managed to get myself and Kelso onto the seat next to an indignant Ellis.

"How dare you!" he said, trying to open the car door. "Unlock this at once! We are American citizens, and—"

"Shut up," Carlo said, pointing a very real gun at Ellis, who gasped and blanched.

Giovanni, I was unhappy to note, was behind the wheel of the car, his emotionless eyes moving from Carlo to the rearview mirror, and back to Carlo, his gaze never resting very long on any one thing.

"Look, I imagine you think something is happening that hasn't actually happened," I said when Carlo dismissed the third man, and got into the car. "But I can assure you that my friend here has nothing to do with Merrick."

"So you admit you are working with him." Carlo's voice was silky smooth. It gave me the shivers, and not the good kind.

"Not at all. What you saw on the video screens was Merrick kidnapping me. I didn't know who he was before that. Well, that's not strictly true," I said, my conscience prompting me into full disclosure. I blamed my time in the cult for my inability to lie. "But it's the first time I met him."

Carlo's eyes narrowed until they were little slits of anger. "You came to my house under the guise of my cousin's daughter, when all along you were trying to infiltrate my home for the Dark One?" His voice was as flat as Giovanni's eyes. "I see the truth now. You are to be congratulated on your deception. You are quite the actress."

"I'm not!" I objected. Ellis made a wordless noise of protest, and gripped my arm. "I'm a horrible actress. Just ask anyone! I didn't know you were Victor until Merrick told me after he kidnapped me."

"Victor," Carlo said slowly, allowing the syllables to roll over his tongue. "Is that what the Dark One thinks? How very interesting."

"You're not him? Er ... Victor?" I shook my head. "Now I'm lost. If you're not the big bad guy, then why did you kidnap us? Why did you show up at Merrick's hotel? Why did you leave your house in such a hurry with pictures of Merrick and me plastered all over your video screens?"

Carlo turned around to face front, clearly done with the conversation.

"Where are you taking us?" Ellis asked, his voice a bit higher than normal. "We're Americans! You can't just abduct us like this."

There was no answer from the front seat. I exchanged glances with Ellis, and tried my door, but it was locked.

Kelso curled up between us, his head resting on my lap.

I slumped back, wondering what plans Carlo had, and how we could escape.

We stopped about an hour later. Ellis was asleep next to me, slumped sideways, snoring, his face mashed against the window, where he was drooling slightly. Kelso was also sound asleep, although his ears and feet twitched as if he was chasing something in his dreams.

Only I was awake when we slowed down and pulled into a gas station. We were still in France, or so I assumed because we hadn't passed over a border. I'd given up trying to get Carlo to talk to me, and instead made and discarded any number of escape plans.

I could knock down whoever opened the car door, and run away ... except that would leave Kelso and Ellis behind.

I could wake up Ellis, whisper the plan, and have a firm grip on Kelso's leash when the car door was open, then burst out of it, knocking down whoever was there, and then fleeing. But still ... high heels and running did not equal good fleeing skills. Could I go barefoot?

I looked at the gritty asphalt, and discarded that idea.

What if I hit Giovanni on the head with something while he was driving, and escaped that way?

I looked around the backseat, but there was nothing there but the bag slung across my chest, which was hardly a blunt weapon.

I couldn't even call Merrick, since Carlo had my phone.

I kicked Ellis with my toes a couple of times until he snorted, murmuring sleepily.

"Wake up," I whispered in his ear. "Ellis, wake up!"

He murmured again, and turned his back to me, the jet lag clearly having caught up to him. I nudged and kicked him a few more times, but he just mumbled and started snoring again.

There was nothing for it—I couldn't see a way to save Ellis and me, but if I got away from Carlo, then they'd be likely to dump Ellis somewhere. They wanted me, not him, so I was fairly confident that they wouldn't want to be bothered with a captive who had no use.

They might kill him, Inner Tempest pointed out, but I reminded her that Carlo had had the chance to do that already, and hadn't, which boded well for Ellis.

I had a strong feeling I was in a different situation, which meant I couldn't just sit back here and wait for them to use me to get to Merrick.

I turned my head slightly to look out of the window. Giovanni stood outside the car, filling the gas tank. In front of me, Carlo had leaned back in his seat, if not asleep, then clearly relaxed.

Giovanni finished with the gas and, with a stretch, bent down to say something through the window to Carlo. The latter just grunted. Giovanni headed for the gas station building, probably to use the bathroom. It was now or never.

Without telegraphing my intentions, I suddenly flung myself forward, slamming my fist into the side of Carlo's head and causing his head to knock painfully into the window. He snarled in pain, one hand up to the eye I'd punched, the other scrabbling at nothing. He was effectively trapped by his seat belt when I scrambled over the seat, but turned to look when I snatched up my phone, which sat next to him on the seat. I punched him again, snapping his head back with a dull crack, and climbed out of the car, unlocking the back doors as I did so.

"Ellis! Wake up! This is our only chance!" I jerked open the door, and tried to pull him out, but like Carlo, he was strapped in tight. "ELLIS!"

He just mumbled something, and returned to snoring. With no time left, I snapped, "Kelso, come!"

The dog leaped over Ellis and came straight to me, his tail up and ears alert.

"Good boy. Let's go." I grabbed his leash but, in doing so, dropped my phone, which bounced under a display stand of various grades of motor oil. I paused for a moment, wanting my phone, but knowing it was more important that I get away. Carlo started shaking his head groggily, which decided for me. We ran for the street; all the while I half expected to hear Carlo bellowing for Giovanni at any moment.

We made it down the block before we heard the sound of an engine roaring and tires squealing. Since we were in a quasi-residential area, I immediately turned off the street, and ran for the side of the nearest house, hoping to get in the backyard before Carlo's car passed. We didn't quite make it, but a small waist-high stack of chopped wood provided Kelso and me with cover. We crouched behind and peered around it, watching as the car sped past.

"We're staying here," I whispered to Kelso, urging him to lie flat on the ground. "I bet they'll come back looking for us, and if we try to go, they'll see us."

Sure enough, five minutes later, the car crawled past, obviously looking for signs of us. Evidently they didn't feel the woodpile was suspicious, although they drove by four more times in the next few minutes. I sat cross-legged with my back against the house, and decided to wait a half hour before venturing out.

"I just hope Ellis is OK," I said softly, stroking Kelso's head. He gave me his paw, which I gravely shook.

The sun was beginning to set when we finally left our hiding spot. Just as we emerged from the side of the house, a car pulled up and a family of five got out of their car, all of them staring at me.

"Hi," I said, waving awkwardly as Kelso and I shuffled toward the road. "Sorry, my ... uh ... dog ..." I gestured toward the side of the house just as if that explained everything, and added, *"Bonjour! Ça va! A bientôt."* And then I hurried off in the direction of the gas station, where I hoped my phone would still be under the display of oil.

CHAPTER TWELVE

The odd feeling came while Merrick was about an hour outside Nice, accompanying the thief taker.

"Yes, I'm fairly certain we're on the right track," Savian said, examining the ground outside a small café. "There's definitely signs of him here. I'm willing to bet you that he was originally headed for Nice."

"We just came from there," Merrick objected, trying to pinpoint why he was suddenly uneasy.

"Yes, but we were following the trail the wrong way. That or he doubled back over his track, and I don't see why he'd do that." Savian looked up and down the highway, just as if the answer were written there. "Then again, maybe he did. Hmm. If I had to guess, I'd say ..."

Merrick waited, struggling with his impatience. He glanced at his phone, but there was no message from Tempest. He had no doubt she'd text him if she was in any trouble ... or had a question ... or even just to say something outrageous.

Damn, but he wanted to hear from her. He wanted to know what she was thinking. And doing. And he wanted to touch her. The taste of her was still fresh in his mind, and dwelling on it had the hunger that growled around inside him roaring to life.

"I'd say they went that way." Savian pointed away from Nice. "The signs are just a smidgen fresher that way."

"I still don't understand how you can see a trail from someone in a car," Merrick couldn't help but say, getting into the car nonetheless.

"Remember when I said that you lot shed an arcane-based blood residue? That stuff gets everywhere. It's like a superfine powder that flies out the window, or is spread when the door is opened, or even when air is cycled through the inside of the car. It's lying on the road like a faint copper shimmer," Savian replied, nodding in the direction that led toward Monaco and, beyond it, Italy. "I wish you could see it. It's really quite lovely."

Merrick felt like all he'd done for the last few days was travel the same stretch of road over and over. "I just want to find the man. I don't care about scenic Dark One residue."

They drove on, Merrick puzzling over his odd feeling that something was wrong—and, more importantly, his need to know that Tempest was well—until a traffic delay gave him a moment to consult his phone. He pulled it out and frowned at it, lost a mental struggle, and finally texted her.

To: Tempest
What are you doing now?

There was no answer, a fact that left him feeling oddly bereft. Damn the woman, didn't she know he was busy, and if he texted her now, it was obviously of importance?

"Wait." Savian, who had been humming to himself and staring at the road ahead, suddenly lifted up his hand. "Can you pull over?"

Merrick did so. Savian got out and ran down the shoulder of the road a few yards, before standing with his hands on his hips, staring first in one direction, then the other. Merrick wondered if he dare get out to see what was the matter with the thief taker, but as there was no shade on the side of the road, he stayed put.

After a minute or two of the thief taker's odd antics, he returned to the car. "We need to go back."

"Why? Did you lose the trail?"

"No, it's on the other side of the road, but it's not here. There was a sign a little ways back, wasn't there?"

"Yes. It was for the road going north."

"Let's go back and see if that's what happened."

Merrick said nothing, but he was annoyed. The whole purpose of getting the thief taker was to eliminate errors.

They retraced their route, and Merrick duly turned onto a new highway, Savian urging him forward. "This is it. See that? Waves of sanguine all over the place. Bet they had a window down somewhere. There's something else there."

"What?"

Savian was silent for a minute. "It's hard to describe. It's like there is a second sanguine, only it's different from the first one."

Merrick said nothing, his mind still on Tempest and the texts. Why hadn't she answered him? Was it a ploy to make him worry? Or had something happened to her, something that prohibited her from reassuring him that she was all right?

Dammit, he disliked worrying about her. This was one more reason against ever having a Beloved.

"Hold up."

Still thinking dark thoughts about women who made you care about them, Merrick obligingly pulled over next to a petrol station. Savian got out and made a brief search of the area around one of the pumps. Then he stood next to the car and looked down the road, a confused expression on his face.

"What's wrong now?" Merrick asked, wishing he hadn't engaged the thief taker. The man clearly had no idea of how to track people who weren't immortals.

"Nothing's wrong other than there are now multiple trails. That way, I think." He pointed down the road, and got back into the car.

"Are you sure you are on the right trail?"

Savian flashed a grin at him. "Not impressed, eh? Well, don't worry, you will be. Left here. No, right, go right. We'll follow the new trail."

"What new trail? I thought you said there were multiples?"

"There are, but this one is newer. The shimmer has a bit more gold to it. And another right turn up here."

Merrick frowned as Savian instructed him through a residential neighborhood, the streets of which were full of children and dogs playing. He had the highest doubts that Victor would place himself into such a scene.

"And a left ahead. Very fresh trail now."

Merrick turned the corner, and instantly hit the gas. Up ahead, he caught sight of a woman leading a white dog.

"Whoa! I can't follow the trail if you drive like this—ack!" Savian was thrown forward against his seat belt when Merrick came to a quick stop.

He was out of the car and had his hands on Tempest before the fact registered in his brain. "Where the hell have you been? What are you doing here? Why didn't you answer my text?" The need to kiss her grew until it was unbearable.

"Merrick! Oh, what are you doing he—" Tempest was forced to stop speaking when he gave in to the demand, and kissed the words right off her tongue. Her mouth was as hot and sweet as he knew it would be, and immediately, he wanted more.

"Wowzers," she said when a tingling at the back of his neck warned him that he'd left the car without grabbing his hat. "That was ... hoo, baby! That was quite the greeting. Ack! You're turning red. Merrick! What are you doing out in the sun!"

To his mingled amusement and annoyance, she started shooing him toward the car. Part of his mind protested that if he wanted to stand out and get burned by the sun, then he would do so, but luckily, sanity overrode that stubborn idiocy, and he hustled her and the dog into the car before taking his seat behind the wheel.

"Hullo," Savian said, turning around in the seat to look at Tempest. "Savian Bartholomew at your service."

"Hi, Savian. I'm Tempest Keye. Merrick, your neck is bright red. Do you have some aloe vera?"

"No. It will be fine." He shot a little glare at Savian to warn the man to stop ogling Tempest. "Why didn't you answer my text?"

She held up her phone. It was cracked and dirty. "A car ran over it. I had to use a stick to get it out from under an oil stand at the gas station, and just my luck, someone pulled in at the same time that I got it free. I don't suppose my text got sent? The one telling you we were kidnapped?"

Merrick sighed softly to himself, and once again pulled off the road. "Would you mind changing seats with Tempest?" he asked Savian.

"No," Savian said slowly, his eyebrows high on his forehead as he looked first at Merrick, then at Tempest. "Not at all. Happy to. Er ... the dog won't mind?"

"Kelso is very chill. He seems to like most people," Tempest said, and went around to take the front passenger seat.

Merrick waited until everyone was settled before asking, "Who was kidnapped?"

"I was. Well, Ellis and Kelso and me." She leaned forward, putting her hand on his arm, sending streaks of heat rolling through his body. He breathed deeply to try to get a grip on the sensations that filled him, but that just heightened his awareness of the scent of her, sun-warmed, with hints of wood and petrol. "But that's not the worst of it."

What was wrong with him? He used to have perfect control of his emotions, and now a few minutes with a woman and he was as uncontrolled as a youth.

"Ellis and I were checking into the hotel—oh, I should talk to you about that, since I don't want to have to sleep with Ellis—and all of a sudden, boom, there he was!"

He touched his forehead. Wasn't that how mortals determined if they had a fever? He didn't feel ill—Dark Ones didn't sicken, as a rule, unless they were suffering from poisoning—but perhaps he'd been in contact with some virus that affected his kind.

"Who was there?" Savian asked from the backseat. "This really is a nice dog. He seems to think I have a treat in my pocket, though. Oh, wait, I do have some mints."

He fought the hunger, the need to take Tempest in his arms, and do all those things to her that suddenly became the most important things in the world.

"It was my cousin Carlo." Tempest squeezed his arm. He thought seriously of pulling out his phone and finding the nearest hotel so that he could give in to all those desires.

"Wait ... Carlo is your cousin?" Savian asked.

"Yes. Don't blame me, though. I'm beginning to think that all of my dad's family is a bit off. Merrick?"

No, he couldn't make it to a hotel. He eyed the houses down the road. Perhaps if he offered one of the owners a sizable amount of euros ...

Merrick? What's wrong? Why are you panting? I can feel you thinking, but you must be trying to hide your thoughts from me, because all I get is a sense of you holding something back.

He snarled soundlessly into her head, and let her see just what he was thinking.

"Glorious grasshoppers!" she said on a gasp, and lunged forward, both hands on his face, her lips burning a brand on his, enticing him, driving him insane with need, pushing him almost past the point of control.

With a superhuman effort, he managed to push her back, but took pleasure nonetheless in the fact that her eyes were dilated with desire, she was breathing raggedly, and a sexual flush had washed upward from her chest.

She was desire personified, and it would take a stronger man than him to resist her. He didn't. She was there in his arms again, warm and sweet and satisfying.

"Erm. Should I leave? Apparently you two would like a little private time."

He kissed her the way he wanted to kiss her from that moment on, tasting every last morsel of her, his hands full of her breasts, his mind consumed with the hunger for her.

"I probably should. Perhaps the dog would like walkies?"

It wasn't enough. He needed to feed, but only from her. He needed the taste of her on his tongue, filling all the dark spots inside him with her warmth and light and goodness.

"Walkies, dog? Good boy. I'll just take you out for a little walk, and hopefully by the time you're done, Merrick and Tempest won't be naked and writhing around on the seat. Not that I care what you do in your private time, but you are paying me by the hour, and the trail is getting colder with each passing minute. Well, then! Kelso, is it? Shall we go find a nice spot to take a dump? You, that is, not me, because lucky for all of us, there is a petrol station right there behind us should the need arise. Not that I'd announce to you both that there was that need, because there are some things one should just pull a shade on. You're still going at it, aren't you? I thought perhaps one or both of you would come up for air, but no, I see I was wrong. Right. Well. I reckon that's our cue, my lad. Out we go."

Who is that man?

Merrick, absorbed in thoughts of how he could get Tempest naked, dragged his mind off her luscious, delectable self and onto what she had asked. *He is a thief taker.*

Oh, that's right, you told me about him. Wait, you're stopping? Why?

Merrick realized just how close he was to taking her right there in the front seat, and gently pushed her back to her side of the car. "Because it's still light out, and if I did all the things that you want me to do to you here, people would see. What were you saying about being kidnapped?"

"Hmm? My lips feel like they should be bruised." She touched her mouth, which just made him stare at her lips, wanting to taste them yet again. "Do they look bruised? You are an awesome kisser. Did anyone ever tell you that?"

"Stop tempting me. Who was kidnapped?"

"I told you already. Ellis and Kelso and I were grabbed and stuffed in a car."

"Ah." He dragged his gaze off her mouth.

She gave him a look of disgruntled disbelief. "Ah? Is that all you're going to say? Ah? Just like it didn't matter that I was kidnapped?"

"Were you harmed?"

"No, but …" She waved an arm around in vague gestures of incomprehension. "But in all of C. J. Dante's books, when a heroine is kidnapped, the vampire goes nutso cuckoo. He clutches her to his chest, and declares the kidnapper will die for touching her, and generally slips into super-protective mode. Why aren't you doing that?"

"You say you aren't hurt, and I can see that you are well and able-bodied. I believe in saving my rage for situations where it can be used, not wasted on empty gestures."

"Well, I like that! Dante's vampires don't use empty gestures! They love their Beloveds! They can't live without them." She poked him in the chest. "And they admit it, unlike some pigheaded vampires I could name." She poked him again, evidently for good measure.

"I will repeat yet again that real Dark Ones are not the same as those in Christian's books." He absently watched Savian walk the dog along a strip of grass. "Who kidnapped you, and why?"

"Cousin Carlo." She sounded slightly sulky, but he ignored that to pin her back with a look that would have scared anyone else.

"What? Why didn't you tell me you'd seen him?"

"I did!"

"You did not! I would have remembered if you'd told me that."

"I most certainly did tell you. I told you just a few minutes ago, when you were doing all that thinking that you didn't let me see. What exactly were you thinking about so deeply that you didn't hear me?"

He looked away, feeling somewhat martyred.

"You were thinking smutty things about me, weren't

you?" She looked downright delighted. "The sorts of things you let me see right before you made me kiss you."

"I was not," he answered; then something compelled him to correct himself. "It was only a few of those things. Others were added once you lunged at me."

"It was a good lunging," she said, smiling smugly to herself. He let that go, honking the horn until Savian returned with the dog.

"Carlo has been spotted," he announced when both man and dog were back in the car. "Tempest will now tell us what happened."

She did so, sketching out a scene that left his blood running cold. If Tempest hadn't had the wits and courage to escape when she did, she could have been lost to him forever. If Carlo wasn't Victor himself, then he must be one of his lieutenants. Either way, he had to find the man. He had to be punished for his involvement with the crimes against Dark Ones.

And for touching Tempest.

"—we were hiding behind—what?"

"Hmm?" Merrick tried for an inscrutable expression, but was unsure of whether he pulled it off.

Tempest frowned at him. "Did you say something?"

"I wouldn't interrupt you that way," he said, allowing a bit of righteous indignation to temper his tone.

"Oh. OK. Well, we were hiding behind this stack of logs, watching for the car to come back—"

Merrick's mind wandered to the things he wanted to do to Victor, but he was very careful to shield them from Tempest.

"—and then we decided the coast had been clear long enough, so we went to get the phone, but it was broken, so we just started walking toward the nearest big town. I figured we'd get a train back to Nice, and are you growling?"

Merrick stopped growling to himself. "No."

"Oh." She looked over her shoulder. "No growlies, Kelso. Savian is your friend."

"Eh?" Savian said, looking confusedly between the dog and her.

"Which direction were they headed before they stopped at the petrol station?" Merrick asked Tempest, starting the car and preparing to head out in chase.

"North, but I don't know what the destination was. It had to be somewhere in France, though, because Ellis's passport was with the hotel, and he wouldn't be able to get across the border. Although I don't think they knew that. Hmm."

Savian pulled out his phone. "Let's see. Nearest large town is Tourrette-Levens, although I don't know that you're necessarily looking for a town."

"We'll go on the assumption that he was heading that way, since your trail indicates the same. Can you track from the backseat?"

"I am the best thief taker in all of Europe," Savian said with a laugh. "I could track blindfolded. Well, all right, not blindfolded, but with one eye patch."

"What exactly are you talking about?"

Merrick focused on his attention on driving while Savian explained his profession and the sanguine trail to Tempest, who, as expected, was delighted by both.

"This is so cool!" She turned to Merrick and punched him lightly in the shoulder. "Don't you see what that means? That trail that Savian was following was me. It shows that we're connected."

"I didn't know you had a mate," Savian said, catching Merrick's eye in the rearview mirror. "It would have been easier to separate the trails had you mentioned that."

Merrick said nothing, his teeth grinding just a little.

Tempest gazed at him with raised eyebrows, finally saying, "Well? Aren't you going to protest that you don't have a Beloved, and you don't need one, want one, or intend to ever have one?"

He unclenched his teeth. "No."

"Really?" He expected elation on her part, but was

surprised when her brows pulled together in a little frown. "Why?"

Does it matter? There are more important things to be discussed now, such as the possible motives of Carlo in kidnapping you. I wonder now if he really is Victor, or if he's fronting for him.

I would prefer to think my cousin isn't a horrible murderer, and don't think I don't know that you're changing the subject, because I can feel how uncomfortable you are at discussing relationships.

"What were you doing in Nice?" he asked aloud in order to keep her from continuing along that particular conversational path.

"Looking for you. Ellis wanted to see you, and I knew you'd like to meet him."

He sensed something in her, a little bubble of emotion that she acknowledged but pushed to the side.

It was anger.

Why was she angry at him? *Why are you angry with me?*

Huh? Who said I was?

I can feel your emotions just as you feel mine.

She looked startled for a moment. *I keep forgetting we are a two-way radio.*

Why were you angry with me enough to leave the safety of my home in order to find me? I arranged for everything you needed there.

Again, the little bubble of anger rose in her. He was genuinely perplexed by it, and wanted to know what was triggering such a reaction when all he was doing was keeping her safe.

It took her a few minutes to answer, and she glanced over her shoulder at Savian, who was engaged with his phone, looking up every few minutes to check the trail before returning to text messages. *You know how I said I lived with a cult?*

Yes. Your father belonged to it, I believe.

That's right. Well, one of the things they were very big on was telling women what they could and couldn't do. Mostly couldn't, because they didn't like us doing anything that came close to making us actual human beings rather than the pretty, brainless little childbearing dolls that they wanted.

Merrick drove on, keeping his thoughts carefully to himself. He noted, however, the sense of anger was replaced by a deep sadness in Tempest.

Even as an adult, every facet of my life was structured. I had times when I had to milk the goats, and times when I had to wash the clothes, and times when I had to be on my knees begging God for humility. I was never allowed to do anything off the schedule, or make a decision for myself, or, merciful deity of your choice, actually live life the way I wanted to.

With a shock, he realized that she had viewed his actions in the same fashion she viewed those of the members of the cult, and he had to admit that when they were seen in that light, she was justified. He had taken away her choices, and given her parameters under which she could live, and no more.

So when you dumped Kelso and me off at your house—

"*Dumped*" *is hardly the word.*

—I decided that I wasn't going to go back to that sort of a life. These last few months have been wonderful, Merrick. I can decide what I want to eat for a meal. I can decide when to have the meal. I pick out the clothes I want to wear, and when I will wear them. And I decide where I will go, and what I will do. She slid him a sidelong look. *Even a Beloved has a right to autonomy.*

Yes, she does, he agreed, enjoying her start of surprise.

That's why we decided to come to Nice, to see you. I'm sure you're angry about that, but I will point out that at least I've seen Carlo, so we know he's still in the area.

I am angry about many things, but you making decisions for yourself is not one of them. Unless it endangers you, and then I reserve the right to feel a little testy.

She giggled in his head. *I'd never imagine you saying the word "testy."*

I am a man of much depth, he said complacently, then added, "What will your friend do if Carlo discards him?"

"Discards as in what? Throws out of the car?" She looked horrified at the thought. "Or thrown away because they killed him? You don't think they killed him, do you? Galloping grape juice, what have I done? I was sure they wouldn't kill him, but now—"

"Calm yourself," he interrupted, not liking the panic and guilt he saw in her eyes. "They have no reason to kill him. He is not an immortal, and he has no ties to me. They do not kill for the pleasure of it."

The image of his sister's broken body rose in his mind, but he ignored the guilt that accompanied the memory. He couldn't think now of how he had failed her. She was dead because he hadn't kept her safe, and that was all there was to it. He had to keep the most important item uppermost in mind.

Protecting Tempest.

No, he corrected himself. Finding Victor was the most important thing. No one, not even Tempest, would be safe until Victor was located and imprisoned.

"Oh, I sure hope so, because Ellis is a nice guy. You'd like him." Her voice was leaching sadness and regret, making Merrick want to take her in his arms again. He wanted to make love to her until she forgot about the world, forgot about the drama in which she'd found herself, forgot about everything but him.

He wanted to be the world to her.

"What exactly has this Victor done, if you don't mind me asking? I know the Revelation is bad news, but I haven't heard anything about him specifically," Savian asked, pulling his head in from where he'd been looking out the window at the trail.

"He is directly responsible for the death of my sister, and twelve other Dark Ones over the last twenty years. The Horsemen were brought together ten years ago in order to combat the threat they pose to our kind." Merrick kept his voice level despite the anger and sorrow that rose at not being able to save his sister.

Tempest rested her hand on his leg, providing wordless comfort.

"I'm so sorry," Savian said, looking horrified. "I had no idea they were killing vampires, and for you to have lost a sister ... that's just terrible."

"Are you sure Victor is the head of the organization?" Tempest asked.

"Everything points to that, although it could be a code name rather than his actual name. That's why it's so vital for us to determine once and for all just what role your cousin has to play in the Revelation. Either he's Victor, or he's one of Victor's henchmen. Or he's a deliberate cover, intending to throw us off the scent of the real man behind it all."

Tempest murmured sympathetic things into his mind, allowing him to push aside the hot spike of revenge that always rose whenever he thought of his sister.

It wasn't long after that they came to a large city, and there, unfortunately, Savian lost the trail.

"It's not so much that it's gone too faint to see," he said after half an hour of running up one train platform and down another. The three now stood at the deserted end of one of the platforms. "It's that it's been dispersed by the large amount of foot traffic. Stirs up the air, you know, and makes all the sanguine particles spread around."

"Then we've lost him?" Tempest asked, her face pale with strain.

Merrick didn't like her stressed. He wanted her happy and giggling, and saying outrageous things into his head while she did the most amazing things to his body.

"I'm afraid so. The best I can say is that he likely got on a train served by this platform. If you like, I can ask what trains have been through here in the last hour or so," Savian offered.

"That would be helpful," Merrick said, hiding his frustration. He'd been so close to Victor, and yet once again the opportunity seemed to slip away.

"I'm sorry," Tempest said, her hand on his arm, instantly flooding him with warmth and understanding and concern. "I feel like this is partially my fault. If I hadn't broken my phone, I could have seen your text, and you could have been after him immediately rather than being delayed."

"We were already tracking him; stopping to pick you up did not delay us any significant time, so you can cease feeling guilty." Merrick fought the hunger that her nearness triggered. He reminded himself that he was a Horseman. He was a stranger to softer feelings, and had no intention of changing his ways now.

Dammit, but she smelled good. Like a glass of golden sunshine, warm and slightly floral and very heady.

"What are we going to do now?" she asked, frowning at nothing. "We have to find Carlo. Not just because he's probably Victor, but he also has Ellis, or at the very least knows where Ellis is."

It was on the tip of Merrick's tongue to tell her to return to the safety of his home, but in time he remembered her anger at being dominated. He very much disliked the idea that she would put him in the same group as the men in the cult, but at the same time, he wanted her protected and kept safe from the viciousness of which he knew Victor was capable.

It was as if she were a little bird, standing on the edge of the nest, trembling with excitement at the world that lay beyond, but with fledgling wings that he wasn't sure would support her.

"I know you are concerned about your friend. Would it make you feel better if I asked the thief taker to search for him?"

She sighed with obvious relief. "It would, it really would. I want to go help him—Ellis—but I don't know where he is, and I don't know how to help him if I can't find him."

"I will have him direct his search for your friend, although, being mortal, he will be harder to track," Merrick said.

She beamed at him, making him want to kiss her again. "Thank you. That would make me worry less to know Savian was on the trail."

"While he's searching, it would be helpful if you could make yourself available to being contacted, say at the hotel in Nice where Carlo tracked you," he said slowly, picking the words carefully so that she didn't feel like he was telling her what to do. "In case he wishes to speak with you. With your mobile phone not functioning, he will need some other method of contacting you."

Tempest had been about to protest the idea of returning to Nice, but paused instead to consider it. "That makes sense, although do you really think it's likely he'll try to call me?"

"If he went to the trouble of kidnapping you, yes, he will want to find out if you are in Nice or are somewhere else. And assuming he took a train out of the area, he can't check on you himself."

She squinted up at him. "Do you believe that's what he was doing at the hotel? That he followed me there specifically to kidnap me?"

Again, he had to pick his words carefully. "I believe his plan is to use you to get to me, yes. As for following you ... describe again what happened after you and the dog got away from his car."

She ran through the events again. At the end, he nodded to himself. "Let me see your phone."

"It's broken," she said, pulling it out of her pocket and handing it to him. "It won't even turn on."

"I don't believe it needs to." He pried off the back cover, flipping it over to find exactly what he expected to see. He held the back cover out to her, nodding toward it. "There's a tracking chip here."

"A what, now?"

"It's a chip that allows someone to track the location of this phone. Did you, at any time, leave your phone while you were in your cousin's house?"

She thought for a moment. "Yes. I left it in my room the first day I was there, when I went to the pool. And of course, I took a couple of showers. And now that I think of it, I left it upstairs when we had dinner. But would that be enough time for someone to doctor my phone?"

"Certainly. The question is why they would do so before they had an idea you were connected with me."

"I didn't even think of that," she said, her fingers tightening on his arm. "I know I've been sheltered until the last four months, but that's not normal behavior, is it?"

"No." He puzzled over the question for a minute. "You did not mention seeing C. J. Dante at all, did you?"

"No. Were you thinking he knew you and I had met, even if we hadn't really met?"

"Possibly." He glanced at his watch. "It could be something as coincidental as general paranoia on his part. You did contact him out of the blue."

"Good point," she said, nodding. "But if he knew where I was, and that I was with you, why didn't he try to get us at your house?"

He smiled. Oh, it was a grim smile, to be sure, but he felt he deserved credit for mustering up any form of smile. "My house has protection against such things. The best they'd be able to do is trace us to the town, and then you would effectively disappear. Likely they waited until they had a strong signal they could follow."

"Which was in Nice," she said, sighing. "Who would have thought Carlo had that in him?"

Merrick said only, "What do you wish to do? Go back to Nice or somewhere else?"

She slid a look up at him that had him wanting to shut them both away in a room for a day or two. Possibly a few years. "What happened to Bossy McBossypants telling me that I'm going to your house and will stay there and be safe, because clearly when I go out on my own, things happen like I get kidnapped?"

"You are a grown woman." He ignored the spurt of fear that accompanied the reminder of just how close she had been to a man who very well might turn out to be the murderous Victor. "If you do not wish to return to Nice to be available for contact, then I can hire someone to do the same."

She seared him with a scornful look. "Are you kidding? This is *my* adventure. I'm not letting someone else have it."

"Tempest—" he said warningly.

She stopped him with an upraised hand. "I know, I know—it's not all fun and games, and Cousin Carlo is probably a super-bad man who hurts people, so I shouldn't be flip about it. And I'm not, although it sounded like I was. I'm very well aware after the last few hours that he does not have my best interests at heart."

"Good. See that you stay that sensible."

"I plan to. This isn't just a ploy to get me out of the way?" she asked when they maneuvered through the incoming crowds to the ticketing area. "Because I'm so going to have some things to say to you if it is."

"He knows where to find you. The hotel is definitely not a place of safety," Merrick pointed out. "Sending you there is risking your life, so, no, it's not a ploy. It's a way for you to help locate a man who has the potential to destroy a great many people."

"I am so with you on that," she said, lifting her chin and looking determined. "And I'm glad you've finally realized that I'm the ideal person to help find Carlo, so if you'll tell me what train to take, Kelso and I will head back to Nice."

He bought her a ticket and was just giving her instructions when Savian appeared and headed their way. "Be sure to pick up a new mobile phone and send me the number. And don't leave it anywhere."

She smiled and gave him a swift kiss that he felt like the kick of a mule in his gut.

Dammit, he would *not* fall for this woman. His life was simply too dangerous for that.

CHAPTER THIRTEEN

"Well, this is just as anticlimactic as all get-out."

Kelso panted at me. I patted his head, and obligingly stopped skulking around the building across the street from the Hotel Mad Goats, and ignored Kelso while he had a little personal time on the grass verge. I was a bit disappointed, to be honest, that there were no men in black cars parked obviously on the street, or street vendors who just happened to lurk outside the hotel's entrance. Instead, it was business as usual with the bright lights of all the nightclubs and restaurants making the town positively glow, while a dull throb of bass came from a bar a few doors down. People dressed in varying degrees of fashion wandered up and down the streets, laughing, calling to one another, and generally creating a party atmosphere. There was nothing sinister about any of it.

I checked the cheap phone I'd picked up at the Nice station to see if Merrick had texted back a response to me telling him my new number, but the phone was just as uninspiring as the rest of the evening.

"And just when I was set to be Bond, Jane Bond," I told Kelso when he was finished, using a bag from the Nice station shop to scoop up his offering and deposit it in a nearby trash can, before glancing around one last time.

No one cast so much as fluttered an eyelash our way. We peered in through the glass door of the hotel, but the lobby was empty. The same clerk was at the desk, though, and he looked just as bored as he had the first time I'd seen him.

"Hi," I said, giving him a firm look and a friendly smile. *"Bonjour."*

"Bonsoir," he answered, pursing his lips slightly.

"I have here a note from my ... er ... boyfriend, Merrick Simon, authorizing me to use his room." I handed over the piece of paper that I'd made Merrick write before I got on the train. "You see it asks you to give me a key of my own, and honor any requests of a room service nature. Speaking of which, my dog and I are starving. Do you still have my luggage?"

"Oui, madame." He read the note and made a face that expressed polite disdain.

"Good. If you would bring those to my room—which is Merrick's room—then I can feed my dog. I'd appreciate it if I could get dinner, too, if it's not too late."

He looked scandalized. "But it is only ten of the clock, madame! Of course food is available."

"Sorry. Silly me and my American ways. I'll just go up to the room and consult the room service menu, then."

I will say this for Merrick—he might have picked out a weirdo hotel to stay at, but the accommodations were mighty fine. The room was a decent size, with a high, airy ceiling, a huge bed on a pedestal and swathed in mosquito netting, pale blue furnishings and accents, and a large balcony with a complete set of patio furniture.

We checked out the room, consulted the menu, and placed an order for scampi and salad, and a big plate of chopped beef for Kelso.

"Now, I want you to use your nose," I told him. "If you smell anyone like Carlo and Giovanni, let me know. Bark, whine, do your best Lassie telling someone that Timmy is once again in the well—I always wondered why that kid was always falling in—just so you make it clear that you smell one of the baddies."

Kelso tipped his head at me.

"You are so cute. I can't believe someone just dumped you on the side of the road. Oooh. That must be dinner."

We dined, and by the time I crawled into bed, and invited Kelso up to snooze with me, there was still no answering text from Merrick. I decided to prod him.

To: Merrick
Are you staying at a hotel? Are you finding the trail? Will you come back here? Warm me if you do because I put chair in front of door.

From: Merrick
I'll warm you, all right.

To: Merrick
That was a typo, silly. Although can I add a hoobaby? I think I will. Hoobaby. Did you find the trail?

From: Merrick
No. Savian called in two sprites and another thief taker while he searches for your friend. The sprites should pick up the trail for us.

To: Merrick
Um. Do I want to know if sprites are little fairylike creatures with wings, and bags of fairy dust?

From: Merrick
No bags. They use saltshakers these days. Distributes the dust more efficiently.

I gaped at my phone in openmouthed surprise.

From: Merrick
Close your mouth. And go to sleep. I won't be back in Nice until morning at earliest.

I gaped even more, finally turning to Kelso. "How on earth did he know my mouth was open?"

Kelso chose that moment to lick his genitals, and thus offered no insight worthy of consideration.

I fell asleep making a mental note to grill Savian about these sprites that Merrick mentioned, and whether they could make people fly.

The sound of a chair falling woke me up even before the light flashed on, instantly blinding me, and causing me to blink wildly while clutching the nearest weapon I could find, which just happened to be Kelso.

"Woof," he barked, then promptly ruined the effect of killer guard dog by wagging his tail, and rolling onto his back when two men strolled into the room.

"Help!" I screamed, and, releasing the dog, threw myself across the massive bed to where both my cell phone and the hotel phone were sitting. "Help, help! *Aidez-moi!*"

Before I could blink, one of the two men was sitting on the side of the bed, pinning my arms down so I couldn't reach the nightstand.

"Now, now, none of that, my sweet," the man holding me said, his voice rich with a French accent. He had black hair that was swept back off his brow in movie star fashion, and a matching light dusting of beard stubble. He was dressed completely in black, and would probably be considered quite handsome, but I didn't think he held a candle to Merrick's austere gorgeousness. "We don't want people to get the wrong impression, do we?"

"On the contrary, I think I *do* want them having the wrong idea. I want them all to have the wrong idea. Who are you?" I asked, squirming in the bed when I realized with my arms captured as they were, I couldn't pull the sheet up. I was wearing a deliciously wicked nightgown made from a lovely apricot satin, and positively dripping with champagne lace. I knew it would have my father spinning in his grave, not just because of the price, but because it left little to the imagination where it concerned my front parts. "Let go of me! And stop staring at my breasts."

"Really?" The man glanced from my chest to my face, laughter visible in his eyes. "You wear *that*, and don't want me to look?"

"Let go of me," I repeated, trying to kick my legs out from under the sheet at the same time I twisted my arms in his grip. "If you don't, I'll have my dog attack, and he goes for the noogies first. They taught him that at attack-dog school."

"Would this be the same dog that is currently having his belly scratched?" The man loosened his hold on my wrists, allowing me to jerk my hands free. Instantly, I grabbed the sheet and hauled it up to my chin, glaring first at the man sitting next to me, then at the other man at the end of the bed, who was, indeed, scratching Kelso's hairy white belly.

"What are you doing here? If you intend to kidnap me, I will warn you that I won't go easy. I will scream the hotel down, and Kelso—for the love of heaven, dog, stop moaning in happiness. These are intruders! Kelso will attack if I give him the command to do so."

"Do you know—" The man sitting next to me spoke in a companionable voice. "That sort of a threat simply makes me feel like a gag would be a good idea. What do you say, Ciaran?"

The other man slid a glance toward me and shrugged. "Not into that, myself, but if it makes you happy, I have no objections."

I had gasped in horror when the first man mentioned a gag, but when the second man didn't try to dispute such a heinous idea, I immediately switched my attention to trying to figure out how I could escape the room.

"It's not my preference at all. At least, not for sex, which is what I assume you're implying."

Would it be better to try to knock the man next to me out with the lamp, and then call down to the desk for help, or should I smash him with the lamp, then run out of the room, racing down the hallway trailing expensive satin and lace in the best gothic heroine fashion?

"Assuming makes an ass out of you and me," the second man said with the air of one delivering a bon mot. I stared at him in surprise. What sort of kidnapper trotted out the type of saying that a grandmother might use? The man didn't seem to think anything of it, though. He just glanced around the room while still scratching Kelso. "Are you sure you got the room number right?"

Pickle juice! The plan for calling the front desk was clearly out, because if I bashed the man sitting on the bed on the head, Mr. Likes Dogs was sure to do something other than stand there and scratch Kelso's belly.

It would have to be the bash and dash plan.

"Fairly certain, yes." The man sitting next to me looked at me, his eyebrows high. "And who might you be, my lovely one?"

I took a deep breath as if I was going to answer him, instead suddenly lunging forward, shoving him off the bed at the same time I grabbed for the lamp and yelled, "Your worst nightmare!"

The lamp was bolted onto the table. I lay half off the bed, staring in horrified surprise at the lampshade that came off in my hand.

"Hardly that," the man who had been with Kelso said, strolling over to stand over his buddy. "I know the sorts of nightmare Han has, and they don't often include scantily clad redheads. What do you intend to do with that shade? Beat him about the head and shoulders with it? I applaud your intentions, but have doubts as to the effectiveness of the plan."

"I ... the lamp ..." I gestured toward the object in question with the lampshade. "It's stuck on the nightstand."

The man on the floor was laughing openly, wiping his eyes before accepting his friend's hand and getting to his feet. "I can't say that I've ever been beaten up with a lampshade, but if anyone can do it, my money is on you."

"Well, poop nuggets! You don't have to be so smug about it." I thought about throwing the shade at the two men who were now looming over me, but decided that would do no good. Instead, I resolved to make the biggest scene ever when they tried to take me out of the room. Unless there was some other method of escape. My gaze roamed around the room, looking for inspiration.

"Now, perhaps you wouldn't mind answering a question or two—" The second man paused, and frowned, then leaned forward a little and sniffed. "Han."

Perhaps if I made it out onto the balcony, I could climb down the three floors?

"Hmm?" The man in black was brushing off the white dog hair that he'd no doubt picked up from his time on the floor.

"Take a whiff of her."

Climbing down from the balcony didn't seem very likely—hey! I turned my gaze back to the two men, and glared. "I *beg* your pardon! There is nothing to whiff about me. I had a long soak in the tub after Kelso and I had dinner."

To my annoyance, the man named Han leaned forward, too, and took a couple of exploratory sniffs. I clutched the sheet to my chin again, and made mean eyes at them both.

"Holy shit," Han said, his eyes widening.

"Language!" I snapped.

He looked curious. "Pardon?"

"Your language. There's no reason to be so rude," I said, and returned to my plan of escape. Maybe if I screamed and banged on the wall, the person next to me would complain, and the manager or someone would come up to see what was going on.

"So you smell it, too?" the first man, whose name I gathered was Ciaran, asked his friend. "I wasn't just imagining it? It's pretty faint."

"You didn't imagine it." Han leaned forward and sniffed again. "It's not terribly strong, but it's there. Holy everlasting shit. Who'd have thought?"

"Right, that's it," I said, standing up right there on the middle of the bed. With a dramatic flourish, I pointed to the door. "Out! I've had enough of you both! It's bad enough that Giovanni, or that man who threw me into the car like I was a sack of groceries, or Carlo, or whoever hired you to kidnap me, has sent you in here to ogle my frontage and scatter profanities like they were wildflower seeds, but you needn't be insulting, as well!"

"I never insulted your breasts," Han said, giving them a considering look. "On the contrary, they're quite nice. Merrick is a lucky man."

"I don't care what you—" I stopped, the words finally filtering through my brain. "Wait, what did you say?"

"Merrick is a lucky man." He smiled and sat on the edge of the bed again, and patted the sheets. "Make yourself comfortable, sweetness. We have a few things to talk about."

Slowly, I knelt down, wary of him.

"Talk about what?" A horrible thought occurred to me. "You haven't done anything to Merrick, have you? Because if you've hurt him—"

I didn't let the thought finish. I threw myself forward onto Han, knocking him down off the bed again, but this time I went with him, slamming my fist into his nose at the same time I tried to knee him in the groin. My knee missed the mark, but my fist hit true, and I had the pleasure of seeing blood on his face.

"I swear by all that is holy if you've hurt him—" I got my hands into his hair with the intention of slamming his head on the floor when I was summarily yanked backward.

"That will be quite enough," Ciaran snapped, jerking me against his body when I lunged forward, intent on beating the truth out of Han. "Stop fighting me, woman. I don't want to hurt you."

"You ass," I yelled, snarling with frustration, and struggling to get free of Ciaran's hold on my arms. "He hurt Merrick. No one does that and gets away with it!"

"I haven't hurt Merrick in decades, but that's only because he refuses to box me since I broke his nose sometime in the 1930s." Han sat up, touching a finger to one nostril that was leaking blood.

"I remember that match," Ciaran said. "Didn't he break your collarbone and three fingers?"

Han got slowly to his feet and waved away the idea with a bloody hand. "Possibly. I don't remember the exact details. Luckily, our fiery little morsel of delight didn't *quite* break my nose, although it hurts like hell."

"I am not your fiery morsel of delight." I almost spat the words at Han. "I'm Merrick's morsel, and so help me, if you have done anything to him—"

"That's three times she's threatened you," Ciaran told his friend.

"Shut it."

"And knocked you down twice."

"I said shut it."

"And she got in a punch." Ciaran released me and gave me a shove that had me stumbling backward to the bed, where I sat down suddenly. He gave me a little nod. "You ought to be proud of yourself, Red. It's not many people who say they have bested a Horseman."

"I wasn't bested," Han said with a roll of his eyes. "You think I can't defend myself from a woman?"

"Hey," I said, the anger that had blinded me with rage slowly fading. It was as if my brain had gone into a reboot mode, and now it was done and back to normal function. "Horseman? You're one of the Four Horsemen?"

"Two of them, actually." Han nodded toward Ciaran, who was going through a leather satchel that held Merrick's clothing. "The fourth is on his way, although what he's going to make of a Beloved, I don't know."

I sat up straight at that and stared openmouthed (I was doing a lot of that lately, but there was a lot to be stunned by during this past week). "You know I'm a Beloved?"

"Yes, we know." Ciaran looked at Han, who was now in the bathroom dabbing at his nose with a wet washcloth. "What comes as news is that you are Merrick's."

"I'm not a possession," I said stiffly, and got to my feet, snatching up a T-shirt to pull over the nightgown. "Merrick and I have an—" I stopped, the word "understanding" on the tip of my tongue. But I couldn't say it, because there was no real understanding. Merrick refused to accept the role I had in his life.

"You have a what?" Ciaran asked, pulling out his cell phone.

"None of your business. If you're Merrick's friends, what are you doing creeping around his room, scaring the grass balls out of me?"

"Grass balls?" Ciaran shook his head. "We were to meet him here. I take it he left you to tell us where he's gone?"

"Not exactly ..." I bit my lip, not sure how much to tell them. "I'm sorry, but do you have some sort of identification saying you are Merrick's friend? A Four Horsemen card or something?"

Han laughed when he emerged from the bathroom. "Now, there's an idea for the future. We need identity cards, cousin."

"You're cousins?" I asked, looking from the dark Han to the strawberry blond Ciaran. The latter had a faint English accent, but sounded mostly American to me. "Real cousins, not just ... er ... Horseman cousins?"

"Yes, we are real cousins, although Ciaran is a good three hundred years older than me. Where is Merrick ... er ..."

"Tempest," I said, wondering what I should do. "Tempest Keye. I'm sorry, but I can't tell you where Merrick is. For one, I don't know, exactly. And for another, I don't know that you are who you—"

"Just got a text from him," Ciaran interrupted, tapping at his phone. "He says he's a few hours north of here, and on his way back. He should be here before the sun is up."

"Tell him we approve of his Beloved," Han said, smiling at me.

I narrowed my eyes at him in return. He was just too smooth.

Ciaran tapped rapidly at the phone, then gave a short bark of laughter.

"What?" I said, suddenly worried. "What did he say?"

"I don't think you want to know," he said drily, showing his phone to Han, who snickered.

"I'm Merrick's Beloved," I said, jumping up and stomping over to him. "According to C. J. Dante's books, that means he can't lie to me, he can't live without drinking my blood, and he basically has to do everything I say. Let me see what he said."

Han and Ciaran exchanged glances before the latter flipped his phone around so I could see the face.

Don't encourage her was Merrick's reply.

"Mothballs," I swore, and, before Ciaran could stop me, snatched his phone and typed in, *If you don't start being nicer to me, I'll leave you and then you'll be alone and have to drink blood from strange cows and you'll die alone in your pretty house with no one to care about you.*

Ciaran crossed his arms over his chest, and gave me a long-suffering look while I waited for Merrick's response.

It wasn't long in coming, but it was in Italian.

"What does this say?" I asked, showing the two men the phone.

"It says to give me back my phone." Ciaran suited action to word, and tucked it away in his pants pocket. "Do not touch my phone again without my permission."

"Or what?" I said, feeling a bit obstreperous. I didn't like Merrick's friends much. They seemed far too arrogant and unyielding. I disliked both attributes in a man ... except for Merrick. He managed both well. "You can't do anything to me. I'm a Beloved."

Ciaran gave me a slow smile. "Not yet you aren't. Not fully. And until then ..." He stepped forward until he was a hairsbreadth away from me. "Until then, you're entirely mortal."

"I will not be threatened," I said with a little spike of fear in my belly.

"I believe you just were," Han pointed out.

"No, I wasn't." I lifted my chin and stared down Ciaran. "Because to be threatened, I have to give you the power to frighten me. And I'm not frightened. I might look weak to you because I'm a woman, and most men think women are weak, but you're wrong. I have taken self-defense classes. I know how to shoot a gun. And I am an almost Beloved, which means if you did something to me, Merrick would be pissed." The last was a shot in the dark based on C. J. Dante's books, but I was hoping it was true.

"What makes you think I care about Merrick's state of mind?" Ciaran leaned closer, his eyes all but firing lasers into my head, but I stood my ground, and after a few seconds of attempted intimidation, he turned away. "Bah. He is welcome to you and your self-defense classes. We have more important things to discuss."

I smiled to myself, not wanting to gloat over the fact that he'd backed down, but pleased with myself nonetheless. Everything was going to be just fine, I decided. All I had to do was hope Savian could find Ellis so that I could rescue him, help track down my cousin, and convince Merrick he couldn't live without me.

Easy-peasy, right?

I sighed. My pep talk to myself did nothing but make me feel just how far from perfect my life really was.

CHAPTER FOURTEEN

Merrick's arrival wasn't everything I had hoped it would be.

I'm sorry if I'm disappointing, he said, giving the two men in my room a fist bump.

You're not—wait, did you just fist-bump your buddies?

I greeted them, yes.

"But you fist-bumped them," I said, inadvertently interrupting Han when he was in the middle of asking Merrick about Carlo's journey north. "Sorry, Han, didn't mean to stop the conversation, but you fist-bumped. That's modern! Even I know that."

"So?" Ciaran asked, a frown wrinkling his brow.

"She believes what she reads in Christian's books," Merrick said in a mansplaining voice.

"Ah." Both of the other vamps nodded.

I objected to that sort of thing immediately. "Look, I don't like this boys' club attitude where you guys are imagining that you're superior to me, and you can talk down to me."

"You're the one who has problems with us fist-bumping," Ciaran retorted. "You clearly expect us to act like we're living a hundred or more years ago."

"We wouldn't last long if we were like the Dark Ones in Christian's books," Han said, agreeing with his friend.

I glared at Merrick, who just raised an eyebrow.

Well? I asked at last.

Well what?

Aren't you going to jump on the Horseman bandwagon and tell me how wrong I am about you guys?

No.

I smiled at him, thinking to myself just how handsome he was. How any woman could look at him and not want to fling herself on him was beyond my understanding, but I hugged the knowledge that he was utterly pounce-worthy, and he was mine.

I don't have to tell you, because they just did.

You rat! Just when I was thinking nice thoughts about you, too. I retract them all.

Even the part about other women wanting to fling themselves on me?

"OK, this eavesdropping thing is getting out of hand," I told him, gathering my dignity to myself, and making a mental promise that I wasn't going to think anything smutty about him without first making sure he couldn't hear me.

What a shame that would be. "Have you heard anything from Carlo?"

"No." I had been sitting on the edge of my bed while we waited for Merrick to arrive, but got to my feet and retrieved my phone from where I'd placed it next to my bag. "I texted him my new number, though, in case he wants to explain why he kidnapped me, and where he is now."

Merrick, who had been about to ask something of his friends, shot me a startled look. "You did what?"

"Was there a reason I shouldn't?" I pulled a small notebook from my suitcase. "I had his number written down, so I figured I'd just text him my new number, and tell him that my old phone was destroyed, and that we found the tracking thingie, and that I really didn't appreciate it, but if he wanted to explain, I'd be willing to listen. It ended up taking about ten text messages to type it all out, but you said it was important to make sure I was available for contact, so I figured it was worth the effort."

The two other Horsemen slid him unreadable looks.

Merrick's lips tightened.

"And then I texted Ellis the same thing, only without the accusations of kidnapping, and asked him to call me when he could and tell me where he was, but I haven't heard anything back from him, either." I bit my lower lip, concern about Ellis ruining the joy at seeing Merrick again. "I hope he's OK. Merrick, we have to find him. I can't just let him be kidnapped by my cousin without making sure he's alive and well and unharmed."

"What's this?" Han asked, his head snapping around to glare at me. "Cousin? Victor is your *cousin*?"

"Possibly my cousin—" I started to explain, but Merrick interrupted by storming over to me, and inexplicably shoving me behind him so that I was staring at the back of his head.

What the Heckle and Jeckle? I gave his shoulder a little shove. *Why did you do that?*

Self-preservation. I don't want to have to feed from cows and die alone in my pretty house. Stop shoving me. I don't like it.

And I don't like being pushed behind you to stare at your big fat head, either!

My head is not fat, and stop poking my shoulder. I know you are unhappy, but right now, I have something more important to deal with.

I stopped my hand in midpunch to his shoulder, and asked, *Like what?*

Keep the other Horsemen from sacrificing you.

"Your Beloved is cousin to Victor?" Ciaran asked, his face furious. He stalked forward, which just made Merrick growl. "You knew and you didn't tell us?"

"Do you have any idea how much time and trouble this would have saved us?" Han asked, his voice a near shout. I had been about to move next to Merrick to show them I wasn't afraid, but I've always had a dislike of men shouting. It went back to when I was a small child, and my father had just joined the cult, and I was constantly being "corrected."

"Stop shouting. You are upsetting Tempest," Merrick said, his voice low, but with an edge of menace in it that caused me to glance at the back of his head with new respect.

I'm not actually that upset, but thank you for thinking of me. Just out of curiosity, if one of them tried to attack me, would you fight him?

Of course.

Even though they're your besties?

I don't have a friend, let alone a best friend. They are compatriots, nothing more.

But you'd still fight them?

Yes. I heard the exasperation even though he hadn't spoken aloud.

Would that be because I'm your Beloved?

I don't tolerate anyone attacking those who are weaker, he answered, sidestepping the question. *It offends my sense of honor.*

"But you knew!" Han said, jabbing a finger in Merrick's chest.

"We aren't certain that her cousin Carlo is Victor; we believe he might be one and the same, but until we know for a fact that he is, we're treating him with extreme caution."

I laid my hand on his shoulder blade, and beamed warm thoughts at him.

What are you doing? he asked, startled.

Being supportive. Showing you how much I appreciate your protective streak. Letting you know that I have your back.

Han snapped something in a language I didn't recognize, and stormed over to the door, then back, running a hand through his hair. I peeked around Merrick to watch them, decided that although both men looked furious, they weren't going to attack.

You have a very odd view of Dark Ones if you think we are steeped in chivalric manners and yet would attack an unarmed woman.

Han yelled. I could tell he wanted to yell at me.

I frequently find myself in just such a situation, he thought drily.

Yeah, but that's because we're a couple. I want to shake you sometimes, too, I said, pinching his back.

He reached back and wrapped an arm around me, pulling me against his side.

"The solution is easy," Han said, still pacing. Ciaran was tapping on his phone, no doubt tattling to the fourth Horseman. He came to a stop in front of us.

"No," Merrick said before Han could continue.

"Tempest lures Victor into a rendezvous."

"No," Merrick repeated, this time shaking his head.

"That's not a bad idea, if it would work," Ciaran said, at last looking up from his phone. "But will Victor be drawn out for her?"

"No!" Merrick said louder. "Christos, how many times do I need to say no? She is not bait. You are not using her to do anything, let alone risk her life."

"She's your Beloved," Han said, nodding toward me. "He'd have to really try hard if he wanted to kill her."

"That's right," Ciaran said, nodding. "He'd have to take off her head."

"Drawing and quartering would work, too," Han said helpfully. "Or cremating her alive."

"And then there's disemboweling—"

"Hey!" I said, my amusement at watching Merrick in full protective mode fading. "Do we have to get specific? I have a blood aversion."

Both men burst into laughter. Merrick gave me an odd look. *Is that true?*

I don't lie unless it's a matter of life and death, and even then, I don't know if I could pull it off very well.

"But you like Christian's books," he said with a little mental shake of his head.

I shrugged. "They aren't gory, and when he mentions blood, he makes it sound like spiced wine."

"It is like spiced wine. To us, at least," Merrick said, then turned back to his friends. "I know what you're going to suggest, and the answer is no. We will find some other way."

"You know, maybe they have a point—" I stopped when Merrick's phone sang a few bars of "Pour Some Sugar on Me."

He glanced at it. "It's the thief taker. He might have some news."

"About Ellis? Oh, thank goodness. I have been so worried, and so frustrated that there's nothing I can do to help find him. Where is he? I can take a train out to get him wherever he is."

"This is the second thief taker, not Savian. I've heard nothing from him other than he's rounding up more sprites."

Disappointment caused my shoulders to sag.

"Who is Ellis?" Ciaran asked when Merrick moved off to take his call.

I explained about our connection, wanting to complain about Savian not doing a good job, but knowing that it wasn't easy to find someone who was kidnapped. It wasn't Savian's fault if it took more than a few hours. "Our plan is definitely going to work," Ciaran said, nodding to his buddy.

"What exactly *is* this sure-thing plan?" I asked.

"We just told you. You tell your cousin to pick you up, and we'll grab him," Han said, eyeing me as if I were a particularly choice pigeon, and he a hungry wolf. "It will be easy."

"Not as easy as you think," I said, mulling the idea over. "I don't see why Carlo would fall for it. I mean, he knows I'm with Merrick, and he's sure to suspect a trap. That's assuming he'd go to any trouble to capture me again, which I don't know that he would. I got away from him awful easily, after all."

Merrick returned, his eyes lit from within. I could feel the excitement in him, the tensed muscles that reminded me of a lion about to spring. "The second thief taker has found Carlo. He's at an airport booked to fly to Rome."

"Rome?" I asked, surprised. "But he lives in the north of Italy. Was Ellis with him?"

"That's where he's flying to regardless. The thief taker says there are only two men, and that neither matches the description of your friend," Merrick said, tapping on his phone. "The flight will leave in an hour. If we take a portal, we can be in Rome before him."

Neither of the other two men said anything—they just turned and walked out of the room.

"Hey!" I said when Merrick started to follow them. "Wait a minute—aren't we even going to talk about this?"

He frowned. "What is there to discuss?"

"Well, like what am I going to do? Am I going with you to Rome? If so, then I need to walk Kelso first. And what about poor Ellis? What if Savian doesn't find him?"

"I've already instructed the other thief taker to join Savian in searching for Ellis." He paused for a few seconds before adding, "The portal company will not allow animals through."

I was relieved another person would be looking for Ellis, but was momentarily distracted by what Merrick said. "Really? Why not?"

He shrugged. "I am not privy to their rules other than they refuse to portal animals. If you wish to accompany me, you will need to leave the dog behind."

"I can't leave him," I said, clasping the furry white head to my side. Kelso leaned into me, making my heart melt. "He was abandoned on the side of the road."

"You don't know that for sure."

"Well, someone let him go, or dumped him, or just didn't care enough to make sure he was safe and secure, and I'm not going to abandon him now."

"Fine." He glanced at his watch. "You stay here. Carlo's plane lands in less than three hours. I'll be in contact."

Then he, too, turned and walked out the open door.

I hurried over to it and called after him, "And what am I supposed to do while you're off chasing Carlo?"

"Whatever you like," he said, with a little dismissive wave at me before disappearing down the stairs.

"Gah!" I said loudly, so loud that the door opposite me opened a crack, and an eyeball stared out at me.

"Sorry. Pardon. It's just that men ... gah!" I returned to my own room, and sat on the bed next to Kelso, and contemplated my immediate future.

It didn't look particularly rosy.

"And to think I was looking forward to being a Beloved ... oh, maybe that's him now, apologizing." I dashed around the bed to where my phone was charging, my eyebrows lifting at the name of the caller. "ELLIS! Where are you? Are you OK? What's happened to you? Did Carlo hurt you? Is Savian with you?"

"Darling, slow down! I can hardly make out what you're saying because it's all coming out one big noise."

I relaxed against the headboard, so relieved to hear Ellis sounding hale and hearty that I was willing to forgive any amount of snark. "Thank the heavens you're OK. I was so worried that Carlo would strike out at you because I escaped. He didn't, did he?"

"Not in the least, although he certainly did swear up a blue streak, and made several cutting remarks about your life choices of late. Now, darling, I don't have long to talk because the reception here in St. Gennevier is bollocks, simply bollocks—isn't that a divine phrase? I got it from dear Armande—but I wanted to tell you that you were right."

"Of course I'm right," I said absently, my mind busy with thoughts of how to get wherever Ellis was. I'd simply have to drive the car to him. My phone's GPS should help with that. And I'd have to let Savian know Ellis was safe so that he could stop searching, and cancel the other thief taker. "Who's dear Armande?"

"A very delicious Englishman with one of the best accents you've ever heard. But don't let's talk about him or I won't be able to stop, and I have to tell you something important."

"That I'm right? You already said that. What exactly am I right about this time?"

"Vampires, lovely one, that's what I'm trying to tell you, only you keep distracting me with smutty thoughts of Armande!" His voice rose a little when the sound of cheering broke out in the background. "I have to hurry, darling. The wet T-shirt contest is about to start, and I'm the judge because I'm the newest. Now listen closely—vampires are real."

"I know that, you silly," I said, somewhat exasperated. "I have Merrick, after all. Well, not *have*, but we're connected. Who is holding a T-shirt contest? Just where are you?"

"In St. Gennevier. I told you that!" Now he sounded just as exasperated as me. "You have to listen to me, Tempest. I'm in the basement of the house your cousin Carlo was renting. But he's gone now, and I wanted to call you before things got too crazy here, and tell you not to worry about me, and that you were right, and that I know now that vampires are real."

"It sounds like you're having a party." I paused when something struck me. "Wait, why are you so insistent on telling me vamps are real when you didn't believe me about Merrick? You said I was letting my lust see him through vampire-tinted glasses."

"I know for a very good reason. Yes, yes, I'm almost done, Armande. Tell the boys to go ahead and line up. I'll be there in two ticks of a leg shake, or whatever it is you adorable Englishmen say. You still there, Tempest?"

"Yes, although I'm confused about what you're talking about."

"Darling, if you would just listen! I'll say it as plainly as I know how: I know vampires are real because I *am* one. Carlo demanded that dear Armande turn me, and he did, and it's all really rather exciting. There goes the music cue—must dash, sweetie. Don't want to miss the first contestants! Smooches to you and Kelso."

I stared in stark, absolute disbelief at the wall across from me, unable to believe my ears.

What the Jolly Green Giant was going on?

CHAPTER FIFTEEN

"Right," I told Kelso a half hour later, consulting a map of France on my phone. "Savian says driving there is too far, even though it looks close on the map, so driving to the town where Ellis is being a vampire is out of the question. We'll have to take the train. Luckily, we can catch one in half an hour. Done pottying?"

Kelso wandered over from where he had been watering a shrub, and snuffled my shoe. I took that as an assent, and went inside to order a taxi to the station. A short while later, we were seated, the countryside slipping past us in a hypnotizing blur.

From: Merrick
What are you doing?

To: Merrick
Right now? Sitting on a train looking out of a window, and trying to ignore the woman across the aisle who is glaring at Kelso sitting on the seat next to me.

From: Merrick
Where are you taking a train to?

To: Merrick
St. Gennevier. It's the town that Carlo had a rental house. Ellis is there. Didn't Savian text you? He said he would.

From: Merrick
No. What is he texting about? Why aren't you at the hotel?

To: Merrick
Ellis called me. He's fine, so I told Savian to stop looking, and to cancel the other guy. I'm so relieved that Ellis is OK. Which ... uh ... reminds me that there's something I need to tell you.

From: Merrick
Are you insane? You can't go there by yourself! Get off at the next station, and go back to Nice. I'll return as soon as your cousin lands in Rome and we capture him.

From: Merrick
You're making a face, aren't you?

To: Merrick
Yes.

From: Merrick
I knew it. I would apologize for sounding domineering, but you know as well as I do just how dangerous Carlo is. You can't go to his house alone.

To: Merrick
I'm not alone.

From: Merrick
The dog doesn't count.

To: Merrick
Now you're being an ass, and I don't want to talk to you anymore. And before you text me again demanding that I stop doing what I'm doing, which you know full well annoys and irritates me, just remember that my cousin, if he is Victor, is on a plane heading straight for you.

From: Merrick
We don't know who he left behind.

To: Merrick
We'll know soon enough. And you might want to brace yourself for some news about Ellis. He called and in between telling me about this man he met, and a wet T-shirt contest he was going to judge ... well ... never mind. I'll tell you in person.

Merrick didn't answer after that, and I spent the next couple of hours alternating between wondering what was happening in Rome, and considering whether Ellis was in his right mind.

The town of St. Gennevier was small, barely worth stopping at, or so I thought as I surveyed one main street, and a few scattered houses that seemed to crawl up one side of a mountain. Green terraced fields indicated grapes were a primary form of agriculture, but other than that, and a very ruined castle on the top of a big hill, there wasn't much to see.

Luckily, I had managed to get the name of the house out of Ellis before he hung up, so I stuffed Kelso and myself into a tiny little taxi, and we headed out to see what was going on.

"This isn't very much like a villa that has a dungeon, is it?" I asked Kelso when we were deposited at the entrance to what looked like a modest rambler set against a sheer rock face that led upward to several terraced fields. To one side stood a small shed, outside of which were a couple of goats, who stared at me with bored eyes.

The house didn't even have a fence to keep people out. I glanced around, didn't see anyone other than the goats, and, with a mental shrug, went up to the door and knocked. "Stay with me, though, just in case something bad is going down that we don't know about," I told Kelso. We waited for a couple of minutes, then knocked again. Faintly, a woman's voice could be heard approaching, and after what seemed like another two or three minutes, the door opened to reveal a short white-haired wizened woman.

"Oui?" she asked in a husky voice, then proceeded to fall into a coughing fit.

She wobbled and weaved like she was going to fall down, so I hustled forward and, taking her by the arms, got her onto a wooden bench just inside the door.

"Are you OK? Man, that's a dickens of a cough. Can I get you something? A glass of water, maybe?"

The woman hacked up a few more times, then waved one gnarled hand at me, and said in heavily accented English, "You are American?"

"Yes, I am."

"I have met Americans before," she said, pausing to cough a little more. "The Americans liberated our town. They were very nice, very pleasant."

"I'm glad to hear that. Are you sure about the water? Is there someone I can call for you?"

"Non, non, I am well. It is my lungs, they do not march, you know?"

"Uh ... sure." I glanced around the inside of the house, but like the outside, it was perfectly innocuous, with open doors showing what must be a sitting room, where a TV burbled loud commercials, while farther down, the hall opened into a big country kitchen. "How about some water?"

She shook her head, and gave me a curious look. "Guy, my grandson, will be here soon for supper. Who are you?"

"Sorry, we didn't get to introductions, did we? I'm

Tempest, and this is my dog, Kelso. Er ... what's your name?"

"Belloir." She got to her feet, her knees popping loudly as she did so. She barely came up to my shoulder, so must have been under five feet tall.

"It's a pleasure to meet you. You wouldn't happen to know of another American who is supposed to be here, would you? His name is Ellis."

"Another American? From the liberation?"

"No, no, one like me, only male. He said he was at Villa Pinoir."

"This is Villa Pinoir," she said, nodding, and, grasping my wrist to brace herself, shuffled into the room with the loud TV. "There is no one here but me. Not until Guy comes home."

"Oh." My shoulders sagged a little when she released me to plop down in a padded rocking chair. "Either I got the name wrong, or he did—"

"There are the Dark Ones, of course, but they are below," she said, gesturing with a tissue toward the floor. "In the wine cellar. They were not here during the war."

I gawked at her for the count of ten before I managed to get my wits gathered up again. "You have vampires in your wine cellar?"

"*Oui.* Monsieur Carlo, he arranged for them to stay there." She clutched a remote control, and changed the channel. "Ah, it is time for my shows. Close the door behind you when you leave. Guy tells me never to leave the door open in case the Dark Ones try to escape."

My head was spinning a bit at the matter-of-fact way she was speaking about vampires. "Would you mind if I made a quick visit to the wine cellar? My friend might be down there."

"It matters not to me," she said, her gaze glued to the TV, which was displaying some sort of game show with scantily clad men and women. "The key is next to the door. Don't let them out. Guy would not like that."

"I will do everything in my power to keep Guy as happy as

a clam," I said, feeling the full weight of the surreal situation. I found the key next to a wooden door that opened into the kitchen. There were three chain locks on the door, all of which I unhooked before using the key, and opening the door just a smidgen.

I don't know what I was expecting—maybe a group of vampires clustered on the other side of the door just waiting to knock me down in their haste to get out of their prison— but there was on no one on the stairs.

A deep pulsing beat of music could be heard, however.

I looked down the wooden stairs, dimly lit by a naked bulb dangling overhead, and back to the kitchen.

"There is no way I'm going to go down there when the door can be locked against me," I told Kelso, and, after a moment's thought, took one of the kitchen table chairs and wedged it under the doorknob.

"There. Now no one can trap us. I'm so glad I watched all those horror movies last month, or I wouldn't have thought of the door. You ready, boy?" Kelso, who had been watching me with interest, wagged his tail. "That's as good a yes as I'm going to get. Onward, my brave one!"

We descended into the near darkness, an odd thumping noise seeming to come up from the ground. I really wished I could reach Merrick by mind-radio, but he hadn't answered when I tried earlier. The noise was creepy enough it gave me goose bumps.

"It's like it's a heartbeat," I whispered to Kelso, glancing around once we arrived in the cellar. There was not a lot to be seen, certainly not a wet T-shirt contest full of partying vampires. A few wooden crates lined one wall, while the other bore a massive black iron coal furnace, a hot water heater, and a fuse box.

The heartbeat continued to throb. "Just like we're at the heart of the house. OK, now I'm freaking myself ... what are you doing? Leave it, whatever it is. Kelso!"

With one eye on the still-open door at the top of the

stairs, I shuffled over to where Kelso was pawing and snuffling something on the ground. The dim light just barely revealed a metal ring set into the stone.

"Clever dog," I praised, patting Kelso on the head before curling my fingers around the ring. "Let's pray that Ellis is under here, and not some horrible disembodied heart beating away."

I was expecting to have to fight the trapdoor, but it swung upward without too much effort. I staggered back regardless, not due to the effort, but from the blast of pounding music that exploded upward.

I peered down into the hole to see a dirt floor, colored lights flashing around in a simulation of a rockin' nightclub, and six men spraying one another with bottles of what looked like champagne. "Ellis?" I shouted over the pulsing techno music. "Ellis, are you there?"

"Darling!" One of the men in the back pushed forward, dancing an intricate step until he was directly under the trapdoor. "You rescued us! How thoughtful. Everyone, this is Tempest, one of my oldest friends, and vamp hag."

"Hey!" I said, fluffing up my hair. "I might be a little disheveled, but 'hag' is a bit harsh—"

"Sorry, love, it's just a term the boys tell me is all the rage. Can you grab the rope ladder? I haven't yet learned how to master the art of turning into a bat."

"Dark Ones don't turn into bats," I scoffed, and retrieved a bit of rope that poked out behind the water heater. It turned out to be a somewhat motley rope and wood ladder. "At least I don't think they do. What are you guys doing down there?"

It took a good five minutes before I got the answer, because first everyone climbed up, but then one man realized he'd left his phone below, then another wanted to grab some of the champagne just in case they got thirsty, and finally, Ellis had to go back to retrieve his shirt, which he said he'd taken off in order to keep it from getting stained.

It was then that I realized I'd met one of the vampires before.

"Spiky Pink!" I said, astonished when the vampire turned out to be the one who had dropped off Merrick.

He wrinkled his nose at me. "Eh? Do you have a problem with my hair?"

"Not at all. I know you!"

"I don't think I've had the pleasure—"

"You don't remember me? I saw you when you left Merrick off at C. J. Dante's castle."

For a moment, the man looked terrified. "Shite! That was you?"

"Yes, but don't worry, I'm not going to tell your boss that you were merciful instead of killing Merrick. Far from it, I'm very grateful you did so."

He looked faintly embarrassed. "I just didn't like to kill one of my own, you know? And Giovanni would have done so had he not been called back to Carlo. As it is, I had to lie and tell them he overpowered me when they found out he was still alive. It was a close thing for a few minutes, let me tell you. I'm sorry, I'm babbling, aren't I? It's just that Ellis says you're a good 'un, and that you would never give us away."

"Never," I said. "I'm glad you didn't get in any trouble over Merrick."

Spiky looked mollified. "I won't say Carlo is happy with me, but that's why when he demanded I turn your friend, I made no protest. And I don't think Ellis minds terribly that I did so, do you?"

"It certainly doesn't seem like he does. In fact, he looks very happy."

By the time I herded the six men upstairs, my brain and ears were buzzing with their constant chatter, jokes, teasing, dramatic explanations, and occasional bits of song lyrics.

"I'm so glad to see you," Ellis said once we had taken over the kitchen of the villa, the door to the old lady's room remaining firmly shut. The other vamps were milling around, poking into drawers and opening cupboards. One of them found a huge pair of shears, and immediately announced his intention to give himself a pair of booty shorts. "I thought I was a goner once you bailed out, and then of course, Armande turned me, and that was high drama, let me tell you! You do not know the value of your bladder muscles until you have a vampire chomping down on you."

"I've been chomped on several times and not had any bladder issues," I said smugly.

"Yes, but you're a girl. You have superior bladder parts."

"What I don't understand," I said, idly watching the others as they all stripped out of their jeans in order to make shorts, "is why Carlo wanted you to be a vamp. What does that do other than make you allergic to garlic and burn up in sunlight? Is that his way of punishing you?"

"Don't you know? I suppose you don't, although I'd think that vampire you've been doing the sheet tango with might have told you. Your dear cousin Carlo and that dead-eyed henchman of his are building a vampire empire."

"A what?"

"Just what I said. The boys here are hired out to attend parties. Special parties for only the very rich."

"You have got to be kidding me." I stared at him in disbelief.

"It's god's honest truth, I swear! Armande's team—that's him there with the pink hair—gets sent to super-exclusive parties of the rich and wannabe famous, and then they feed off everyone. Armande says the people get their jollies off of being with a real vampire, and the boys get fed, and your cousin rakes in the cash."

"Who in their right mind would want a vampire to feed off—" I thought of what it was like when I was feeding Merrick, and stopped speaking.

"That's right," Ellis said, nodding, and flashing a grin at Armande. "When I say the mortals get their jollies, I mean they *get their jollies*."

"I don't know whether to point out that's awfully close to prostitution, or to just let it go because it's none of my business."

"Do the latter. It's much easier on your blood pressure," he advised.

"We do not like that part, being intimate with the mortals." Armande paused when passing us. "We want to have a dance troupe, you know? All male dancers." He did a couple of pelvic thrusts and a triple spin. "Like the Chimpendales."

"Chippendales, darling," Ellis corrected, and applauded when Armande did a split jump. "Such lovely thighs you have. I think a dance troupe is much nicer than having to service all those dreary mortals with their vampire obsessions."

"You were a mortal yourself half a day ago," I pointed out.

"And life is so much better now," he said, blowing me a kiss.

Armande had been doing a few more pirouettes before saying, "Yes, the dance troupe will be good. We have practiced many routines during our years working for Carlo, and all we need are a few costumes, and then we will be megastars! If we can get Carlo to agree to it, which I know he will not do. Jon-Marie! What are you thinking? You cut out the heart over your left butt cheek, not your right cheek."

I shook my head when Armande bustled off across the room to fix whatever fashion faux pas one of the other vamps was about to make. "It's kind of hard getting to grips with the idea that your own cousin spends his days pimping out vampires. I wonder if Merrick knows the sexy stuff goes on."

"Oh, Carlo doesn't just send the boys to parties," Ellis said, shaking his head when one of the men offered him the scissors. "Armande, tell Tempest what you told me about the research groups."

"It is true. Carlo and Giovanni take the vampires who refuse to cooperate, and auction them to labs." Armande frowned as one of the others paraded by in a very short pair of cutoffs.

"What sort of labs?" I asked, torn between suspicion and fear.

"Ones where they research the ways of the Dark Ones, naturally," Armande said with a shrug. "It is why we, in general, do as Carlo says. We do not want to be sent to the labs. Instead, we go to parties and pretend to make love to the mortals, and they let us drink their blood."

I forestalled any comments about the morality of such a thing and focused on what was important. "Where does Carlo send the other vampires to?"

"No clue. I only know they round them up every month or so and sell them to the highest bidder."

I looked at Ellis. He cocked an eyebrow at me.

"I think we need to talk to Merrick," I said after a moment's thought, and despite doubting it would do any good, sent out a mental call. *Hello, Tempest calling Merrick, Tempest calling Merrick. Come in, Merrick.*

There was no answer from him, not even the feeling of him touching my mind.

"I must be out of range. Text it is."

To: Merrick
I just found Ellis. He's OK.

Three minutes later I received the response:

From: Merrick
Good. Go back to Nice. I'll meet you there once we've got your cousin.

To: Merrick
I have a lot to tell you about what he's doing. Ellis, not Carlo.

From: Merrick
Tell me later. We've followed Carlo to a villa, and Han is about to break through the security system.

"Troubles?" Ellis asked when I made a face at the phone.

"Not really. Merrick is in Rome busy breaking through Carlo's security so they can storm his villa, which means he's incommunicado right now. The big poop. You'd think he'd want to hear your news, since it is all about Carlo and what he's doing."

Ellis stilled for a few seconds before taking my arm in a grip that was borderline painful. "Say that again."

"Say what? That Merrick is a poop? I suppose that's unfair, but he is the sort of man who likes to protect people rather than keep them informed—"

"No, the part about him being in Rome and breaking into a villa. What villa?"

"I don't know, and you're going to leave bruises if you keep squeezing my arm like that."

Ellis clicked his tongue, but released me, turning to call across the room to Armande, "What was the name of the villa where Carlo sells the vampires to the vivisectionists?"

"Villa Luna," Armande answered without even glancing toward us.

Ellis turned back to me.

"On it," I said, my blood suddenly sporting little icebergs of pure dread.

To: Merrick
What's the name of the villa you're at?

From: Merrick
I told you that I'd talk to you later. We're going in.

To: Merrick
WHAT'S THE NAME?

From: Merrick
Villa Luna. I'm turning my phone off now. I'll call you when we have him.

"Jumping giant green frogs and all their little tadpoles."
I lifted eyes that I knew were filled with fear to Ellis. "He
turned off his phone."

"He's there?" Ellis asked, his normally sunny expression
somber.

I nodded.

"God help him."

"Maybe they'll be OK. If it's just Carlo and Giovanni,
the three vampires should be able to take them."

Ellis stared at me, his expression turning to horror.

I gasped as a thought occurred to me, and turned to
where the other vampires were putting final touches on their
cutoffs. "Armande! You said Carlo auctions off the vampires.
Where do they do that?"

"Usually in Rome," he answered, pointing to a spot
one of the others had missed trimming. "No, no, François,
not that short. Your balls are hanging out now. No one
wants to see hairy balls. If you shaved them like I told you,
then it would be acceptable. But as it is?" Armande *tsk*ed.
"Deplorable."

An iron hand seemed to grip my insides, squeezing
everything until I wanted to scream with frustration. "They
walked right into it, Ellis," I said in a hoarse whisper. "They're
walking into some horrible vampire auction, and Carlo will
capture them, three of the Horsemen, and will sell them to
the highest bidder. If they don't kill them outright."

"Lordisa, I hate to agree, but ..." Ellis's Adam's apple
bobbed a couple of times. "We should think positive. Perhaps
they know what goes on there, and they'll be cautious."

"They don't, or they would have said something. Sweet,
glorious grape juice, they're sitting ducks!" I swayed for a few
seconds, seriously thinking of swooning, but just then Kelso
bumped my hand with his wet nose.

I patted his head, and strength returned to me, strength
and the determination to do whatever it took to save
Merrick. "No one touches my vampire and lives to tell about

it!" I swore, then lifted my chin and said loudly, "Vampires, assemble! We have to get our butts to Rome and fast. I have a hunky man to save, and you guys are going to help me do it!"

CHAPTER SIXTEEN

"I'd just like to know," I said in an undertone to Ellis while we were on the outskirts of Rome, riding to Villa Luna, "why Merrick felt it was OK to lie to me about the portals."

"Oooh, he lied? Interesting," Ellis said, eyeing me, his voice also lowered so that the taxi driver wouldn't hear us. "Do we think the honeymoon is over already? Has the bloom gone off the rose so quickly? Is it your blue coochie that drove him away?"

I poked him with an elbow. "No to all of those, and there's nothing blue down there anymore, as you well know since you helped me pick off all the lint."

"What did Vamp Boy lie about, then?"

I patted Kelso, who had his nose out of the window and was snuffling like crazy. "He said portals wouldn't take animals, and the shop we went to said that only applied to animals being sent solo, and so long as I was holding tight to Kelso, he'd be fine. And he is. And while we're on the subject, jumping beans, was that portal neat. I wish I'd known about that before, because I'd have put that right at the top of my bucket list."

"It certainly was interesting. Have you tried your walkie-talkie again?" Ellis asked.

"Huh? Oh. I'll try it again, although he didn't answer

when I tried at the portal shop." *Merrick, I know we're not super near each other, but I'm twenty minutes away, and surely that's close enough for you to hear me.*

Silence was my only answer.

Dammit, don't shut me out like this! I'm so worried about you that my stomach is all wadded up into a little ball, and I think I may throw up. Please, just say hi, just one word to let me know you're OK.

"Well?" Ellis asked.

"Nada," I said with a sigh, worry clamping down tight on me until I felt like I couldn't draw a proper breath. "What if he's ..."

"Armande assures me that it's hard to kill us. Us being vampires, that is." Ellis patted my knee. "If the boyfriend is protective, maybe he's just not answering in order to keep you from fretting."

"I don't know," I said, trying to feel Merrick's presence. There was nothing. It was as if I was on the edge of a deep abyss filled with a complete absence of Merrick.

Armande, who was sitting in the front with the taxi driver, turned around to say, "What are we going to do when we get to Carlo's villa? It's fine for you to say that we're going to fight Carlo, but we have no weapons. We have nothing we can use to fight him or the dreadful Giovanni. We are dancers, not soldiers."

"You're vampires," I told him, trying to sound like I had confidence in them. In myself. "You're immortal. You drink people's blood. You can ... er ... I'm not sure what else you can do, because Merrick is kind of reticent to tell me that sort of stuff, and Dante doesn't mention anything like that." I glanced at Ellis. "Do you have other powers?"

"You're asking entirely the wrong person, darling," he answered, shaking his head. "I'm just the comic relief in this scene. A dashing and urbane comic relief, but one nonetheless. I do like a plan, though, so let's figure out what we're going to do once we get to the villa."

The rest of the journey was spent arguing over whether it would be better to go in with (metaphoric) guns blazing, or if a stealthy attack would be best. In the end, we decided on a three-pronged approach.

"Think of yourselves as bloodthirsty pirates," I said in a little motivational speech when we were deposited at the villa. "Imagine yourself about to pillage a rich vessel, a dagger clutched between your teeth, and your trusty scimitar at your side."

"But we don't have any weapons," said one of the dancers (the one whose testicles were still visibly noticeable through his booty shorts).

I averted my eyes from his nether bits, and gave them all an encouraging look. "Pick up whatever you can find outside the house, and use it to your advantage. Be creative! Be resourceful! But above all, take down those auction dudes."

"Yar!" one of the men shouted, and although we had to immediately hush any further such noises, I promised them all they could yell as loudly as they liked when the actual attack took place.

"I know some karate," Ellis offered. "I used to do it after school so that I could keep from being beat up by all the homophobes. I must have watched *Karate Kid* at least a hundred times back then. Do you remember, Tempest?"

"I remember you swanning around in a white outfit whenever you got a new belt, but that's about it," I admitted.

He tried to look modest. "I went all the way up to a brown belt before my mother took me out of the class."

"Good. You and Armande can attack from the side opposite our dancing pirates."

We synchronized our watches, and scattered.

"Hello," I said a minute later when the front door of the villa was opened. It wasn't a huge house, smaller than Merrick's, but I could see the turquoise glint of a swimming pool behind it, and a stepped yard that dropped down to reveal a view of Rome in the distance. Huge, deep fuchsia bougainvillea lined a crazy tile walkway up to the door, filling the air with its heavy honeysuckle scent, while the villa itself rose with cream stone magnificence three stories above my head.

The man who answered the door was short, stocky, and had the sort of cauliflower ears that made me think he spent a lot of time in a boxing ring. "Who are you?" he asked, suspicion fairly dripping from every pore.

"I'm Tempest, and this is Kelso. I'm here to ask if you've seen my boyfriend. Well, fiancé, really, although he hasn't asked me, but I'm not going to shack up with him without being married, because I think marriage shows a certain level of commitment, don't you? Besides, getting married is number twelve on my bucket list, and if there's anything I'm serious about, it's crossing things off my bucket list."

Cauliflower Ears stared at me like I was a two-headed blue whale, then started to close the door. Praying that the other two prongs were doing their things, I pushed my way past the man before he could shut me out.

"Did I mention that Carlo is my cousin? No? Well, he is. COUSIN CARLO!" I bellowed the last few words while taking a few steps into a foyer that had beautiful mosaic tile on the floor. "I thought you'd be worried about me, so here I am!"

To the left, double doors were flung open and Giovanni appeared, his dead, flat eyes narrowed. "What are you doing here?" he asked, shifting to block me when I tried to peer around him. Kelso growled, distracting Giovanni for a moment.

"Oh, I think we both know what I'm doing here, so you can just tell me where Merrick and his friends are, and we'll be on our way." *Merrick? You here? I know you must be, because I can feel something warm in my brain, and that can only be you, so you might as well answer me.*

Giovanni glowered.

Merrick?

Several things happened at that moment. First of all, I was mentally forming a scathing sentence to let Merrick know that if he was conscious and able to answer me, but chose not to, he had a few things he was about to hear, and none of them were any too nice. Second, Giovanni, evidently deciding that capture was the better part of valor, grabbed my arm and jerked me forward into the room. And third, Kelso's low growl became a savage snarl when he leaped forward and flung himself at Giovanni.

All hell broke loose then. There was a crashing of glass and several bloodcurdling whoops as the vampire dance squad flung themselves into the room, brandishing various garden implements. Behind me, from the opposite side of the house, I heard Ellis give his best *Karate Kid* yell, and the loud urging of Armande for Ellis to beat the tar out of the man at the door.

I had a brief glimpse of my cousin Carlo and another man at the back of a long narrow room filled with two rows of chairs, from which a half-dozen men in dark suits were in various stages of rising. Beyond them, a big black table lurked, and upon that table was the trussed-up form of a man. For a moment, my heart leaped, but the man's hair was blond, not as black as a crow's wing.

Carlo took one look at me and escaped out a door on the far end, his buddy looking startled for a moment, but following. The man on the table didn't move.

It was a glint of metal in Giovanni's hand that pushed me over the line. I had started past him to rescue whoever it was who was tied up, but from the corner of my eye I saw Giovanni twist away from Kelso and pull out a switchblade.

"No one hurts my dog!" I roared in a voice that surprised even me. Before I knew what I was doing, I'd kicked Giovanni's knee, flinching at the horrible crunching sound that followed. He collapsed and started howling, but I stomped on his hand twice until he released the knife, at which point I snatched it up and ordered Kelso to follow me.

The vampire dancers moved in, shouting and waving garden tools at the men who were still gathered around the chairs. I paused long enough to leap to a chair and yell, "Let them go if they'll leave peacefully. If not, take 'em down, boys, take 'em down!"

The vampires whooped and moved forward en masse. The men, who I gathered were there to purchase vampires for nefarious purposes, glanced at one another, and all lifted their hands in surrender.

I hopped down to check the man on the table. It was Ciaran, and I sagged a little in relief when I realized he was breathing, although he appeared to be unconscious. I used the knife to cut through the zip ties binding his hands and feet and, with a mumbled apology for leaving him, ran to the door through which Carlo had escaped, Kelso on my heels. We emerged in some sort of a back hall, with a staircase on my left, and a closed door on my right. I took a quick glance through the door, but it led to an empty kitchen.

"Up we go," I told Kelso, and we leaped up the stairs, the switchblade in my hand, and my heart in my throat.

Please tell me you're all right, Merrick. Please don't be dead. Not now, when I realize that I'm falling in love with you, and that I need you, and more importantly, that you need me so you won't be a sad, lonely old vampire who lives by himself with no company but fifteen cats and a stray otter named Aloysius.

I would never name my otter Aloysius.

Joy flooded me at the soft voice in my head. *You're alive!*

Yes. Barely. I feel like I was hit on the head with a piano.

Where are you? I paused at the top of the stairs, looking wildly up and down a hallway filled with closed doors.

I don't know. It's dark, and my hands are tied. I don't appear to be able to move.

I looked at the doors, and glanced upward where the stairs continued. "Attic," I told Kelso. He looked as eager as I felt when we dashed up a second flight of stairs, and started down the hall throwing open doors as we went.

Merrick was, indeed, in an attic room tucked up way under the eaves, lying on the floor under a rickety iron bedstead. On top of the bed was Han, also tied up, and unresponsive.

"What happened?" I asked Merrick as soon as I cut away his bonds. I winced when he rolled over and I saw his face was splattered with blood. "Glorious grand geese, Merrick! You're bleeding!"

Unable to stop myself, I covered first his face in kisses, then went for his lips. His mouth was warm, and wonderful, and tasted like he'd been eating cloves. He moaned as his mouth parted, allowing my tongue to make tentative little dabs inside. *This is so … I've never done this before! With my tongue in your mouth, I mean. It's … mrowr!*

It would be better if my head didn't hurt so badly, he said.

I released his hair. *Oh. Sorry. I didn't know I had grabbed your head.*

"It's all right. The kiss was worth it, although …"

"Although what?"

"Nothing."

"You know I'm not going to be happy with a 'nothing,'" I pointed out.

"I know that very well, but it'll have to wait." He winced when he touched his forehead.

I *tsk*ed. "You poor thing. What happened?"

"Your cousin happened. Or one of his men. Ciaran and I were ambushed while Han and Nico were disabling their security."

"Who's Nico?" I asked, helping him sit up before moving over to remove Han's bonds.

"Another Horseman." Merrick wiped blood from his face, and glanced around the room, stiffening. "Where are the others?"

"Ciaran is downstairs. He's out, but he's breathing, so I assume he's OK. I don't know where this Nico person is."

Merrick leaped to his feet, an act that he clearly regretted when he wobbled a little, clutching me for a few seconds before regaining his balance. "Where is your cousin?"

"I don't know. He ran out when we attacked."

Merrick, who had given Han a fast examination, had turned and started for the door while I was speaking, but paused to look back. "We? Who is with you? And speaking of that, what are you doing here?"

I pointed the switchblade at him. "Do not even think about telling me I should have stayed in Nice, because you know that's only going to piss me off."

He thought about it for a moment.

I can tell what you're thinking, you know.

I know, he said with a mental sigh. *God help me, I know. Just as I know that I'd move heaven and earth to keep you safe all the while you're going to be running headlong into danger. You're going to lead me a merry dance, aren't you?*

I smiled, and handed him the switchblade. "That depends if you like to dance."

He started to leave, checked himself, then scooped me up for a kiss that fairly scorched the hair right off my head. *You're going to exasperate me, annoy me, and fill my days with danger, but I wouldn't have it any other way.*

I love you, too, I said, kissing him with enough passion to ignite a bonfire.

He froze. *Tempest …*

I know. Loving you wasn't on my bucket list, but it just kind of happened. One moment we were friends with beneficials, and then boom. I knew it was love. Not the movie star sort of love, either. This is bigger. More encompassing. I want to share everything with you, even when you're making me angry. Stop making that face like you're annoyed, because I can feel how warm and squidgy the fact that I love you makes you feel.

It's not wise at all.

"Like that stopped anyone from falling in love?" I smiled at him, allowing him to feel the blossoming love that started in the tiniest atoms of my being, and grew out until it filled my body. "And don't think I'm going to demand that you tell me you love me, too, because I'm not. I know you're fighting centuries of conditioning to not feel anything for anyone. I'm content to wait until you come to your senses and realize that you can't live without me."

He sighed dramatically. "I have no doubt you'll remind me of that daily until I tell you something suitably romantic, like the fact that you brought light and warmth to a life of despair and hopelessness, that you fill my thoughts until nothing has much meaning unless it can please you, and how the merest thought of you can ease the pain that is my constant companion."

I widened my eyes. "Was that a declaration of love, or were you saying that's what you will say when you realize just how much you love me? Because if it was the former, it was the most romantic thing ever, even better than something that one of C. J. Dante's vampires would say. I think I might cry. Or tear off your clothes and have my womanly way with you."

One side of his mouth twitched. "Much as I'd like that, we can't stay up here if Carlo is about."

"You're right," I said, putting aside the need to kiss and touch him, and tell him again how much I loved him. "Let's go catch my evil cousin so we can turn him over to the cops."

There was a whisper in my mind, a faint shadow of a thought that said, *He won't end up with the mortal police,* but I decided it was better if I ignored that and focused on being helpful.

There would be time later for me to molest Merrick as he so very much deserved.

Wrapped in a warm glow of happiness, I helped Merrick check all the rooms on both the top and second floors. Ellis and his friends had cleared the ground floor of the auction people, and had Ciaran propped up, giving him copious amounts of advice.

"Beefsteak. Beefsteak is the answer to any crisis, or so my daddy used to swear," Ellis was saying when we entered the main room. "Mind you, he said the same thing about Jack Daniel's, cocaine, and trips to the local strip club, but the man knew how to take the redness out of a black eye."

"He doesn't have a black eye," Armande pointed out, *tsk*ing when Ciaran, still obviously a bit rummy, brushed a clumsy hand over his twisted-up shirt. "No, no, you are making it worse. Allow me."

"How are you?" Merrick asked his friend. Ciaran looked up and grimaced, putting his hand to the back of his head.

"Something hit me."

"Carlo?" Merrick asked him.

Carefully, Ciaran shook his head. "I don't think so. I could see him in the doorway when we came in the back. There was someone behind me. Behind Nico and me. Another man."

"I had the impression of two men, as well." Merrick eyed the vampires collected. *Who are these Dark Ones? I don't know any of them.*

The one in the yellow shirt is my friend Ellis.

He shot me a look of surprise.

That's what I wanted to tell you. Carlo had Ellis turned into a vampire.

Dark One.

When I rescued Ellis, he was with Armande and his band of dancing vampires.

I beg your pardon?

That's what they want to do—be exotic dancers. Vampire ones. They don't like being prostitutes.

Merrick rubbed his face. *I must have been hit harder than I thought. Prostitutes?*

I patted his arm. *I know it sounds unlikely, but to be fair, the whole day has been weirder than …*

An otter named Aloysius?

You got it. "Ellis, have you seen Carlo at all? Or that other man who was with him?"

"No. We put Michel on door duty at the back. Michel? Has anyone tried to leave?" Ellis called.

"*Non,*" came the answer.

I looked at Merrick. *Do you think he's still here?*

We searched the two upper floors. He glanced around with speculation. "The one on the couch, who is he?"

"Giovanni the sociopath. I see Ellis and friends tied him up. He's Carlo's henchman, so it was probably he who attacked you guys. Although there was another man with Carlo when we burst in."

"A third man." Merrick eyed Ciaran, and said, "Perhaps one of the Dark Ones would help you upstairs to check on Han. He was not awake yet, but should be coming around soon."

"Sure," Ciaran said, groaning when he slid off the table to his feet. One hand was gingerly feeling the back of his head. "I'd like to know what they hit us with."

"Monsieur needs help?" one of the dancers asked, giving Ciaran a long look. "I will be happy to be of service."

"Thank you," Ciaran said politely, then added as the two men started up the stairs, "Is there a reason you have hearts cut out over your arses?"

"Is there a basement to this house?" I asked Merrick, puzzling over where Carlo and the other man had gone.

He didn't answer me, one hand absently rubbing dried blood off his face.

Penny for your thoughts.

Hmm?

I asked you if this villa had a basement.

Ah. I don't know.

What were you thinking so hard about?

I was wondering what happened to Nico. He was here with Han. I wonder if they captured him, too, or if he escaped?

"Oh man," I said, suddenly sick to my stomach. "What if they already auctioned him off?"

"Auctioned?"

Ellis and I quickly explained what Carlo was up to.

"Laboratories," Merrick said slowly, then stiffened. "Genetic experiments. No, he wouldn't..."

He spun around and ran off toward the back of the house.

"Merrick?" I blinked a couple of times, then looked at Ellis.

"Should we go after him?" he asked.

"I guess so." *Merrick, should we go with you?*

No. It's dangerous.

"Come on," I said, gesturing to the vampires. "Sounds like we're going to be needed."

"To battle!" Ellis called as I ran out of the room, the sound of several vampires following when I rounded the corner into the kitchen, where Merrick was wrenching open a door. One of the vampires, Michel, squeaked something unintelligible from his vantage point at the French doors that led out onto a patio, but I didn't stay to find out what it was.

Kelso ran ahead of me down a flight of stone stairs into a fully finished lower level, clearly set up as a theater room. Opened doors on either end had me pausing for a moment, straining to hear. The sound of dog toenails scrabbling on a tile floor sent me running off to the right. "Go the other way," I yelled over my shoulder to Ellis. "Kelso and I will do this side."

I ran through a series of rooms, one opening onto the other, until I came to a closed door. Kelso stood outside it, whining and snuffling at the bottom of the door.

"OK," I whispered to him. "We're going to take them by surprise. Whoever's in there, that is. When I open the door, you leap in and bark and I'll disable anyone who might be hurting Merrick."

Kelso gave me a look that said he didn't have a lot of faith in my disabling abilities. Since I shared that opinion, I amended the statement. "Fine. We'll provide the distraction and Merrick can do the disabling and disarming. Better?"

Kelso wagged his tail, and whined, looking expectantly at the door.

We're coming in.

What? No, don't! Nico is here, and I'm trying to talk some sense—

I flung open the door and charged into the room, screaming at the top of my lungs while waving my hands around in the very best "distract the bad men who might be holding your vampire" method.

Before I could skid to a stop, there was a dark blur and a man with dishwater blond hair had Merrick against the wall, a wicked dagger at his throat.

Beyond them, Carlo was stuffing a laptop and a handful of thumb drives into a black leather satchel.

"Who is this?" the man with the dagger snarled.

Yeah, who is that? I asked Merrick.

Nico, the fourth Horseman.

Oh. Is he normally this testy?

Testy doesn't quite cover it. "This is no one, Nico. Just ignore her, and tell me why you've betrayed us. Betrayed your own people."

Look, I know you said that because you're trying to protect me and divert his attention from me, but just so you know, that shit don't fly.

Tempest, he said, amused. *Such language.*

"Do you think I will be fooled by such obvious rot? This is your woman, isn't it?" He sniffed the air a couple of times. "She's a Beloved!"

Oh my stars and heavens! I clapped a hand over my mouth even though the words hadn't emerged from there. *Now I've got a potty mouth! Hey. Why aren't you worried?*

"She is, but I don't want her. I've told her so frequently, haven't I, Tempest?" *About Nico? I can take him.*

"Daily, if not hourly," I said, nodding, my gaze flickering over to where Carlo was emptying out the contents of a few drawers into his bag. "He's become a big pain in the ass, and I've decided I don't want him, either." *What about my cousin?*

If I was to ask you to leave—

No. You want me to sic Kelso on Carlo? I don't want him getting hurt—Kelso, that is—but if it gives you a distraction, I'll rush Carlo myself.

"I don't give a damn what you think of each other. I'm done taking orders from you," Nico snarled, and a line of red appeared under the knife. "You can be as self-sacrificing as you like, but I'd rather have a life, one filled with all the things I've wanted. And I'm going to have it, too. I'm going to have—"

Now! I shrieked in my head, and, without warning, leaped forward, yelling for Kelso to attack with me. I flung myself across the desk and tackled Carlo without much of an idea as to what I'd do once I got him, which of course meant that approximately ten seconds later I lay facedown on the floor, my arm twisted up behind me in a way that brought tears to my eyes, and Carlo snarling over me.

"Stay back, or I'll blow her brains out." A cold object touched my temple.

Did you disarm Nico?

Yes, although I wish you'd given me a little more warning that you were going to do that. I had the situation well in hand.

Where is he?

On the floor. Unconscious. With a broken nose and collarbone. There was a distinct sense of pleasure in Merrick's voice that I couldn't help but approve.

"Now here's what's going to happen," Carlo said, his voice as cold as the gun pressed to my head. "You're going to carry my bags out to the car parked in the back, and I'm going to take your little playmate with me to make sure you don't get any ideas."

Don't listen to him, Merrick. I'm a Beloved, so according to C. J. Dante, I'm now immortal, too. That means his bullets can't hurt me. Go ahead and grab him.

Er ...

My eyes widened. *Why are you concerned about me? I can feel you are worried. Wait, what do you mean by thinking "irreparable brain damage"? I'm immortal now, aren't I?*

Considering the fact that you must have taken in some of my blood when you kissed my face, and thus have completed the steps to Joining, yes, you are a Beloved.

Is that why you tasted so spicy? Wow. Do you have your soul back?

No.

What? Why not?

I don't know, and now is not the time to worry about it.

He had a point, although I felt oddly cheated. *What are you going to do? I don't want to go away with Carlo. I want to stay with you and make you say those romantic things over and over again until you can easily admit that you love me. You do love me, don't you? Just a little bit?*

He sighed in my mind. *Would I risk sounding like I should be in one of Christian's damned books if I didn't?*

I giggled at him, something Carlo evidently found objectionable.

"Up," he snarled, jerking me up to my knees. He caught my hair in the process, yanking on it painfully while he tried to pull me upright. A little exclamation escaped me, and suddenly, my mind was filled with rage, a red, boiling rage, and just as suddenly, I was free.

I spun around to see Carlo against the wall where minutes before Merrick had been, only Carlo was a good two feet off the ground, and was being throttled. His face was blotchy and he struggled against the one hand that Merrick used to hold him.

"Wow, that is seriously impressive, Merrick. I can't believe you can hold him up like that. But don't you think you should, you know, let him have a bit of air? Otherwise he'll die, and we won't have the satisfaction of turning him over to the police."

"We aren't turning him over to the police," he answered, but loosened his grip and allowed Carlo to slide down the wall to a gasping heap on the floor. "Both Nico and he will be going to see the Council."

"What council?" I asked, moving over to *tsk* at the thin line of blood that had dribbled down Merrick's throat. "Wait, back up a bit. I don't understand why your Horseman guy is here. Was he trying to get Carlo?"

"No. He was working with him. What are you doing?"

"Dabbing at your neck."

He had stopped me when I pulled a tissue from my cleavage and was fussing over his slight wound. "Why?"

"Because it's what a Beloved does. We worry."

A corner of his lips twitched. "Did you get that from Christian's books, too?"

"No."

I leaned forward to kiss him. His mouth was as hot and sweet as I knew it would be, and just the taste of him was enough to make me want to strip off every bit of his clothing, and rub myself all over him.

I'm quite willing to let you do that, but I would suggest you wait until we are in a less public place before doing so.

Stop reading my smutty thoughts.

Why? You are enjoying them.

Yes, but you'll think less of me if you know I want to lick you. All over. Hoo baby.

He laughed aloud. "I assure you that I enjoy your smutty thoughts as much as you do, and I would never think ill of you. Now if you're done wiggling against my cock in a manner guaranteed to make me throw you on the nearest couch and do exactly what you're thinking about doing to me, then I really should make some calls and have these two bastards taken into custody."

I glanced over at Carlo's now empty table and thought seriously about making love to Merrick.

"Tempest," he said in a warning tone, but there was laughter and heat in his eyes.

"What? Your buddy is out, and I bet we could knock out Carlo easy enough."

"Garg!" Carlo said from where he was prone on the floor, wheezing like an elderly bulldog.

You're a bloodthirsty little thing, aren't you?

Just in love, my darling vampire.

Dark One.

"If you want me to keep my hands off you, you're going to have to distract me," I said when he hauled the still unconscious form of Nico over to a corner, and swiftly used the man's own tie to bind his wrists behind him. "Are you certain your buddy wasn't trying to capture Carlo?"

"I doubt that he was." Merrick's voice was grim. He glanced up when Ciaran, with his arm around a stumbling and bleary-eyed Han, appeared in the door. "I think Nico sold us out to Victor."

"So Carlo is Victor?" I asked.

"I don't think so. He would have had many more men at his disposal if he led the organization. I think, judging by the fact that he was taking the laptop and records, that he was in charge of this arm of the Revelation."

I felt a tiny bit of relief that my cousin hadn't been ultimately responsible for the death of Merrick's sister. "That means Victor is still to be found?"

"Yes," Merrick answered. "Unless Nico can tell us where he is, and somehow, I doubt if he was given that information."

Ciaran looked from Carlo on the floor, to me, then over to Nico. "Bloody hell. That would explain a lot."

"Money," Han said, letting Ciaran assist him to the chair behind the table. "Nico always wanted money. Never was happy with what he had. Always wanted more."

"To the point of turning us over to the enemy?" Ciaran shook his head, winced, and put a hand up to the back of it.

Han made an aborted gesture toward the traitorous Horseman. "I agree that he's a bit unbalanced, but if he was working with Victor, he has the blood of several dozen Dark Ones on his hands."

Ciaran walked over to where Nico was slumped, and squatted next to him. "If he's betrayed us, betrayed our own people, then he should die."

"That's not for us to decide," Merrick said, a note of warning in his voice. "We'll leave it to the Council to weigh the evidence and make a decision. I have no doubt they'll find he's guilty, though. He's always preferred to go it alone, and never wanted us to come to search in Italy or France."

Ciaran squinted down at the prone form. "Let me kill him just a little."

"No," Merrick said firmly.

"Just a few pokes with a knife. Or a sword. Han, you have a sword?"

"Not on me, no. My gun was taken away when someone bashed in the back of my brain. Ow. There's a huge lump there. And speaking of being bashed ..."

"That was probably Nico, as well," Merrick said, his jaw tight. "No one else could have taken us unaware. He knew we were coming here, and obviously got here before us, lying in wait to pick us off one at a time. Tempest says they had Ciaran ready to be handed over to one of their buyers."

Ciaran grimaced, but sent a grateful look my way. "I'm delighted you interfered when you did. I will be forever in your debt."

"Stop looking at her like that," Merrick said, his lips thinning.

Oooh, are you jealous?

Not in the least. He simply needs to stop looking at you like he has the right to do so.

I laughed in his mind. *You are beyond adorable.*

"I guess that means we're now the three Horsemen," Han said, looking a lot less groggy. "We'll have to recruit a new member."

I raised my hand.

"Absolutely not," Merrick said, glowering at me.

"Oh?" I lifted my chin and glared right back at him. "You wouldn't be trying to tell me what I can and cannot do, would you?"

"No." His jaw worked a couple of times. "It might seem like I am, but the simple fact is that you can't be a Horseman. You're not a Dark One."

"I'm a Beloved!"

"But not a Dark One. I know full well you'd be able to fight even the worst threat to our people, but Horsemen must be Dark Ones. It is from that we draw our strength."

"Hrmph," I said, unconvinced.

I was about to point out that there was no valid reason for them not allowing me to join their group when Merrick, who had been keeping an eye on Nico, suddenly spun and leaped forward, calling out, "Tempest, move!"

I turned, and time seemed to do that slow-motion thing that you see in the movies. Carlo had crawled over to where his gun was, and was rising up on one knee, aiming it at Merrick and Han. I knew with every ounce of my being that he was going to shoot Merrick in the head, and that it wouldn't be a wound he could recover from. Without being aware I was moving, I dove forward toward Merrick, intent on knocking him out of the way.

A ridiculously loud explosion hurt my ears, followed almost immediately by a searing, burning pain in my left arm.

Merrick flashed past me, slamming Carlo into the wall, clearly intent on bashing the ever-living life out of him. Han and Ciaran pulled him off before he could do more than knock Carlo out, but I felt the rage in Merrick, rage and anguish and, oddly, a sense of brilliant gratitude.

What is that? I asked, wondering at the lightness that filled him, driving out the dark stain of despair and pain that had filled him ever since I had first met him.

A soul, my goddess. You've given me back my soul. Instantly I was pressed up against Merrick, his arms hard around me. *Are you hurt? You're thinking hurt thoughts. Why are you thinking hurt thoughts? How bad is it? I refuse to let you die, do you hear me? You're my Beloved now, and thus you cannot leave me, so stop thinking about pain and go back to thinking about molesting me with your tongue. Christos, I will never forgive myself if Carlo's harmed you. I should have picked up that gun he dropped.*

I'm OK. I think ... I pushed back from Merrick and looked down at myself. A patch of blood bloomed against my sleeve, and was growing at the same rate as the burning pain. "I think I'm about to strike number seventy-seven off my bucket list."

"Being shot?" Merrick asked, tearing my sleeve off in order to examine the wound.

"No." My voice seemed to come from quite a distance away. I weaved, unable to keep the black splotches that appeared in front of my eyes from spreading. I gave in to their promise of insensibility; the last thing I heard was my voice saying, "Seventy-seven is fainting."

EPILOGUE

From: Ellis
Darling! We're in Monaco, having used the money your dishy Merrick gave us to buy a theater club.

To: Ellis
Oh, good. He said he was going to give you guys the reward money that the vamps ponied up for the capture of Carlo.

From: Ellis
We hope to put on a musical version of Dracula. Don't you think that would be awesome?

To: Ellis
I'm surprised it hasn't already been done.

From: Ellis
I'm sure it has, but we're doing it with actual vampires!

To: Ellis
Good point. You're happy there? You're not going back home?

From: Ellis

Happy as a clam in tomato sauce, darling. You? Did you work things out with your hunky bit of beefcake?

I looked up from my phone across the bedroom to where Merrick was having a videoconference with Han and Ciaran, and smiled.

What?

What what?

I feel you smiling at me. What have I done to make you do so?

I don't know. Maybe just being magnificently arrogant. And stubborn. And reluctant to admit just how crazy about me you are.

Is this about the otter again? I told you that the swimming pool is not a suitable habitat for an otter, not that they are indigenous to this part of the world.

I laughed aloud. "All right, but if we get a house back in Oregon, I want to have an otter sanctuary. Kelso would love that."

Do you really wish to return to Oregon?

Yes, but I'm willing to split our time between this house and one back home.

As it happens, Han seems to think there's a facility in northern California we should investigate, he said, looking thoughtful. *A home on the West Coast might be very beneficial.*

I'll start looking up what it takes to open an otter sanctuary. I leaned back against the headboard of his bed. Outside the French doors, the twinkling lights of the town below us glittered like diamonds set in onyx.

Life, I decided, my gaze going back to Merrick, was shaping up to be everything I hoped it would be.

It is now that you are in it, he said, sending me a look of sapphire heat that shone as brightly as the lights of the town.

I picked up a small notebook. "Item number one hundred fourteen, name an otter Aloysius. Number one hundred fifteen, lick every inch of Merrick."

Abruptly, he closed the lid of his laptop and stalked toward me, pulling off his clothing piece by piece. "Number one hundred and sixteen, allow Merrick to indulge every fantasy he can think of, and, my darling Tempest, I have a very good imagination."

I giggled, and tossed the notebook to the side as the vampire of my dreams fulfilled that promise.

And how!

DARK ONES CONNECTIONS

The following is a list of the Dark Ones books, and how the characters are connected (if applicable).

A GIRL'S GUIDE TO VAMPIRES
Dark Ones, Book 1
Originally published 2003; reissued Jan. 2011
Hero and Heroine: Raphael St. John and Joy Randall
Secondary Character: Christan Dante
Comments: Christian! Christian! Christian! I wrote him just for myself, but decided I would share with everyone. First mention of GothFaire and Miranda Ghetti, Francesca's mother.

SEX AND THE SINGLE VAMPIRE
Dark Ones, Book 2
Originally published 2004; reissued April 2011
Hero and Heroine: Christian Dante and Allegra Telford
Secondary Characters: Noelle the Guardian, Asmodeus the demon lord, Sebastian Mercier
Comments: The first introduction of a Guardian and demons. Joy, Raphael, and Roxy from Girl's Guide also appear in this book.

SEX, LIES AND VAMPIRES
Dark Ones, Book 3
Originally published 2005; reissue Sept. 2011
Hero and Heroine: Adrian Tomas and Nell Harris
Secondary Characters: Sebastian Mercier, Asmodeus
Comments: Christian and Allie appear in this book. Also included are the first references to polters.

EVEN VAMPIRES GET THE BLUES
Dark Ones, Book 4
Signet (May 2, 2006)
Hero and Heroine: Paen Scott and Samantha Cosse
Secondary Characters: Finn, Avery, and Daniel Scott;
Noelle the Guardian
Comments: The first book where you get to "see" a
polter. Avery later found his Beloved in the Unleashed
novella in Cupid Cats.

BRING OUT YOUR DEAD novella Dark Ones, part of
the series
2006
Hero and Heroine: Sebastian Mercier and Ysabelle
Raleigh
Secondary Characters: Adrian, Nell, and Damian, as well
as Noelle the Guardian, and Asmodeus.
Comments: This short story picked up where Sex, Lies,
and Vampires left off, and was intended to satisfy people who
wanted to see Sebastian and Noelle together. Noelle refused
to cooperate.

THE LAST OF THE RED-HOT VAMPIRES
Dark Ones, Book 5
Signet (April 3, 2007)
Hero and Heroine: Theondre (Theo) North and Portia
Harding
Secondary Characters: Christian Dante, Noelle the
Guardian
Comments: This was the first Dark Ones book with a
hero who wasn't a vampire at the beginning of the story.
Noelle is present in the guise of a test proctor, while
Christian is there as the head of the Moravian Council.

CAT GOT YOUR TONGUE short story in MY BIG FAT SUPERNATURAL HONEYMOON anthology
Dark Ones, part of the series
St. Martin (Dec 26, 2007)
Hero and Heroine: Raphael St. John and Joy Randall
Comments: This short story was written to satisfy readers who wanted to know why Raphael was so wigged out by werefolk.

ZEN AND THE ART OF VAMPIRES
Dark Ones, Book 6
Signet (Dec 2, 2008)
Hero and Heroine: Kristoff von Hannelore and Pia Thomason
Secondary Characters: Alec Darwin, Christian Dante, Sebastian Mercier, Ulfur the ghost
Comments: The first part of a two-book story that introduced two new elements into the Dark Ones world: reapers, and the Moravian Council. Christian and Sebastian have cameos.

CROUCHING VAMPIRE, HIDDEN FANG
Dark Ones, Book 7
Signet (May 5, 2009)
Hero and Heroine: Kristoff von Hannelore and Pia Thomason
Secondary Characters: Alec Darwin, Christian Dante, Allegra Telford, Sebastian Mercier
Comments: The second part of Pia's story, with a look at how Allie and Christian are doing, as well as longer appearances by Kristoff's brother and cousin. Ulfur the ghost is also present in this story.

UNLEASHED novella in CUPID CATS anthology
Dark Ones, part of the series
Signet (Jul 6, 2010)
Hero and Heroine: Avery Scott and Jacintha Ferreira
Secondary Characters: Paen Scott and Samantha Cosse, as well as Jas's sister Cora
Comments: This novella sets up the story of how Alec Darwin finds his Beloved despite the fact that she was killed some five centuries before. It's also the story of one of Paen Scott's brothers, and the first time I deal with Moravian finding his Beloved (i.e. Avery has his soul before he meets Jas). Trivia: Jacintha owes her nickname "Jas" to my beloved dog, who died a few months before I wrote this story. More trivia: all my proceeds from the sales of this anthology goes to three local animal charities: Purrfect Pals, Old Dog Haven, and Save a Forgotten Equine, in memory of my dog.

IN THE COMPANY OF VAMPIRES
Dark Ones, Book 8
Signet (Nov 2, 2010)
Hero and Heroine: Benedikt Czerny and Francesca Ghetti
Secondary Characters: Miranda Ghetti, Eirik, Finnvid, and Isleif (ghosts), Imogen, Loki
Comments: The long-awaited adult story with Ben and Fran, set five years after Circus of the Darned. Ulfur the ghost (now a lich) is in this story, and makes mention of Pia and Kristoff. Two characters seen for the first time are David and Petra, who will be given their own book.

GOT FANGS? and *CIRCUS OF THE DARNED* in the *CONFESSIONS OF A VAMPIRE'S GIRLFRIEND* omnibus
Dark Ones, part of the series
YOUNG ADULT
NAL (Nov 2, 2010)

Hero and Heroine: Benedikt Czerny and Francesca Ghetti

Secondary Characters: Miranda Ghetti, Eirik, Finnvid, and Isleif (ghosts), Imogen, Loki

Comments: First printed in 2003 and 2004, these two books were released as YAs, and brought back the GothFaire introduced in A Girl's Guide to Vampires.

MUCH ADO ABOUT VAMPIRES
Dark Ones, Book 9
Signet (Oct 3, 2011)
Hero and Heroine: Alec Darwin and Corazon Ferreira
Secondary Characters: Kristoff Hannelore and Pia Thomason, Ulfur the lich, Bael, Sally, and Christian Dante

Comments: Jacintha's sister Cora's story, including the uber short story My Heart Will Go On And On, and explaining how Alec could have a Beloved when she was killed 500 years before.

A TALE OF TWO VAMPIRES
Dark Ones, Book 10
Signet (Sept. 4, 2012)
Hero and Heroine: Nikola Czerny and Iolanthe Tennyson
Secondary Characters: Benedikt Czerny, Francesca Ghetti

Comments: This is the story of Ben's father, who supposedly "died" a few centuries ago. Ben, Fran, and Imogen all feature heavily in the book.

SHADES OF GRAY novella in the UNDEAD IN MY BED anthology
Dark Ones, part of the series
Pocket Star (Sept. 25, 2012)
Hero and Heroine: Grayson Soucek and Noelle the Guardian

Secondary Characters: Michel de Nostradame, ghostly cousin of the infamous Nostradamus

Comments: A novella that finally gives Noelle her Dark One.

THE VAMPIRE ALWAYS RISES
Dark Ones, Book 11
Keeper Shelf Books (April 25, 2017)
Hero and Heroine: Merrick Simon and Tempest Keye
Secondary Characters: Ciaran, Han, and Nico (Four Horseman), Ellis, Kelso the dog

Comments: A return to the Dark Ones with Tempest Keye, niece of Roxy from A Girl's Guide to Vampires and Sex and the Single Vampire. All Tempest wants is to meet a real vampire...fortunately for her, Merrick is dumped at her feet. Literally.

ABOUT THE AUTHOR

For as long as she can remember, Katie MacAlister has loved reading. Growing up in a family where a weekly visit to the library was a given, Katie spent much of her time with her nose buried in a book.

Two years after she started writing novels, Katie sold her first romance, *Noble Intentions*. More than fifty books later, her novels have been translated into numerous languages, been recorded as audiobooks, received several awards, and have been regulars on the *New York Times, USA Today,* and *Publishers Weekly* bestseller lists. Katie lives in the Pacific Northwest with two dogs and a cat, and can often be found lurking around online.

You are welcome to join Katie's official discussion group on Facebook, as well as connect with her via Twitter, Goodreads, and Instagram. For more information, visit katiemacalister.com

OTHER BOOKS BY KATIE MACALISTER

Dark Ones Series
A GIRL'S GUIDE TO VAMPIRES
SEX AND THE SINGLE VAMPIRE
SEX, LIES, AND VAMPIRES
EVEN VAMPIRES GET THE BLUES
BRING OUT YOUR DEAD (novella)
THE LAST OF THE RED-HOT VAMPIRES
ZEN AND THE ART OF VAMPIRES
CROUCHING VAMPIRE, HIDDEN FANG
CUPID CATS (novella)
IN THE COMPANY OF VAMPIRES
CONFESSIONS OF A VAMPIRE'S GIRLFRIEND
MUCH ADO ABOUT VAMPIRES
A TALE OF TWO VAMPIRES
THE UNDEAD IN MY BED (novella)
THE VAMPIRE ALWAYS RISES

Aisling Grey Guardian Series
YOU SLAY ME
FIRE ME UP
LIGHT MY FIRE
HOLY SMOKES
DEATH'S EXCELLENT VACATION (short story)

Silver Dragon Series
PLAYING WITH FIRE
UP IN SMOKE
ME AND MY SHADOW

Light Dragon Series
LOVE IN THE TIME OF DRAGONS
THE UNBEARABLE LIGHTNESS OF DRAGONS
SPARKS FLY

Dragon Fall Series
DRAGON FALL
DRAGON STORM
DRAGON SOUL
DRAGON UNBOUND

Time Thief Series
TIME THIEF
THE ART OF STEALING TIME

Matchmaker in Wonderland Series
THE IMPORTANCE OF BEING ALICE
A MIDSUMMER NIGHT'S ROMP
DARING IN A BLUE DRESS
PERILS OF PAULIE

Contemporary Single Titles
IMPROPER ENGLISH
BIRD OF PARADISE (novella)
MEN IN KILTS
THE CORSET DIARIES
A HARD DAY'S KNIGHT
BLOW ME DOWN
IT'S ALL GREEK TO ME

Noble Historical Series
NOBLE INTENTIONS
NOBLE DESTINY
THE TROUBLE WITH HARRY
THE TRUTH ABOUT LEO

Suffragette Historical Series
SUFFRAGETTE IN THE CITY

Paranormal Single Titles
AIN'T MYTH BEHAVING
DEATH'S EXCELLENT VACATION (short story)
MY BIG FAT SUPERNATURAL HONEYMOON
(short story)

Mysteries / writing as Kate Marsh
GHOST OF A CHANCE

Steampunk Romance
STEAMED

Young Adult / Writing as Katie Maxwell
CONFESSIONS OF A VAMPIRE'S GIRLFRIEND
EYELINER OF THE GODS

Emily Series
THE YEAR MY LIFE WENT DOWN THE LOO
THEY WEAR WHAT UNDER THEIR KILTS
WHAT'S FRENCH FOR "EW"?
THE TAMING OF THE DRU
LIFE, LOVE AND THE PURSUIT OF HOTTIES

Printed in Great Britain
by Amazon